BURNT ISLAND

BURNT ISLAND

KATE RHODES

**SIMON &
SCHUSTER**

London · New York · Sydney · Toronto · New Delhi

A CBS COMPANY

First published in Great Britain by Simon & Schuster UK Ltd, 2019
A CBS COMPANY

1 3 5 7 9 10 8 6 4 2

Simon & Schuster UK Ltd
1st Floor
222 Gray's Inn Road
London WC1X 8HB

Simon & Schuster Australia,
Sydney

Simon & Schuster India,
New Delhi

www.simonandschuster.co.uk
www.simonandschuster.com.au
www.simonandschuster.co.in

A CIP catalogue record for this book
is available from the British Library

Hardback ISBN: 978-1-4711-6599-3
Trade Paperback ISBN: 978-1-4711-6600-6
eBook ISBN: 978-1-4711-6601-3

Typeset in the UK by M Rules
Printed and bound by CPI Group (UK) Ltd, Croydon, CR0 4YY

MIX
Paper from
responsible sources
FSC® C020471

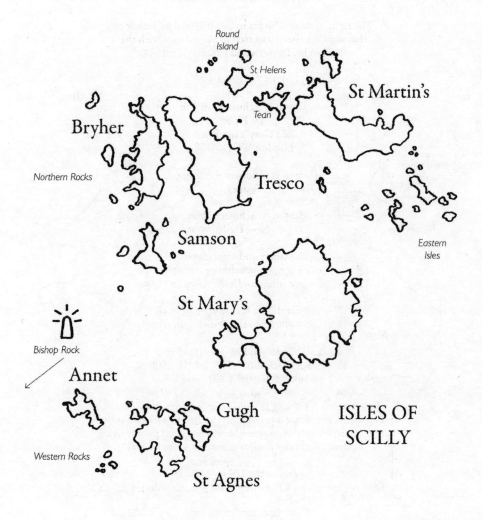

Round
Island

St Helens

Tean

St Martin's

Bryher

Northern Rocks

Tresco

Samson

Eastern
Isles

St Mary's

Bishop Rock

Annet

Gugh

ISLES OF
SCILLY

Western Rocks

St Agnes

St. Agnes

Gugh

Burnt Island

Big Pool

Porth Killier

Quay

Holiday Cottage

Carlyons' house

Kittern Hill

Blanket Bay

Lifeboat house

Lower Town

Helstons' Farm

Turk's Head Pub

Porth Conger

The Bar

Obadiah's Barrow

Lighthouse

Higher Town

The Cove

Keith Pendennis's Cottage

Middle Town

Cove Vean

Garabeara

Troytown Maze

Tolmans' house

Naomi Vine's house

St. Warna's Cove

St Warna's Well

Tolgillian

• *Boy's Rock*

Wingletang Down
•
Devil's Punch bowl

N

Beady Pool

**ST. AGNES
AND
GUGH**

0   Mile   1/4

Horse Point

PART 1

'To be silent and consumed by fire is the worst punishment on earth.'

'Blood Wedding and Yerma',
Federico García Lorca

PART

The sun is rising when Jimmy Curwen sets out on a cold November morning. He passes the lighthouse first, its tall form looming over St Agnes like a winter ghost. The building is one of his favourites, even though its light was removed years ago, but there's no time to stop and admire it. Jimmy's friends are waiting and he can't disappoint them. He takes his usual route to the lake, with his binoculars hidden in his pocket.

He walks north through Middle Town, where the stone faces of a dozen houses observe his progress, keeping his head down to avoid the blank stares of shuttered windows. He only relaxes once he reaches open country, where no one will disturb him. The meadow is crisp with frost, grass crunching under foot, his heart lifting when he spies the Big Pool. Today, the expanse of water is as flat and shiny as polished glass, tinted pink by early sunlight. Yet none of his friends have come to greet him: the sky is empty, not a single cry of welcome.

Jimmy is about to return home when seagulls descend suddenly in a swirling cloud. The flock circles overhead, close enough to touch, bawling out raucous greetings. When he throws scraps of bread into the air, they battle for each crumb.

He can smell brine on their wings, wet feathers caressing his cheeks. The birds stay long after the food supply is exhausted before disappearing back into the sky, leaving few of his favourite creatures behind. Oystercatchers wade towards him through the shallows, absorbing his attention.

His fingers are numb with cold by the time he slips his binoculars back into his pocket. There's an odd smell on the air – a stench of burning fuel mixed with a sweetness he can't identify. Now that the birds have gone, he notices smoke billowing from Burnt Island, as if someone is sending him a signal. He leaves the pool and picks his way across the sandbar that stretches from Blanket Bay.

Jimmy's pace slows as he scrambles uphill, towards the source of the fire. The smell is stronger now, its sickly taste irritating the back of his throat. He's panting for breath by the time he reaches the top. The sight that greets him makes little sense at first: a mound of charred sticks glowing a dull red, paraffin cans abandoned on the grass nearby. When he looks again, small flames surround a blackened mass at the heart of the bonfire. His stomach rolls with nausea. A face leers up at him from the ashes, melted flesh hanging from exposed cheekbones, empty eye sockets fixing him with a direct stare. The dead body appears to be begging for help and Jimmy can't refuse. Another life slipped through his fingers years ago; this is his chance to make amends.

'I'll find out who hurt you,' Jimmy mutters. 'I promise.'

He can't even tell whether the corpse is male or female. The sight sends him reeling backwards, desperate to escape, but his conscience keeps him rooted to the spot. His fingers catch on a rocky mound as he steadies himself. Letters have been scratched into the stone beside the bonfire, but he has never learned to read, forced to rely on the instructions of others. His gaze soon returns to the embers. Jimmy recalls something his mother used to say: always leave something for the dead, to show respect. His eyes smart with smoke and tears as he throws his sheepskin coat over the body, extinguishing the last flames. Jimmy recites the start of his mother's favourite prayer. *Our Father who art in heaven, hallowed be thy name.* His words vanish in the smoky air, his grey hair flying on the breeze as he stumbles towards safety.

1

Friday 5 November

My thirty-fifth birthday arrives without fanfare. It's a work day like any other, with an evening duty to complete. The winter air chills my skin as the ferry struggles to land on St Agnes at 6 p.m., tonight's riptide too fierce to dock near Higher Town. The island releases its familiar smell of woodsmoke and freshly turned earth as I step onto the old quay at Blanket Bay. Granite boulders are littered across the long horseshoe of sand, beside piles of razor shells and seaweed from the last high tide. St Agnes is the wildest and most secretive place in all the Scillies: just two miles long and half a mile wide, it lies furthest from the mainland with dozens of hidden coves and a pair of small islets clinging to its coastline. There are no cars or motorbikes to disturb the peace. The only vehicles here are a handful of tractors, golf buggies and rusting bicycles.

My dog Shadow seems happy with his new surroundings, even if I could use some more excitement.
The hectic pace of my old job working undercover
for the Murder Squad in London has been calling to
me lately, but my dog is in his element, sniffing every
stone and refusing to follow instructions. Shadow is a
two-year-old Czechoslovakian wolfdog with pale grey
fur, eyes the colour of sea mist and a strong sense of
mischief. He only materialises at my side again when
I head inland, our walk bracing enough to dispel my
reluctance to spend my birthday overseeing the island's
firework display.

St Agnes appears deserted this evening, steadying
itself for an influx of visitors in a few hours' time. I
walk uphill towards the hamlet that lies at the heart of
the island without seeing a soul. Middle Town is home
to most of the community's eighty permanent residents;
the village so picturesque that it often features in the
tourist board's glossy brochures, advertising the joys
of Cornish holidays. The island's lighthouse still dom-
inates the settlement from the top of a low hill, despite
being decommissioned years ago.

It's only when I drop down to Covean Beach that I
catch sight of a gang of people building a bonfire on the
rocky shore, hurling pallets, logs and driftwood onto
a six-foot pile, their laughter rising from the darkness.
Another party is rigging fireworks to a metal platform,
and more volunteers are slaving over a lavish barbecue.
My arrival dampens the atmosphere by a few degrees.

Despite having known most of the islanders all my life, they are still adjusting to my new role as Deputy Commander of the Scilly Isles Police, their chatter quietening as they register my presence. Just seven officers oversee the islands, but some inhabitants view us with suspicion, preferring to solve disputes by themselves.

I'm surprised to see one of the island's newest residents, Naomi Vine, helping with preparations. Vine is a sculptor with an international reputation. She moved to the island just over a year ago, but tonight she's using her hands for less glamorous purposes: breaking up pallets for firewood. Her slim figure is swaddled in a winter coat, most of her short red hair tucked under a woollen cap, her face animated. The community buzzed with gossip when they heard she was buying the island's old mansion house, but the sculptor's abrasive behaviour has caused controversy ever since. The crowd are keeping their distance from Vine, apart from one islander who seems unmoved by her reputation as a troublemaker. Rachel Carlyon is a native of St Agnes, a tall, ungainly woman who prefers to stay in the background, but tonight she looks relaxed while chatting with her new friend. The only common ground the two women appear to share is that they're both in their early forties, but odd allegiances can spring up when you live in a minute community at the edge of the world.

Sergeant Eddie Nickell stands on the far side of the crowd, dressed in full uniform, epaulettes gleaming on the shoulders of his coat. My deputy hasn't missed a single opportunity to wear formal regalia since he was promoted last month. He's just twenty-five, but making faster progress than me in his private life. The sergeant has got a two-month-old daughter with his fiancée Michelle, and seems happy in the flat they're renting in Lower Town. Wind has teased a few blond curls from under his cap, his choirboy face blanched by the cold. Eddie is perfectly capable of managing a family event on a winter evening with a good-natured crowd, I just need to check that safety measures are on track. We walk further up the beach so that we can hear ourselves over the buzz of conversation.

'You're putting me to shame, Eddie.' His pristine uniform makes my donkey jacket, jeans and walking boots look shabby by comparison.

He grins in reply. 'If you've got it, flaunt it, boss. It took me two years to earn these stripes.'

'Are we all set for tonight?'

'It's looking good. We've got twelve marshals and two safety officers with St John's ambulance training.' His voice is so earnest it sounds like he's expecting a royal visit.

'Great, I'll go down and thank them.'

My godmother, Maggie Nancarrow, appears at my side as I trudge across the shingle. She's come over early from her home on Bryher, never one to miss a party. I feel like a giant beside such a petite woman, her small face framed by a cloud of grey ringlets as she gazes up at me through wire-framed glasses.

'Happy birthday, you handsome devil.' She bounces up to kiss my cheek. 'I've got a present for you.'

'You cook for me all the time. There's no need.'

She presses a small package into my hand. 'This was my dad's. Why not see if it fits?'

The box contains a vintage Rolex, undamaged, apart from a few scratches on its handsome steel casing. It slips onto my wrist like it was designed for me to wear.

'This is too much, Maggie.'

'It's only gathering dust at home. Read the inscription for me.'

I flip the watch over. *'Time waits for no man.'*

'Remember that, Ben, or you'll get left behind.' Maggie's grin sweetens the cryptic message before she scurries away, her super-charged energy blazing a trail through the crowd.

I catch up with the party's organiser, Steve Tregarron, as strings of lights are hung from posts on the beach. Tregarron has been landlord of the Turk's Head for decades, but looks more like a roadie after a lifetime of hard tours. His grey hair is tied in a ponytail, deep lines bracketing his mouth, his leather jacket made characterful by dozens of scratches and stains. The landlord is courteous but keeps our conversation brief, soon marching away to help his wife Ella stack crates of beer by the safety cordon.

I watch the islanders carry out a last check on the fireworks before spotting a familiar face: Liam Poldean is hauling wood for the bonfire across the beach. He's a local builder, around my age, with scruffy brown hair and a friendly, capable manner. I got to know him last spring when he came over to Bryher to fix my leaking roof. He drops an armful of logs onto the woodpile, smiling as I approach.

'I thought you'd be running the fireworks, Liam.'

'No chance, DI Kitto,' Poldean uses my title with friendly mockery. 'Those rockets can maim someone if they're lit wrong. I don't want that on my conscience.' His face grows serious as he scans the crowd. 'Have you seen my kids running around?'

'Maggie's entertaining them.'

'That's good news. Gunpowder and small boys don't mix.'

'They're fine; the safety barrier's up already. I hear the display's even bigger than last year.'

'Fingers crossed,' he replies with a relaxed shrug. 'Fireworks are unpredictable bastards, but Steve's spent a fortune, so this lot should be okay.'

The crowd expands as ferries deliver partygoers from neighbouring islands. People stand in gaggles outside the pub, others drifting towards the beach, eager for the display to start. The bonfire is roaring already, brightening the darkness with orange flames. Three giant straw figures stand beside it, propped against hay bales, their stiff forms decorated with black cloaks, broomsticks and painted grins. Each one is around fifteen feet tall, the wind tugging at their woven limbs. It's an island tradition to destroy bad spirits each year before the winter deepens. The bonfire is growing fiercer by the minute, its flames brighter and more powerful than before, the crackle of burning logs carried by the breeze. The smells drifting towards me trigger memories of every Guy Fawkes party I attended as a boy: saltpetre, beer and excitement.

I'm about to warn Eddie to keep the fire under control in case sparks fly into the crowd, when someone taps me on the shoulder. A tall brunette beams up at me, her heart-shaped face so attractive it takes time to collect my thoughts.

'Zoe?'

'Have you forgotten me, big man? Pity, I flew all this way for your birthday.'

'Your hair's changed. I didn't recognise you.'

'Is that your best welcome?'

I grab her in a rapid hug. 'I wasn't expecting you till next month.'

'It was cheaper to come now than at Christmas. Let's stand by the fire, I'm bloody freezing.'

'Okay, but I'm on duty; the display starts in ten minutes.'

She wrinkles her nose in disapproval, the ease of a friendship that's lasted since childhood still intact, even though she bears little resemblance to the blonde bombshell that ran her parents' hotel on Bryher until six months ago. Her dark eyes are more watchful than before, but her new life in India seems to be suiting her well. Zoe's skin glows with health, and she's put

13

on a few pounds, making her hourglass curves harder to ignore.

I squash my attraction back into its box as she shows me a photo on her phone of her new workplace. The school in Mumbai is a square concrete box with no trees to camouflage its ugliness, but the pupils lined up in the playground are all grinning for the camera. They're street children, thrilled to live in clean dormitories and receive three meals a day. It's Zoe's job to teach them music and rebuild their confidence. In the past six months she has campaigned alongside the other staff to keep the place open for another year. My own job seems much less worthwhile. All I've done recently is hand out a few cautions for anti-social behaviour and arrest a teenager for setting fire to a neighbour's barn.

'Stay there, Zoe. I'll get the ball rolling then buy you a drink. Steve's gone to light the first flare on Burnt Island.'

The event always starts with a nod to the past. Centuries ago, the women of St Agnes climbed to the highest point on its northern coast, carrying burning torches to guide local fishermen back to the harbour. Zoe and I are still chatting when a man barrels towards us through the dark. One of the few advantages of being six foot four is the ability to scan every face in a crowd, and this man's distress is obvious as he flails past bystanders, not caring who he shunts out of his way. Steve Tregarron's leather jacket is flapping in the wind, his skin reddened by exertion, but it's his eyes

14

that worry me. They're so wide open it looks like he's forgotten how to blink.

'Something's wrong,' he splutters, his voice a rough smoker's growl. 'I saw it on Burnt Island just now, on top of the hill.' He's heaving for breath as shock overtakes him.

I lead him away from the crowd to talk without being overheard. 'What did you see, Steve?'

'Human remains, or what's left of them. It can't be a stray animal.'

'Are you sure? Things can look different in the dark.'

He shakes his head vehemently. 'Come and see for yourself.'

I make a snap decision based on the information in front of me: the crowd are growing restless, impatient for the night's entertainment. If I cancel the display, over 300 people will wander round the island, polluting a potential crime scene. It's better to corral them here, keeping warm by the bonfire. I instruct Eddie to start the event in ten minutes and not allow anyone off the beach, before following Tregarron inland.

The sky is pitch-dark as we jog north, our torch beams drawing white lines across uneven ground. The path takes us round the Big Pool, where kids sail model boats every summer, but tonight it looks ghostly. Its surface reflects clouds chasing overhead and the moon's blurred outline. Tregarron seems too distressed to speak; I can hear his breath rattling, and my concern grows. If he has a coronary I'll have two corpses on my hands, but he ignores my advice to slow down. I'm still not fully convinced that he's found a body. It's more likely that a lone sheep has scrambled up the hill then broken its neck in a fall.

'Hurry,' he calls over his shoulder. 'Before someone else finds it.'

We've reached the north-western coast of St Agnes, with the black outline of Burnt Island rising from the sea before us. Moonlight spills onto the narrow cause-way – later tonight the islet will be cut off by racing currents, until the tide drops again at dawn. The path seems to be afloat on the water's surface already, as the currents rise.

Tregarron scrambles up the rocky hill so fast his boots release a stream of shale. The man finally comes to a halt at the peak, but I can't see anything suspicious, just a granite cairn built so high it could tumble with the first strong wind.

'It's over there,' the landlord says. There's a tremor in his voice and I can tell he'd love to be wrong. I don't know whether it's a failing or a strength, but ten years with the Murder Squad in London have dulled my sense of horror; my first reaction when confronting a new crime scene is curiosity. Whatever I'm about to witness can't be worse than finding a Russian gang member's body crammed inside the boot of his car after being left to fester throughout a long hot summer.

Tregarron keeps his face averted as I shine my torch onto a heap of blackened wood. I realise immediately that he was right – we're witnessing a murder scene. My first concern is for the landlord; the man's skin is paler than before, his hands shaking.

'You did well bringing me here, Steve. Are you okay to walk back alone?' He gives a rapid nod. 'Don't tell anyone about this until I make an announcement tomorrow.'

The landlord rushes away without a backwards glance, clearly desperate for safety. Once he disappears I examine the scene again. It looks like the killer prepared the fire, then laid the body on top while the flames raged. No distinguishing features are left, except a layer of blackened flesh covering the poor creature's skull. My guess is that someone returned to the scene to lay fabric over the fire, damping the flames so no one would see the smoke. The poor sod must have died hours ago; the embers are cool when I touch the charred wood at my feet. When I straighten up again, the sky ignites with colour. The wind carries a muted cheer from Covean Beach as rockets blaze gold and silver trails across the night sky. There's nothing I can do for the time being, so I turn my collar against the wind and watch Catherine wheels spin in dizzying circles until darkness returns. Whoever took the victim's life could be miles away by now, sailing towards calmer waters, or mingling with partygoers on the beach below.

I call Eddie to explain what's happened before contacting the only pathologist in travelling distance. Dr Gareth Keillor retired to St Mary's after his Home

Office job ended, but he's still licenced to act as our consultant when required. He doesn't answer when I ring his home number so I leave him a voicemail. My final call is to the county forensics team in Penzance. I'm expecting another answering machine, but someone picks up immediately, even though it's after 10 p.m. The woman at the end of the line introduces herself as Liz Gannick, Cornwall's newly appointed Chief of Forensic Services. She listens in silence as I ask for assistance. Her northern voice is crisp when she promises to catch the first plane over tomorrow, then abruptly hangs up. It surprises me that she will visit the scene herself, rather than sending one of her minions. I've never met Gannick before, but she's known as a tough operator; her expertise could make or break my investigation into how the victim died.

I hunker behind a boulder, aware that my birthday this year will be memorable for all the wrong reasons. But being stranded here is nothing compared with the victim's suffering. When I look back at St Agnes, the fire on the beach is still burning at full strength, a patch of gold against the sky's blackness. The revellers stand in huddles, watching the ritual sacrifice; burning the straw men is meant to sear away bad spirits on a night of revelry, but seeing the effigies go up in smoke only adds to my discomfort. Flames ravage the cloaks swathed around the witches' bodies while my eyes return to the funeral pyre at my feet. The victim's death must have been lonely as well as agonising, and the killer clearly enjoys symbolism. It looks like he wanted the burned remains found at the very moment the island tried to rid itself of evil.

'Who are you?' I mutter under my breath.

I can't believe that a passing yachtsman would drag a corpse up a steep hill instead of dropping it into the sea with no questions asked. Whoever did this planned to add a vicious threat to a popular local festival. It's likely to be an islander, even though no one from St Agnes has been reported missing, in a place where nothing goes unnoticed.

I leave Zoe a voicemail asking her to look after Shadow until tomorrow. We should be enjoying the party together, but I can't leave a murder scene unattended. By now the tide has almost covered the path leading back to St Agnes. If I requested help a boatload of volunteers would arrive immediately, but they'd trample over valuable forensic evidence, and it's too late for me to risk returning by foot. The churning waters between Burnt Island and St Agnes have claimed the lives of several holidaymakers who misjudged the tides. The darkness seems thicker than before when I crouch beside a granite mound, wishing I'd worn thicker gloves. I'm starting to regret my desire for more excitement at work as the cold sinks deeper into my bones.

2

Jimmy stays at home in his bedsit, avoiding the crowds. At fifty-three years old, he's reliant on charity for the roof over his head, because no one has ever offered him a job. An old-fashioned gas fire keeps the place warm, yet tonight it's impossible to relax. He stares at the objects on his windowsill: bundles of glossy white egrets' feathers, an abandoned swallow's nest and the broken shell of a hawfinch's egg. But even his favourite possessions fail to calm him tonight.

When he peers outside, the bonfire is still blazing on Covean Beach, so he draws the curtains to avoid the spectacle. The flames remind him too strongly of the corpse he found this morning, his window sealed to banish the smell of smoke. Conscience tells him to honour his promise to the figure he saw in the fire, because the death he witnessed as a boy still haunts his dreams. But speaking to the police would terrify him. He can recite the names of every bird species on the island when he's alone, yet words escape him when people are listening. He will have to find the killer without help from anyone.

Jimmy paces around the room, too agitated to relax. He turns on his radio, but strangers' voices discussing things he can't understand set his teeth on edge. Only one thing will settle his mind, so he stuffs a bag of seed in his pocket and hurries downstairs. The air in the yard is freezing, but he doesn't care. The enclosure he built is made from chicken wire and driftwood, the frame rattling as he pulls open the door of the first compartment. Birds caw loudly as he drops food into their bowls, a juvenile puffin pecking at his hand.

'Don't be afraid,' he whispers. 'I won't hurt you.'

An Atlantic gull lets him stroke its wing, his touch slow and cautious. The bird's broken leg is mending and the starving kittiwake will soon be strong enough to release. Jimmy shuts the door of the enclosure, in case one of the injured birds tries to escape before it's healed. He kneels on the mud to watch his friends settling down to sleep on piles of clean straw. The gull's black eyes assess him without judgement, settling Jimmy's nerves for the first time since he fled from Burnt Island. He concentrates on the birds' quiet movements until the corpse's ruined face slips from his mind.

3

Saturday 6 November

I catch a few hours of sleep on the rocky ground, metres away from the corpse, the cold breeze waking me at 5 a.m. My bones ache as I rise to my feet. The sea has become an expanse of silver, ridden by an armada of choppy waves. It feels like I'm standing at the edge of the known world, with nothing except Bishop's Rock lighthouse to interrupt the Atlantic before it laps America's shores. The huge bonfire on Covean Beach is still smouldering, even though the last revellers went home hours ago. The straw effigies have left no trace behind and the tide has receded at last, leaving me free to escape Burnt Island on foot until the next high tide arrives tonight.

When I turn to assess the murder scene again, the sight is worse by daylight. The victim appears to be offering me a broad grin, facial tissue burned away, exposing rows of pure white teeth. The scale of the

22

body makes me assume that it's a man. I can't guess whether he was frog-marched up the hill or came here voluntarily. A sheepskin coat covers his remains from the neck down, burned through in places where fire has scorched it. Two paraffin cans lie beside the pyre, abandoned in a hurry as if the killer feared being caught in the act. The victim's left hand protrudes from under its sheepskin covering. His fingers look like blackened twigs, but it's a relief to see a metal band glinting in the early light: the man's wedding ring could help with identification.

The morning light reveals that shallow marks have been made on a boulder close to where the victim lies. Each capital letter is an inch tall, etched by a knife or chisel, the sentence written in a foreign language. It's possible that some kid was experimenting with a secret code, months or even years ago, but I take a photo of the granite surface just in case, then drop my phone back into my pocket.

When Eddie finally toils up the hill, he's followed by DCI Alan Madron. My boss is a small man with formal manners, always immaculately dressed. Today his boots are polished to a mirror shine, his mackintosh neatly buttoned, the parting in his salt-and-pepper hair so straight it looks like it's been precision-engineered. Eddie looks stricken when he sees the victim, but Madron barely reacts. The DCI's grey eyes scrutinise me with cool detachment.

'I hear you guarded the body all night, Kitto.

Admirable commitment, but you should have requested backup.'

'Evidence would have been destroyed, sir. I'd have needed a boat back to St Agnes and birds could have disturbed the scene if it was left unprotected.'

Madron surveys the victim's remains with distaste. 'The press mustn't get wind of this. Don't announce anything until the pathologist gives his verdict. What do we know about the victim?'

'No one's been reported missing. The body could have been left here by a passing boat, but it's unlikely. I've rung the harbourmaster on St Mary's for a list of vessels on local waters and he's seen nothing unusual. The only identifier we've got right now is the wedding ring.'

'We can't touch it until forensics arrive.' The DCI releases a loud sigh. 'Breakfast's waiting for you at the pub, Kitto. Go and warm up then collect our visitors from the quay. Have you met Liz Gannick before?'

'Not yet.'

'She's an ex-cop, easily riled. Last time I saw her she was in a wheelchair. Make sure you treat her with kid gloves.'

Madron's clipped tone irritates me, but I follow his instructions. The DCI is close to retirement, with little experience of murder investigations, yet loves to draw rank. Our working relationship has remained tense ever since I joined his team earlier this year, my position only recently made permanent. My teeth are still grinding as I walk back to Higher Town. The night's vigil has left me hungry to know the victim's identity, yet my boss has dismissed me from the scene like a naughty schoolboy. There's no one in sight as I walk through the village, only the pristine white lighthouse looming overhead. The place still looks like a rural idyll, an unlikely setting for such a vicious murder.

The back door of the Turk's Head is ajar when I arrive. Ella Tregarron doesn't notice me at first, the landlady keeping her back turned as she labours over the stove in the pub's large kitchen. A cascade of black hair ripples down her back as she pours oil into a frying pan, and the smell of toast wafts on the air. When I clear my throat to catch her attention she spins round in a hurry.

Ella is in her early forties, with a slim build and striking features. Her high cheekbones, pale green eyes and bee-stung mouth look good from a distance, but up close her skin is dull with tiredness. She was a stunner in her youth and her air of mystery remains, but now she carries an aura of quiet disappointment, as if life has failed to match her dreams. I fancied her madly as a boy, but there's no reason why she'd have noticed, when every man on the islands must have felt the same. Ella doesn't fit the stereotype for a pub landlady, her manner contained rather than outgoing.

'Come in, Ben. You must be hungry.' Her voice has such a thick Cornish accent it sounds like she's never travelled past county limits.

'You're a lifesaver, I'm starving.'

'Cold, too, I'm guessing, after your night outside.'

She gestures for me to sit at the steel-topped table, loading my plate with more fried eggs and toast than two men could consume. Ella remains silent as she pours coffee into a pair of white mugs, then sits down opposite, her gaze lingering on my face. She's so watchful that I feel certain her husband must have told her what happened.

'What did Steve say when he got back from Burnt Island?'

'Nothing, he just bolted upstairs. I couldn't get a word out of him.'

'Is he okay now?'

'He's been ill, so I made him a hot toddy then helped him into bed,' she replies, setting down her mug. 'Steve doesn't scare easily. Something bad must have happened up on that hill.'

'We'll make an announcement later today.'

Her eyes widen. 'Someone's been killed, haven't they? It's written all over your face.'

'You'll hear soon enough, Ella, I promise.'

'All the villagers from Middle Town were at the party.' She shakes her head in disbelief. 'It can't be a local.'

Ella looks unsettled so I keep the talk general, and she seems calmer by the time I thank her and say goodbye. She waves away my offer of payment, as if a free breakfast is a just reward for trying to keep the island safe.

The hot food and shot of caffeine help me to think more clearly as I follow the path along the beach to Porth Conger Quay. Whoever killed the victim must have spent time and effort preparing for the murder. They gathered piles of driftwood and hauled paraffin up the hill before it took place. I'd like to know whether the killer chose Burnt Island to set the victim alight as his idea of a joke, or as a symbolic location. My walk takes me past Helston Farm, where green shoots are defying the wintry conditions in the nearest field. The rest of the land seems to be lying fallow, but appearances are deceiving. A legion of bulbs is hidden below the surface, waiting to bloom next spring when the island's famous daffodils will be shipped all over the world. The ground seems unlikely to blossom with colour today; all I can see are acres of tilled loam, raked smooth to keep weeds at bay.

The police launch is nowhere in sight when I reach Porth Conger Quay, but the delay doesn't surprise me. They were a fact of life during my childhood, with ferry crossings cancelled frequently due to unpredictable weather. I'm still standing on the jetty when the vessel finally appears, looking worse for wear, blue and yellow flashing peeling from its sides. I'm expecting Dr Gannick to be a grim-faced battleaxe, but there's no sign of a female passenger or a wheelchair when the speedboat approaches the quay.

Sergeant Lawrie Deane is skippering the launch, a middle-aged officer with cheeks glowing from the hard breeze, ginger hair combed back from a face that generous observers would describe as plain. He's a trusted member of DCI Madron's team and was furious not to win the job as his deputy, but his resentment towards me appears to be fading at last. Dr Keillor is seated beside him, the pathologist's expression sombre as he gives me a nod of acknowledgement, his eyes shielded by thick spectacles.

Once the boat moors I spot a small figure hiding in the bow, clad in a black leather jacket, skinny jeans and red wellingtons. Liz Gannick is tapping out a message on her phone, oblivious to my stare. I can't imagine her in white overalls crawling over crime scenes, but she must be outstanding in her field to win the job of running the county's forensics service. Her appearance is elfin, with short hair dyed platinum, a few longer wisps falling across her brow. Gannick has the physique of a twelve-year-old child, but fine lines around her eyes suggest that she's in her early forties. Her pale brown stare is penetrating enough to measure my flaws in a couple of blinks. She offers a rapid handshake, but remains in her seat as I thank her for making the journey.

'Rough seas don't bother me, Inspector. I know the islands well.' Her tone sounds even more brusque than it did on the phone, her northern accent broader than before. 'Help me out of here, can you?'

I could lift her onto the jetty in moments, but the woman's spiky manner indicates that she prefers independence. She uses crutches to lever herself out of the vessel, only grasping my hand for a second as her matchstick-thin legs land on solid ground. She looks annoyed to catch me observing the manoeuvre.

'It's rude to stare, DI Kitto. Didn't anyone teach you?' She makes the statement in a breezy tone, but it's clear I'm being tested.

'I was told you'd need a wheelchair. We'll be crossing some rough terrain. Is that okay?'

'I'm fine on foot.'

'Good to hear. Shall we get moving?'

'Let me give you some advice first.'

'Go ahead.'

'Treat me like a fully functional human being. If we're working together, it'll make life easier for us both.'

'Sorry, I didn't mean to insult you.'

Now she can see me squirming there's a glint of amusement in her eyes. 'Believe me, I've had worse. There are overshoes and Tyvek suits in that box. I'll grab my kit, then you can give me the details along the way.'

Dr Keillor waits in silence as Gannick gathers her equipment, his expression world-weary, as if examining corpses is a waste of valuable leisure time. He walks ahead with Deane while I accompany the forensics officer. The pair of us must make an odd spectacle: a lumbering giant carting a case full of equipment for a minute woman wielding her crutches at a rapid pace. The scientist's questions are laser-sharp; she absorbs my answers in silence, storing away facts to analyse later.

When we reach Burnt Island, Gannick makes no complaint about the steep climb. Dr Keillor marches ahead while she navigates between boulders with deft agility. By the time we reach the top, I'm embarrassed to have doubted her strength. The chief of forensic services isn't even out of breath when she greets DCI Madron and Eddie, who are still guarding the body. My boss offers her and Dr Keillor a formal welcome; he's a stickler for protocol, and their seniority has put him on his best behaviour. Gannick ignores the DCI's old-fashioned courtesy, remaining in the background while Keillor approaches the murder scene, but I can tell she's itching to get started.

The pathologist focuses on the victim's face when he lowers himself to a crouching position. 'Someone's made a mess of you, haven't they, my friend?' he mutters under his breath.

Keillor draws on sterile gloves, then peels back the sheepskin carefully. Eddie is swaying on his feet, eyes glassy as he observes the corpse, but at least he remains upright. Fire has melted the victim's flesh, arms fused to his torso where fragments of bone are visible, shreds of blackened muscle still clinging to the legs and ribcage. Dr Keillor is too busy studying the remains to pass comment. Silence thickens around us and I'm about to request his verdict when he turns to face me.

'The victim was male with an average build. It's too soon to tell his age.' He leans forward to study the skull more closely. 'There's a fracture in his parietal bone, but the blow could have been inflicted posthumously.'

'Can you give us any more details?' Madron asks.

'I'll need to do a full post-mortem first. His arms and legs must have been bound or else the heat would have forced the muscles to flex at right angles. The lab will have to analyse the embers to explain how the fire started, but you'd need petrol-based firelighters as well as paraffin and solid fuel to create such intense heat. It would have taken a minimum of three hours to destroy so much tissue. The coat was thrown over the body after the event. If everything goes to plan, I'll do the post-mortem this afternoon and will take X-rays for a dental records match.' He turns to face Liz Gannick. 'I'm afraid you'll struggle to find the killer's DNA; we've had rainfall since the man died.'

'I can work miracles, Dr Keillor, didn't you know?' The forensics officer's grin is a direct challenge to anyone who questions her ability. 'Put a sterile tent over the body immediately, please. I'll get started before my colleagues arrive.'

'Thanks for coming all this way, Dr Gannick,' Madron offers. 'You've had a long journey.'

'No problem, Chief Inspector. I've got relatives on St Mary's; this gives me a chance to visit them.'

The DCI and Lawrie Deane escort Keillor back downhill to the waiting boat, leaving me and Eddie to find the white polythene tent in Gannick's box of equipment. My deputy's expression stays blank as he studies the remains again, as if he can't believe that a murder has been committed half a mile from his flat in Lower Town. Once the canopy is securely in place, I use sterile gloves to ease the victim's wedding ring from his blackened hand then drop it into an evidence bag. The design is unusual – white gold, etched with stars and crescent moons.

'Take a picture, Eddie, then see if Marie can identify it.' His older sister works as a goldsmith in the only jeweller's shop on the islands.

The young sergeant looks relieved to be given a specific task. His fingers are white when he grips his phone, as if he's clutching a lifeline. I call some of the islanders while he's busy speaking to his sister, asking them to spread the word that there will be a public meeting in the old lifeboat house at two o'clock. Liz Gannick is on her hands and knees beside the corpse, running a UV light across the ground, its blue beam tracing every rock and pebble. When I ask what she's expecting to find she offers a look of barely controlled irritation.

'Blood spatter, obviously. Contrary to popular opinion, rain doesn't destroy all trace evidence. The torch picks up microscopic splashes, and blood's thicker than water, as they say. It often clings to the undersides of stones.'

I let her continue in peace, noticing that Eddie's face is sober when he finishes his call.

'Alex Rogan commissioned that ring last summer,

with a matching one for his wife. But someone could have stolen it off him, couldn't they?'

'Possible, but unlikely, I'm afraid.'

My thoughts race while I gaze down at the ring, amazed that it survived the flames intact. Professor Alex Rogan was in his late thirties; he'd moved to St Agnes two years ago to marry an old school friend of mine, who now owns the island's shop. The man wore his intellect so lightly I had no idea he was a well-known astronomer until I saw him on TV making a guest appearance on a science programme. When I spent a few evenings in the pub with him and Sally, he came over as a gentle, mild-mannered academic, happy in his relationship, with a wry sense of humour.

Now that he's been reduced to the disfigured skeleton at my feet, a wave of anger is swilling around in my gut. Alex Rogan was newly married, and well-liked here. Why would someone set out to kill him?

4

Forensics specialists bear no resemblance to ordinary human beings. The two scenes of crime officers who help Liz Gannick prepare the victim's remains for transfer to St Mary's Hospital seem fascinated by the corpse's injuries, while I'm more interested in why Alex Rogan met such a terrible death, but I still need to confirm his identity. It bothers me that no one has reported him missing. My thoughts drift as the men in sterile white suits toil over the body, following Gannick's instructions to the letter. One is a portly fifty-something, speaking in monosyllables as he wields his trowel. The other is younger, with a trainspotter's haircut and a gap-toothed smile. He carries a huge camera, stopping to take pictures from every angle. They are working at such a slow pace that I have time to study the letters scratched into the stone beside the murder scene:

AN TIR SANS MA YW DHYN NO AGAN HONAN, GWITHYS GANS MOR HAG EBRON. YNHERDHYORYON OMMA A VEROW YN SERTAN.

I recognise a few Cornish words, so I type the message into a translation website and the result convinces me that it's from the killer:

This sacred land is ours alone, protected by the sea and sky. Intruders here are bound to die.

Eddie says nothing when I show him the translation, his reply a low whistle of disbelief. The killer planned the murder with a cool head – scratching letters into the rock so neatly would have taken hours. Whoever killed Rogan is showing us their deep roots in local soil, and familiarity with a language that was declared extinct ten years ago. Only around 600 people still speak it fluently; Cornish survives now in local place names, although a minority of schools and societies are trying to revive it. The message is surprising too: St Agnes welcomes visitors all summer long, and conflict between islanders and tourists is rare, but someone must be concealing a hatred of incomers.

It takes two hours for the remains to be dug from the ashes and placed in a body bag. The younger SOCO appears ecstatic to discover something inside the pocket of the sheepskin coat. He lays a ruined pair of binoculars on an evidence bag for yet another photo, while I study the fractured lenses and melted plastic. It's not yet clear why an apparently organised killer would leave an obvious clue to their identity at the scene. The younger man gives us a jovial wave as he disappears back down the hill, as though discovering the grim remains has been the highlight of his year.

'Freaks,' Eddie mutters as the SOCOs disappear.

'I couldn't agree more.'

Gannick is too far away to hear, busy scraping soil samples into an evidence bag before levering herself upright with one of her crutches in a single deft move. My respect for the forensics chief has risen through-out the morning; her appetite for work appears to be limitless.

'Over here, Inspector,' she calls out. She's standing near two slabs of granite that tilt together, forming a natural shelter. 'There are blood traces running back to the bonfire. Your victim lay between these rocks. If the blood's his, a superficial wound must have shed droplets as he was dragged along; there's a bigger patch at the base.'

Gannick switches on her light beam again and a fifteen-centimetre-wide smear of blood becomes visible a foot above ground level.

'How did it get there?'

'He probably tried to free his hands by scraping them across the rock.'

I step back to observe the slabs again. They're tall enough to conceal a man's body from local walkers who might venture up the hill on a cold winter's day. 'The poor sod must have been terrified.'

'His state of mind isn't my concern, I just want to know how he died. I'll have the blood samples sent to the lab today. I'm taking leave on St Mary's for a few days; let's talk again when they email the results.' Her pale brown gaze assesses me for an uncomfortably long time. 'Feel free to consult me, Inspector. Once a case starts, I like to get a result.'

'That's good to know.'

I consider offering to escort her back to the quay, but settle for thanking her instead. I'm curious to know why she switched from a police career to forensics, but it's the wrong time for personal questions. Gannick gives a formal smile before setting off, feet barely touching the ground as she descends the hill with the grace of a downhill skier. Once she's gone, I'm left to reflect on the victim's horrible death. He may have been alone for hours, struggling to free himself, before facing the worst end imaginable. Whoever killed him is still on the island, relaxed and fancy free.

My deputy is studying a list of names from the latest electoral role. Seventy-nine people live on St Agnes permanently, with three more on Gugh's tiny settlement. But just over twenty islanders are working on the mainland until the tourist season starts, leaving sixty potential suspects. None of them have ever committed a serious crime, making them unlikely culprits for a cold-blooded murder. We need to visit Sally Rogan urgently. I want to rule out the possibility that another man was set alight with her husband's wedding ring on his finger.

Eddie follows in silence as we walk towards Middle Town. Our ten-minute journey takes us past muddy fields and a herd of goats nibbling winter sorrel. I can see Troy Town Maze in the distance as we reach the hamlet. The landmark is one of the island's biggest mysteries, a scattering of white stones lying in a ragged circle. Some say that early settlers made it, while others claim that a lighthouse keeper built the maze to stave off boredom. I used to love hurling myself from one boulder to the next as a kid, never stopping to question who created the giant spiral of stepping stones. I'd like to walk around the circle and gather my thoughts before talking to Sally, but there's no delaying the inevitable. People of the same age are tightly connected on the Scillies: we're all graduates of Five Islands School on St Mary's, which can be a blessing and a curse. You're never short of friends at the pub, but there's nowhere to hide when tragedy strikes.

Sally's workplace stands in the middle of the settlement. The shop has been in operation for over a hundred years, doubling as a post office. It's a small one-storey building, constructed from local stone, with an apex roof and steps rising to its front door. There's no sign of her as we approach, but my old school friend's improvements are obvious: the window frames are freshly painted, winter flowers are flourishing in a tub by the door. The interior has been painted duck-egg blue, floorboards glossy with new varnish, and the shelves are loaded with hundreds of different items, from packets of soap to a fridge packed with local butter and cheese. Several minutes pass before Sally emerges from her stockroom to stand behind the counter.

My memory spins back to our days at primary school. Sally was a tomboy back then, agile enough to beat most of us boys at football. Later she became Zoe's closest friend when they sang in a band together. By sixteen she was a wild child with a fiery temper and black make-up caked around her eyes. She hated every subject at school, but could play bass guitar with the best of them, despite her dad's attempts to keep her on the straight and narrow. Sally has turned that restless energy into a selling point in recent years. In addition to buying the shop, she's started another business, offering walking tours of the islands. Today she looks more girl-next-door than rock chick, her sandy hair cut into a practical crop. Her attractive face breaks into a smile until she sees Shadow scratching at the door, prompting her to scowl at me in mock disapproval.

'Shadow's smarter than you, Ben. Don't leave him outside.'

It's only when she steps out from behind the counter to stroke him that the penny drops: Sally is expecting a baby, her jumper taut over the dome of her stomach.

We met for a drink at the Rock on Bryher three months ago but she never said a word; the news must have been too recent to share.

'Come and sit down, I'll put the kettle on.' Her smile is burning too brightly, as if she's unaware that two policemen on her doorstep might signal bad news. 'You're not arresting me are you?'

'Not today. Is Alex at home, Sally?'

'He's in London seeing a TV producer, leaving me stranded like a beached whale.'

'When did he leave?

'Thursday morning. His phone must be on the blink, but he's due back tonight.'

'Can you put the closed sign on the door for a minute?'

Sally glances from Eddie's face to mine, as if we're playing an elaborate joke, but she does as I ask. We wait for her in her small stockroom, surrounded by boxes full of tins and packets of coffee until she returns.

'I want you to ring Alex's hotel to check he's okay.'

I stand at her side while she makes the call, her relaxed manner starting to fray.

'The receptionist's been calling his mobile; he never checked in.' Her hand settles on my arm. 'Where is he, Ben?'

'I'm afraid it's bad news. Do you want your dad here while we talk?'

'Are you kidding? I haven't seen him since our wedding. What's wrong? You're scaring the shit out of me.'

I explain that a man's body has been found, which still needs to be identified, but she doesn't let me finish. Her hands flail in the air before landing on my chest. Curses pour from her mouth as she lashes out, as if it's my fault her husband won't be coming home. Her fingernails tear my skin before I can catch hold of her arms. She collapses back onto a chair, while Eddie calls round for local support. Sally's father, Keith Pendennis, is her only relative on the island, but since they've fallen out, Eddie asks one of the island's elders to come to the shop. Sally's cries are so raw, the keening sound is only one notch below a scream. I keep my arm round her shoulders as she weeps. Eddie and I offer to walk her home, but she's too distressed to cover the short distance to the end of the village.

Louise Walbert appears minutes after she's summoned, and I step outside to give her the news. Her wavy grey hair is caught in a ponytail, revealing a round face that looks like it was designed to smile. She's dressed in her usual eccentric style: a scarlet sweater with clashing green trousers and huge earrings that glitter with rhinestones. Despite her bohemian clothes, Louise balances her part-time job as a solicitor on St Mary's with helping her husband Mike to run their farm. She listens in silence to the information about Alex Rogan, her expression stricken, but it's clear we picked the right person to comfort Sally. My friend falls into the older woman's arms immediately, weeping on her shoulder. I'd like to get her home where she'll be more comfortable, but Louise shakes her head.

'We can't rush her, Ben. I'll take her back when she's ready.'

'I'll phone you later.'

Eddie's expression is sober when we finally leave. Sally Rogan was too upset to provide details; all we've learned is that her husband left home forty-eight hours ago to catch the early ferry to St Mary's, carrying only an overnight bag and the kit needed for his short trip. I'm willing to bet that his mobile phone and laptop were incinerated with his body. Eddie's head bows lower when I explain that we must speak to Sally's father next. Keith Pendennis is well-known around the islands, with most people giving him a wide berth. I haven't seen him since his wife's funeral a few years ago, but it seems odd that he's managing to avoid his daughter on such a minute island. The man must go to St Mary's to buy food and plan his outings with military precision, to prevent accidental meetings.

The walk to Pendennis's house takes us through the heart of the island. There's still hardly any breeze, but clouds are massing on the horizon as if the calm conditions are just a temporary reprieve. The landscape is organised into small, orderly fields as we approach Higher Town, with a few sheep observing us over drystone walls until they catch sight of Shadow and skitter away. We walk down to the sandbar that connects the islet of Gugh to St Agnes. It's a larger, greener version of Burnt Island, with half a dozen houses and barns, and a sprinkling of ancient graves and cairns. Gugh is a popular destination for tourists each summer because of its pretty, secluded beaches and its air of secrecy, but you'd need to enjoy your own company to pick the islet as your home. It has only three permanent residents, whose homes are cut off from the main island for hours every day.

Eddie maintains his silence as we cross the narrow causeway, as if he dreads informing the island's toughest inhabitant that his son-in-law has been killed. Only Shadow seems to be enjoying the trip. The dog splashes through the shallows then chases back to join us with a stick between his teeth, begging for a new game.

Keith Pendennis's house is the first dwelling in sight as we step onto Gugh's rocky beach. The building looks uncompromising: a two-storey grey edifice with black window frames and a tarnished steel letter box. There's no sign of the owner when I ring the bell.

'Let's try the back entrance,' I tell Eddie.

Shadow traipses after us at a slow pace when we skirt round the side of the house, only growing lively again when Pendennis's Jack Russell trots out to greet him, the two dogs racing away to explore new territory.

The kitchen is empty when we look through the window, but the door to a small outbuilding hangs open. A rhythmic thudding sound emerges, but no human voices. The outbuilding has been converted into a gym, with free weights and a bench press. The door is open and Sally's father has his back to us, dressed in a vest and tracksuit bottoms, a line of sweat marking his backbone. Leather bindings are strapped across his knuckles while he beats a punchbag that's suspended from the ceiling with steady, rhythmic blows, heavy enough to break an opponent's jaw. He may have aged, but his golden career as a middleweight boxer shows in every movement.

The sight of his brutal workout triggers uncomfortable memories. Keith Pendennis still runs the gym on St Mary's, where I attended his boxing club as a kid until I grew tired of his bullying style of coaching and my interests switched to rugby. I can still remember his disdain when I swapped solitary combat for a team sport that I loved.

Pendennis only notices our presence when he stops to adjust the strapping on his hands. He's average height, but his build is pure muscle, his hatchet-jawed face as lean as his body even though he's in his late fifties. I'm almost a foot taller and twenty years younger, but I'd still hate to receive the full power of his left hook. His bald head is slick with sweat when his dark blue eyes fix on us, then he lets out a bellowing laugh.

'Why are you two skulking there? Are you rating my form, lads?'

'You look fit as a fiddle,' I reply.

The man shrugs. 'I have to keep in shape; it's my livelihood.'

'Can we talk, please, Keith? It's best if we go indoors.'

Pendennis's slow response shows his reluctance to

take instructions from a former pupil. His walk is a rolling swagger as he leads us back to the house. His kitchen has transformed since Zoe and I hung out with Sally here in our teens: all signs of his wife's softness have been stripped away, leaving only black floor tiles, clinical white paint and units that gleam with cleanliness. I'm guessing that the man's reaction to Jeannie's death has been to redecorate his home with ruthless efficiency. He dumps mugs of coffee in front of me and Eddie without asking how we take it, but he looks ill at ease. The sweat on his arms must be turning cold when he finally lowers himself onto the stool opposite.

'You need more boxing lessons, Ben. Someone gave you a pasting, didn't they?' He nods at the scratches his daughter left on my neck.

'It's nothing. We just want a short conversation.'

'Pity,' he replies, shaking his head. 'You'd be a heavyweight contender by now if you'd stuck at it.'

'I never had your speed.' I take a breath before continuing. 'I'm afraid it's bad news about your son-in-law.'

His eyes blink rapidly. 'Sally's husband?'

'He was murdered by an islander yesterday, or the night before.'

A look of outrage crosses his face. 'Why wasn't I told?'

'We only found him last night.'

'What sick fucking bastard would do that?' His voice is hoarse with disbelief, hands fisting at his sides.

'We'll find out, but Sally's struggling. She needs your support.'

He springs to his feet then dumps his mug in the sink. 'I'm the last person she'd want around.'

'She's six months pregnant and you're her only family, Keith. We can walk you there now if you like.'

'Don't give me orders.' Pendennis spins round suddenly, a muscle ticking in his jaw. 'You're a mate of hers; you bloody take care of her.'

My memory dials back twenty years to the way he harangued smaller, weaker boys for making slow progress in the ring. Pendennis may have hated his son-in-law for reasons unknown. It's possible that he disapproved of Sally marrying an outsider, even though he dragged himself along to her wedding. I'd like to ask more questions, but the fitness trainer's lips are set in a hard line. I tell him about the meeting we're planning in the lifeboat house this afternoon, then say goodbye.

Eddie looks shaken once we get outside. 'I wouldn't fancy being stuck in a lift with him right now. He's like a bomb waiting to go off.'

'Do you know why he and Sally rowed? She never said they'd fallen out.'

'I'll ask around, boss.'

My friend ignored her dad's advice often when we were growing up; two strong personalities under one roof led to regular clashes, but she rarely criticised him. Pendennis has spent a lifetime honing his body and his reputation as the island's hard man, but that doesn't make him a killer, unless I can find proof.

5

DCI Madron is waiting for us outside the old lifeboat house, wearing a look of distaste. The building stands above the shore at Bergecooth Bay, its slipway running down to the shingle below, while the rocky outline of Burnt Island looms on the horizon. It's a simple clapperboard barn with the letters RNLI fading on the sign above its entrance. It's stood empty since the island's lifeboat service ended ten years ago, making way for a centralised fleet on St Mary's. The wooden doors that once fell open whenever the rescue boat emerged are starting to splinter.

The DCI seems unmoved by our return from informing Rogan's widow of his death; his sole focus is on police protocol. 'This accommodation's not fit for purpose, Kitto. You can't use it as an incident room.'

'There are no other public spaces on St Agnes, sir.'

'It could damage our professional reputation. I suggest you look again.'

Madron sucks in a long breath as I open the fire

door, his disapproval silenced by the echo of our footsteps. The hangar is empty, apart from the lifeboat's wheel tracks still marking the concrete floor and a row of orange life jackets hanging from the wall. The air feels as cold as the temperature outside, but the room upstairs is more inviting: the observation deck is still intact, with a telescope on a metal plinth, a table and folding chairs stacked in a pile. A panoramic window runs from wall to wall, giving uninterrupted views of the ocean. The grin on Eddie's face is easy to interpret: the space would make an ideal bachelor pad, and it should provide us with a calm environment to solve a case that's crying out for a quick result.

'I thought Naomi Vine wanted this place for an art gallery?' says Madron.

'The islanders aren't keen, sir. They're fighting her application to put her sculptures on the beach, too,' Eddie replies. 'The boathouse would make a great village hall.'

'It would take a fortune to make this place habitable.' The DCI's expression remains thunderous. 'What do you know about Professor Rogan, Eddie? You've lived here six months, you must have the inside track on the community.'

The young sergeant's face sobers. 'Rogan spent holidays here as a kid and fell in love with the place. He was looking for a site to build an observatory for schoolkids and locals to use. He'd persuaded the Science Council to put up half the money and wanted to raise more from his Dark Skies Festival at the end of July. Alex said the Scillies would be one of the best places to see the lunar eclipse. He met Sally when he came down here looking for sponsors and ended up marrying her last summer.'

'What's the festival about?' the DCI asks.

'It's a get-together for stargazers. Apparently there's hardly any light pollution here.'

'That's all well and good, but it doesn't explain Rogan's murder,' Madron replies.

I pull my phone from my pocket to show him the killer's message. 'This was scratched into the rock where Rogan was found.'

My boss stares at the image. 'It's written in Cornish, isn't it? What does it say?'

'He's warning outsiders to keep away. He's claiming that St Agnes is sacred land.'

'Find out who's been criticising incomers.' The man's tension shows in the set of his shoulders. 'I want a word with you in private before I leave, Kitto.'

The DCI's grey stare is colder than the ocean outside when we return downstairs. 'Remember that your conduct as Senior Investigating Officer is under intense scrutiny. The press will spread rubbish all over the tabloids if you put a foot wrong. They'll ask why an eminent astronomer met such a violent death on a small island and we won't get a minute's peace. I expect the highest professional standards from you, Kitto.'

'Have I let you down before?'

'There's always a first time. Sally Rogan's a personal friend of yours, isn't she?'

'A schoolmate; there's no conflict of interest.'

He narrows his eyes. 'It's fortunate that Eddie lives here, but I want you on St Agnes at all times, until the killer's found. That message sounds like the start of a campaign. Go home, pack a bag, then get back here immediately.'

'I was planning to stay till I get a result. There's plenty of room at the pub.'

'Don't allow anyone to visit or leave St Agnes. I'll contact Rogan's parents on the mainland and keep them away until we've got answers.' His gaze lands on my ancient donkey jacket. 'How many times do I have to tell you to smarten up? Get a decent coat and a haircut before the press briefing.'

'Is that all, sir? I need to prepare my talk for the islanders.'

'Liz Gannick knows the Chief Commissioner. He's asked her for a partnership report on the island force. If she writes one negative word, it'll be a disciplinary matter. Make sure you stay in her good books.'

The DCI marches away before I can reply. The man's lack of faith in my ability annoys the hell out of me, but at least he's left me to my own devices. He used to insist on attending every public meeting to monitor my behaviour, so his level of trust must be rising, even though my wardrobe is still failing to impress.

When I get back upstairs Eddie is putting the room

in order. He's busy sweeping dust from the wooden floor, but it feels like the lifeboat crew could return at any minute to reclaim the nautical maps and tide tables covering the walls. Eddie's diligent approach usually makes me smile, but today I have to suppress my irritation. My deputy is performing cleaning duties, and my boss is fretting about his professional reputation, even though a man has died in the worst circumstances imaginable.

Forty islanders gather for the two o'clock meeting. I scan their faces in turn, aware that any one of them could be Alex Rogan's murderer, but their expressions are unreadable. The people of St Agnes have a reputation for toughness. Local families rely on one another when the summer tourists leave and harsh winds race in from the Atlantic. The island is too distant from St Mary's for easy crossings during winter, so the population are forced to be self-sufficient. They are less dependent on tourism than the other islands, with only one pub and a scattering of holiday homes; many of the permanent residents still survive on fishing, farming or growing flowers. Others have become entrepreneurs, selling everything from locally made chocolate to hand-knitted sweaters through shops on the mainland.

The people milling around on the slipway look like nothing could faze them, but their reactions to Rogan's death will be interesting to observe. They can handle life's adversities, but a cold-blooded murder is bound to test their defences. Eddie has laid out some chairs in the hangar downstairs, yet most of the crowd choose to stand, their faces wary as the meeting begins. Keith Pendennis is by himself, arms tightly folded across his chest. The coach has smartened himself up since we spoke, dressed in a heavy winter coat, dark jeans and boots, but his truculent expression remains. He still looks ready to deck anyone who dares to meet his eye.

Ella Tregarron is smiling at me from the front of the crowd. She's wearing a coat with a fur collar, her lips painted a vivid crimson like a fading Hollywood starlet. Her husband appears to have survived his ordeal intact, but the couple's differences are stark by daylight. Steve is still dressed in his scruffy leather jacket, threadbare jeans and cowboy boots, while his wife is perfectly groomed. I notice the man's tight grip on her hand, as if she might slip from his grasp if his concentration lapses. When I scan the faces again, only Liam Poldean looks genuinely upset, his face white with strain as he shifts his weight from foot to foot.

The meeting has already begun when Eddie's fiancée Michelle sneaks in at the back of the room with their baby daughter Lottie slung across her chest. She's a pretty twenty-four-year-old with long, chocolate-brown hair, currently on maternity leave from her job as a nursery school assistant. The young woman's face lights up when she spots Eddie beside me, and gives him an encouraging wave. It crosses my mind that announcing a local murder would feel a hell of a lot easier if someone in the crowd was rooting for me with that kind of devotion, but I've been single for months. I should be used to solitude by now. Silence falls over the room once I rise to my feet.

'Thanks for coming everyone. Most of you know us already; I'm DI Ben Kitto and this is Sergeant Eddie Nickell. I'm sorry there's nowhere warmer for us to meet. You'll have heard by now that a man's body was found last night on Burnt Island. We can confirm that we're treating this as a murder, and that the victim, who we believe to be Alex Rogan, was killed in a fire.'

The crowd's shock hisses around the room like Chinese whispers.

'Alex left home to catch the seven a.m. ferry to St Mary's on Thursday morning, but it appears he never reached the quay. I'll be running the investigation and using this building for our headquarters. This is a murder inquiry – no one can leave St Agnes without my permission. I want all of you to keep your homes secure; lock your doors and windows, and don't spend time alone.'

I take my time passing on selected information, allowing it to register. The islanders' faces are impassive and people seem reluctant to speak. Even though I was born on Bryher and Eddie grew up on Tresco, they're treating us like aliens. Stan Eden is the first to break the silence. Eden is one of the oldest islanders – a former lighthouse keeper with a stout build and a thatch of white hair, his expression solemn. The rest of the crowd watch the old man rise to his feet like he's their best source of guidance.

'Alex was on Porth Killier beach a few nights back, setting up his telescope. I had no idea he was missing.'

'Neither did his wife. His killer wanted him found on bonfire night for reasons we don't yet understand.' I pause to scan the crowd. 'Please speak to me if you know anything about the attack. We'll be visiting every house on the island, and before you leave today please tell Eddie where you were on the fourth and fifth of November. None of you should talk to the press about Alex's death. Anyone who does will be arrested for obstructing a murder investigation.'

The meeting fragments after a few more questions. The islanders seem eager to escape, but their behaviour doesn't stem from rudeness. They have grown used to life with few outside interventions. I'll have to proceed with caution to stop them siding against us. We need all the cooperation we can get.

'One more thing,' I say as the meeting ends. 'We found a coat with binoculars in the pocket at the murder scene. Does anyone know who owns a worn-out sheepskin?'

'The Birdman,' Steve Tregarron calls out. 'Jimmy Curwen wears one all year round.'

The crowd releases another hiss of whispers, the man's guilt already decided.

'Keep watch for him, please. Jimmy may not be connected to the attack, but I want to speak to him.'

'The bloke's an oddball; no other islander would

commit murder.' A male voice reaches me from the back of the room. I can't tell who made the accusation, but plenty of heads nod in agreement. I need to know why they're so quick to assume Curwen's guilt.

'Leave the investigation to us. Trust me, we'll make arrests as soon as we have proof.'

The crowd departs in unison, leaving me and Eddie alone in the freezing boathouse packed to the rafters with unanswered questions. The Birdman has lived on St Agnes all his life; a dishevelled figure patrolling the shore after every high tide, but I know little about his history, except that he was cautioned two years ago for disturbing the peace.

I'm about to go back upstairs when one of the islanders returns to the doorway. Martin Tolman's appearance is distinguished; he's in his mid-forties, grey hair cropped close to his skull, his dark eyes set deep into their sockets. He looks like a character actor playing a particularly intense part, but Tolman is a local architect. I employed him to draw up some blueprints back in the summer when I was thinking of converting my loft; weight has dropped from him since then, exaggerating his sharp cheekbones. He barely manages a smile when I reach out to shake his hand.

'Good to see you, Martin. Were you at the meeting just now?'

He gives a distracted nod. 'I don't know if it's relevant, but Alex Rogan came to my house last Monday night. He was in a dreadful state when my wife opened the door.'

'What did he want?'

'Someone had put burning rags through the window of his study that evening. Luckily he put out the fire before it caused damage. He made me promise not to tell Sally. She was out when it happened.'

Tolman's story fits the circumstances precisely: the killer was so determined to end Rogan's life he tried to murder him on two separate occasions.

'Did Alex see who did it?'

He shakes his head. 'There was no one around when he went outside. The poor chap seemed mystified. Liam Poldean had called by earlier with his kids, but they'd had no other visitors.'

'Were you close friends with Rogan?'

'Acquaintances, really. He came to our church a few times for communion.' Tolman bites his lip. 'Sorry, Ben, I should have reported the incident straight away.'

'It's not your fault, thanks for letting me know. Can we have a longer chat soon?'

'Any time, you know where I am.'

The architect offers a quiet goodbye, his slim form barely casting a shadow when he slips out of the building, but he's the least of my concerns. I need to find out why a coat belonging to the island's most eccentric resident was used to shroud a body at a murder scene.

6

Jimmy hides behind the lifeboat house, peering through a crack in the fire door. He used to love this place when he was a boy. The building reeked of diesel, brine and the rubbery sweetness of oilskin. The crew used to let him peer through their telescope to watch puffins plummeting into the sea, hunting for mackerel, but there's no trace of those officers today. A tall, black-haired man stands where their boat lay, rubbing the back of his neck as if his muscles hurt. Jimmy recognises Ben Kitto and the younger man who waits at his side, his frame so much smaller that the pair look like father and son.

He tries to gather the courage to tell them what he witnessed on bonfire night, but the words turn to dust in his mouth. Jimmy presses his ear to the crack, struggling to follow the conversation. Individual words carry on the still air – suspect, victims, forensics – but their meanings confuse him. Soon the big detective walks closer, his voice reaching Jimmy more clearly.

'We need to find out why Curwen was at the scene, Eddie. No one's seen him since. He could be our killer.'

Jimmy reels backwards, almost stumbling from the ledge. He escapes through the bushes then chases the path back to Middle Town. No matter what happens, his birds need him; he can't neglect them.

When he gets home, the sun has already dropped from the sky. He regrets leaving his coat on Burnt Island because his jumper and thin trousers offer little protection from the cold. Once indoors, he tries to remember what he heard. The police think he's to blame. He must find out who killed the burning man or they'll put him in jail, and the creatures he's rescued will starve. He pulls on another jumper, stuffs his pockets with bundles of feathers from his collection, then packs food in a carrier bag before rushing downstairs.

A tern screams out a raucous welcome, but the gull eyes him calmly as Jimmy refills water dishes and tips seed into their trays.

'I'll find the answer,' he whispers. 'Then I'll come back.'

Jimmy wishes he could spend longer with his birds, but there's no time to waste. He runs until the village lies behind him, uncertain where to start his search. When he reaches the open fields he hides behind a thicket of gorse, his heart jittering with panic.

7

I leave Eddie making phone calls at 5 p.m., checking whether anyone witnessed Alex Rogan's last walk. Eddie's cheeks are flushed with excitement as he crosses names off our list of potential suspects, the field narrowing already, with more than half of the island's residents providing cast-iron alibis. I can see why he's enjoying himself. His duties normally involve travelling between the islands as the friendly face of law enforcement, in a place where few crimes ever happen. He has already visited Jimmy Curwen's flat, but found it empty. The grisly discovery on Burnt Island seems to have energised him, even though it's late afternoon and his fiancée and daughter want him at home.

Tiredness is catching up with me after last night's lack of sleep, but I need to find the Birdman before I attend the autopsy. The best place to get information is at the pub, which doubles as a community centre all year round. The winter dusk is thickening, and my eyes take a while to adjust when I leave the lifeboat house.

I'm following the track towards Middle Town when a torch beam crosses my face and a man's low voice greets me as he steps into my path. Mike Walbert is the owner of Lower Town Farm and was a friend of my father's. He acted as a coffin-bearer at Dad's funeral, a big, avuncular man of around sixty with a bluff manner and skin roughened by a lifetime outdoors. I can tell from the concern on his face that his wife Louise has told him about Sally's ordeal this morning.

'You must be freezing in that boathouse, Ben. Come in and get warm.' The farmer is dressed in a padded coat, a scarf swaddling his throat.

I'm short of time, but offending one of the island's elders could hinder the investigation. Walbert comes from a long-established island family, acting as St Agnes's mayor on several occasions and still heavily involved in local politics. Refusal isn't an option when he puts his hand on my shoulder and shepherds me towards his farmhouse.

Walbert's build is almost as hefty as mine, his walk lumbering. He keeps the talk general as we approach his home, telling me that he's been checking his flock of rare breed sheep, who have a habit of breaking through fences. An appetising aroma greets me when his front door opens, freshly baked bread wafting from the kitchen. The farmhouse bears the hallmarks of Louise's bohemian style – walls painted in vivid colours and adorned with flamboyant paintings of local scenes. I notice some framed newspaper stories from the *Gazette*, too, reporting projects the couple have spearheaded, like building a local playground. The Walberts are childless, allowing them to channel their spare energy into raising money for local causes. When Mike leads me into the dining room, his wife is hunched over a table that's littered with cogs and small pieces of metal.

'You look busy, Louise.'

She puts down her glasses, her eyes puffy with tears. 'I mend things when I'm upset, Ben. This old radio's keeping me busy.'

'It's her idea of relaxation,' Mike agrees. 'Last week she dismantled our washing machine, fitted a new pump, then had it working again in five minutes flat.'

Louise's technical skills don't surprise me because my mother was the same. Island life teaches everyone to make do and mend from an early age.

'How do you remember where everything goes?'

'It's child's play compared to your job right now.' She puts down her screwdriver. 'Ella Tregarron's looking after Sally, but I'll spend the night there, so the poor girl isn't alone.'

'Thanks for taking care of her. Is she up to answering questions?'

Louise shakes her head. 'I'd wait till she gets over the shock. Is there news about Alex?'

'Not yet, I'm afraid.'

'Come and sit by the fire.' Her smile revives when she rises to her feet. 'You must be starving.'

She returns with fruit cake and a pot of tea. Scillonian hospitality relies on good manners, so I thank her warmly, even though I've got no appetite and tea is my least favourite drink.

Mike watches me take my first sip, reminding me that he's keen to help. He offers to put heaters in the lifeboat house to warm the abandoned building. It's only when I look more closely that changes in the farmer's appearance register: he still appears robust, but his expression is bleak. He no longer seems like the confident spokesman who always champions the island's causes with brash good humour on the local news.

'Alex Rogan never hurt a soul,' he murmurs. 'Whoever ended his life must be unhinged. Most people are blaming the Birdman; they say he's the only islander capable of doing it.'

'What do you know about him?'

'Jimmy Curwen's a misfit. He's survived on handouts from neighbours since his mum died two years ago; the Tregarrons give him leftover food.' Walbert shrugs his shoulders. 'He can't hold a conversation with another human being, but chats away to his wounded birds happily enough.'

'Does he seem the violent type?'

'Not to me,' Louise chips in. 'Being alone in the world makes him unlucky, not evil.'

Her husband shakes his head. 'Why would he run off if he's innocent? No one can tell what he's thinking. He chased some lads for destroying a bird's nest years ago and almost got himself arrested. The bloke was screaming these weird noises. Women have kept their kids away from him ever since.'

'He lives by himself, doesn't he?'

'Jimmy's got a bedsit in the lighthouse keepers' cottages. Martin Tolman lets him use one of the flats for free.'

'That's generous of him.'

The farmer nods his head. 'Jimmy hasn't caused much trouble till now, but the bloke's a strange one. If you want help catching him, let me know.'

'Thanks for the offer, but we expect to find him soon,' I reply. 'It's possible that someone tried to torch Rogan's house before he was attacked. Can you think why?'

Louise looks bemused. 'He spent most of his time at Roseland Observatory in St Austell, or here with Sally. Why would that upset anyone?'

'It's too soon to tell. Did he have many close friends?'

'I saw him with Liam Poldean in the pub plenty of times. They hit it off from day one. The only person he clashed with was his father-in-law, but that's not rare. Keith Pendennis is tricky at the best of times.'

'What did they row about?'

'I saw them trading insults on the beach a few weeks back. It looked like it might get physical, but I didn't hear the gist of it.'

Keith Pendennis remains a potential suspect; he has failed to provide an alibi, saying only that he spent the day of his son-in-law's death alone at home on Gugh.

But his clash with Alex Rogan might have escalated to murderous violence.

'Nothing like this has happened before, has it? The place has been crime-free for years.'

'Apart from the fire this summer,' Mike says.

He's busy stirring sugar into his tea and Louise is staring at the polished table-top. They appear reluctant to criticise another islander, but all three of us remember their hay barn going up in smoke in August. The incident has troubled me ever since because the lad I arrested never explained his actions; he protested his innocence until the evidence grew overwhelming and his solicitor told him that pleading guilty would bring a lighter sentence. When Eddie searched the farm's workshop, he found the boy's toolkit packed with firelighters and boxes of matches.

'There's a difference between a teenage prank and cold-blooded murder. Adam Helston did his community service and he's caused no more problems, but he'll be interviewed like everyone else.' The boy struck me as troubled, not dangerous, but I still need to visit his family. The juvenile court left a suspended sentence hanging over him for the damage he caused.

'His dad's so embarrassed he can hardly meet my eye.' The farmer shifts uncomfortably in his seat, as if old grievances are weighing on him. I use the lull in our conversation as my opportunity to leave.

I thank Mike for his hospitality, remembering his certainty that the Birdman could be the killer.

Innocent or guilty, I need to find him fast. Experience has taught me that being different can cause suspicion. When I joined the Murder Squad in London my colleagues spent months mimicking my West Country accent; it took a year before I was allowed into their clan, but Jimmy Curwen hasn't been so lucky. It's clear that he's never been fully accepted by the community. His loneliness and resentment may have hardened into violence.

It's 6 p.m. by the time I continue my journey to Middle Town, trailing my torch beam over drystone walls. There are so few outdoor lights in the Scillies that night falls abruptly; torches are essential to avoid breaking your ankle tripping on a rabbit hole. The drama of nightfall is one of the things I missed most in London. The city sky faded to a dirty brown outside my flat in Hammersmith, with wreaths of smog choking the stars, but the difference between day and night is absolute here, particularly in winter. The sky is midnight blue already, the constellations gleaming.

I'm still questioning why Mike Walbert's confidence has been replaced by anxiety. Shock at Alex Rogan's death seems to have knocked even the strongest community members sideways. The islanders seem unwilling to accept that a vicious murder could occur in a place which has been law-abiding for decades, with the exception of a few petty crimes. I need to remain open-minded at this stage in the investigation. I'll keep a close eye on Keith Pendennis and Adam Helston, but Sally must provide more evidence before I start making assumptions.

I get back to Middle Town and head for the keepers' cottages. They stand in a neat, whitewashed terrace at the foot of the lighthouse, a single light glowing from an upstairs window. The back door of the end house is unlocked, so I climb the stairs. An odd smell taints the air, growing stronger outside the Birdman's flat. A hessian bag of straw almost blocks the entrance to the loft room, releasing a farmyard odour of dust and newly mown grass. I tap on the open door but there's no reply as I step inside.

The room is dominated by Jimmy's passion for the avian species: rows of fractured eggshells crowd the mantelpiece, and different types of feed are stored in tubs and boxes. A few threadbare clothes hang in Curwen's wardrobe. The closest thing to modernity is the Birdman's ancient radio, with no TV or computer in sight. I put through a call to Eddie to inform him that our chief suspect's flat remains empty. Jimmy's absence since the time of the murder places him under strong suspicion. A life of poverty, without any home comforts, may have spurred his violent tendencies, but doesn't explain why he would target a man like Alex Rogan. Further checks must wait until tomorrow. When I glance at my watch it's six thirty, and Dr Keillor will be waiting for me on St Mary's.

'Go home, Eddie,' I say over the phone. 'Curwen will

still be here tomorrow; he can't leave the island without being seen.'

My deputy sounds uneasy when he informs me that no one has provided any useful information about Alex Rogan's abduction. I've spent enough time here to know that the islands yield their secrets slowly, but the first forty-eight hours after a body is found are crucial. Sleeping beside the victim's charred remains has made the vigil personal, my old school friend's grief increasing my need to catch the killer. The case puts the other islanders in danger too. Whoever killed Rogan must be unbalanced; few people of sane mind could stand back and watch someone burn.

A noise stops me in my tracks as I cross the yard, the high squealing of an infant in distress, making me break into a run. It's coming from an enclosure attached to the wall by wooden plinths. But when I get closer, the cage houses a seagull lying on a nest of straw, and half a dozen more birds in separate compartments. One of them screams in terror, wings flapping wildly against the chicken wire, a white bandage encasing one of its claws. I crouch down to inspect Jimmy Curwen's bird hospital and notice that the food bowls are almost full. He must have come back here to feed them since going on the run, but his care for the wounded birds doesn't make him innocent. I still need to find out why the Birdman has disappeared straight after the island's only violent crime in recent history.

8

It's 8 p.m. by the time I sail the police launch into Hugh Town harbour. St Mary's is three times the size of St Agnes, with almost 2000 inhabitants; it seems like a metropolis by comparison, with a handful of vehicles driving through the narrow streets. The island's hospital is one of the smallest NHS facilities in England, and despite being purpose-built, the place looks like a handful of white portacabins thrown together beside a small car park. It contains three treatment rooms, an operating theatre for emergency procedures, and the mortuary where Dr Keillor is waiting for me. He looks unimpressed when I rush through the door. I've witnessed his autopsies before, and communication between us is improving, although he claims to prefer working alone.

The pathologist's suit looks like it was purchased from a gentlemen's outfitters several decades ago, thinning grey hair combed over his bald patch, tortoiseshell glasses reducing his eyes to pinpricks when he glances in my direction. He seems oblivious to the stink of formaldehyde and the fact that his only companion is a corpse waiting beneath a thin white sheet.

'You're late, Ben. My wife tells me it's my turn to cook; she doesn't appreciate being kept waiting.'

'Sorry, I had some loose ends to chase. Didn't you get my text?'

He gives a grim smile. 'The only reason you sent that polite little apology is to stop me whining to Madron.'

'Guilty as charged.' I hold up my hands as if he's pointing a loaded gun at my chest. 'Can I stay anyway?'

'If you keep quiet. Background noise ruins my concentration.'

'My lips are sealed.'

He stands beside the operating table. 'I sent X-rays to dental records and got a match an hour ago: the victim is definitely Alex Rogan.'

The pathologist's face is sober when he draws back the sheet, and the state of the corpse makes me glad not to have eaten recently, my empty stomach somersaulting against my ribs. The sight would trigger nightmares in most of the population; Rogan's body looks worse under the strip lights' glare, his features melted like candlewax, fragments of blackened wood still clinging to his limbs. Keillor's movements are delicate, as if he's treating a living patient. He murmurs a slow monologue for the benefit of the recorder that hangs from the ceiling, but occasional words and phrases reach me: necrosis, oedema, third-degree burns. I only understand half of his terms, but the facts are clear enough: someone set out to cause Alex Rogan an excruciating death.

When I look up again, Keillor is using a long-bladed knife to separate Rogan's ribs and remove the heart, lungs and spleen from the shell of his torso, forcing me to swallow hard to suppress my nausea. Behind the stench of chemicals I can smell the oily sweetness of burned flesh. Once the organs have been weighed and examined, he places them in metal trays, then finally replaces the white sheet.

'At least you stayed, Ben. I hate it when people run screaming from my theatre.'

'It crossed my mind.'

'Full marks for bravery, but I'm afraid your victim had a bad death. His arms were bound with rope that burned away in the fire. He received a heavy blow with a sharp metal instrument, like a pickaxe. The three-inch-deep wound to his skull would have caused a fatal brain injury, but he was alive when he entered the fire.'

'How do you know?'

'The alveoli in his lungs are blackened by tar. If he'd been dead at point of entry, there would have been no smoke inhalation. When the tissue samples come back, I should be able to pinpoint when he died to within six hours.'

'That's the best help I've had yet. The islanders are keeping their cards close to their chests.' I study his face again. 'Anything else?'

'Your killer chose the best way to cover his tracks. Fire destroys all trace evidence at source, if it's intense enough. It can even wipe out DNA.'

Disappointment worsens my bad mood. My journey to St Mary's has only proved that Alex Rogan's killer can't be pinned down. I feel like slinking away to lick my wounds, but a stiff drink might be a better remedy.

'Let me buy you that dinner you missed, or a pint at least.'

Keillor shakes his head. 'My appetite's deserted me. The older I get, the more premature death exhausts me; your victim's the same age as my youngest son. I need a bath and an early night.'

'That's a pity. The Mermaid's got some great local beer.'

He's scrubbing his hands with surgical soap that colours his skin a vivid yellow. 'Liz Gannick's waiting for me there. She wants to discuss my findings, but I'd rather you went in my place. Let's have that drink another time, Ben.'

'I'll hold you to it.'

I head for the pub at a rapid march, keen to find out why the chief forensics officer contacted Keillor without my permission.

The Mermaid Inn has guarded the mouth of Hugh Town harbour for 200 years; the sign above its door shows a brightly painted siren perching on a rock, and the interior is equally characterful. The place was a favourite of mine in my teens for its relaxed atmosphere and high quality beer. It hasn't changed much since then, still doubling as a maritime museum as well as a drinking den. An array of marine salvage hangs from the rafters. Tillers, oars and brass-framed portholes from local shipwrecks dangle above the tables, with mariners' knots and pieces of scrimshaw mounted in frames. I pause to glance at a broken compass that always fascinated me as a kid, its needle still pointing due north.

Liz Gannick is alone at a corner table, poring over a newspaper. She's dressed entirely in black, her bleached hair standing up in spikes, elfin face youthful but careworn.

'Can I join you?' I pull up a stool before she can refuse.

'Where's Keillor?' She looks like an angry sprite about to cast a bad spell.

'I've just watched the autopsy. Why did you set up an unauthorised meeting?' Irritation makes me ignore Madron's warning to keep her sweet.

She stares back at me. 'I pride myself on doing things differently, Inspector. That includes sharing post-mortem notes with the pathologist. I'm a former detective like you, fresh from running a big forensics operation in Leeds. Check my track record online; it's the best in the country. Believe me, a holistic approach solves cases faster.'

'You may be reporting back to the top brass, but I won't let you jeopardise my case.'

'I want the killer found too, in case that slipped your notice.' The air between us hums for thirty seconds, but she blinks first. 'Will you forgive me if I buy you a beer?'

'Throw in some food and I'll consider it.'

Gannick watches me plough through an outsized portion of cod and chips while she sips her gin and tonic. The woman fires questions at me over the next hour, as if I'm being interviewed for a vacancy. By the time coffee arrives she's had my full resumé but revealed little about herself, except that she was born in Leeds forty-two years ago, and now lives in Penzance, visiting her aunt and uncle on St Mary's several times a year. She's as fierce and quick-witted as my old partner in London, but harder to read. I may already have blown my chance of a decent write-up by criticising her approach. I notice that there's no wedding ring on her hand as we finish our meal. Potential partners would need a robust ego to cope with Gannick's critical manner; it's only when she finishes her third drink that her voice finally softens.

'Alex Rogan came here expecting peace, quiet and dark skies.' Her gaze levels with mine. 'You spent the night guarding his body, didn't you?'

'I've had better evenings.'

'Death by fire is the worst ever, and Rogan had special gifts. I heard him on the radio last year; he was a great communicator.' She shakes her head. 'The monster that set him alight is still strolling around St Agnes.'

Her animated tone takes me by surprise. Forensic specialists normally obsess over physical evidence, rarely mentioning the psychology behind a murder.

'Why did you leave the force?' I ask.

'Personal reasons.'

'Cops don't often sling in their day jobs for CSI.'

'The old boys' network stalled me at inspector rank, if you must know. I already had a master's degree in forensic science and it's satisfying work. I can solve cases where ordinary policing fails. Without me, you guys have no hard proof.'

'So my job's worthless?'

'Your words, not mine.' She finally cracks a smile. 'I miss the excitement of a murder hunt, but not the bigots at the top level. My people skills are patchy, but DNA tracing gives me a kick – if it provides answers.'

Gannick carries on discussing how Alex Rogan's body arrived on Burnt Island, but her crime scene analysis has offered little help so far, the fire destroying most of the potential evidence. The woman's approach chimes with mine: once a case starts I struggle to switch off until the killer's found, and she seems determined to maintain her unbroken track record. I get the sense that she's on a mission; no doubt she'd love to convince everyone who thwarted her police career that she made the right decision. We've both had a long day, yet she shows no sign of flagging as she describes tests the lab will conduct to reveal exactly how and when Rogan died.

'How do you sleep after digging a murder victim out of a fire?' The question slips out before I can retract it.

'My loyalties are with the dead, not the living. If you're skilful, a corpse can share all of its secrets.' She levers herself upright then reaches for her crutches. 'Don't get up, Inspector. My aunt's house is a stone's throw away; I'm staying there till the end of the week.'

Similarities between us hit home after she leaves. Many people would view us as freaks: my carthorse build means that women often press their phone numbers into my hand and men square up to me after a few drinks to prove how hard they are to their mates, but fighting isn't my forte. No one would guess that I like to read, unless they saw my collection of vintage American novels. Gannick isn't as tough as she seems either. Most SOCOs become hardened from witnessing fatalities, but emotions churned in her eyes when she described Rogan's suffering. I get the sense that she's alone for the same reasons as me: too proud to risk rejection.

I assess the sea conditions carefully before firing up the police launch's engine. The water is ominously calm, but I limit my risk of encountering a squall by returning to St Agnes at top speed, with a line of wash unreeling behind the boat like a spool of cotton. The journey passes easily, with no clouds to obscure a clean sweep of stars.

*

The Turk's Head is empty when I walk through the doors at closing time. Ella Tregarron is alone behind the bar, polishing wine glasses, black hair spilling over her shoulders, looking more mysterious than the mermaid on the sign outside the pub I just visited. Her gaze is so vacant that I'd guess she's spent the evening knocking back vodka. The smile of greeting she offers is running at half-strength.

'Are you okay, Ella? I hear you spent time with Sally today.'

She gives a slow nod. 'The poor girl's falling apart. This has come at the worst possible time for her; I still can't get my head around it.'

'We'll know what happened soon. Can I stay here for the next few days?'

'No problem, but have a nightcap with me before you go up.'

'You don't need to twist my arm.' I settle on a stool as she pours a double shot of whisky then slides the tumbler into my hands. When she rests her elbows on the bar and gazes up at me, the sensuality in her gaze is hard to ignore. It's just as well I've learned to avoid married women, despite being sorely tempted a few times.

'Are you having any luck finding Alex's killer?' Her eyes connect with mine again.

'We're getting there. In a place this small it won't take long.' I can tell she'd love more details, but instead I take another sip from my drink. 'You and Steve have been helping Jimmy Curwen, haven't you?'

'It's not much.' She looks embarrassed. 'I just give him anything we can't use. Our leftovers would be wasted otherwise.'

'Have you ever seen him act violently?'

She pauses before replying. 'I doubt he'd hurt anyone without a reason, but he gets frustrated when he can't express himself. I've got to know him well over the years. Jimmy knocks on the kitchen door every week, or I leave a box outside his flat.'

'He's lucky to receive so much kindness.'

'Jimmy hates relying on charity, but no one's ever given him a job.' She waves the compliment away with a waft of her hand. 'That must make him angry, too. I'd love to let him wash dishes here, but we'd struggle to pay another wage.'

'Do you know where he might be hiding?'

'He'll be back soon, wherever he's gone. Jimmy never neglects his birds. He'd rather starve than let them go hungry.'

I smile at her. 'Did you always plan to stay on St Agnes, Ella?'

'When I was in my teens I dreamed of leaving. A modelling agency offered me a contract, believe it or not.'

'I'm not surprised.'

'Thank God I stayed, there's nowhere more peaceful than Blanket Bay in summer. That's why I hate all this violence.' Her skin glows for a moment, then the sadness on her face deepens. I'd like to understand why she's in pain, but there's no point in asking until she volunteers an explanation. I've lived here long enough to know that islanders never reveal secrets until they're ready.

'Was Alex a regular visitor?'

'He popped in every week without fail. The guy sat where you are now, reading the paper or chatting to people. Everyone liked him.'

'With a few exceptions?'

'Sally's dad wasn't his biggest fan, and he clashed with Naomi Vine.'

'Did you see them argue?'

'They had a snappy conversation in here last week. Naomi was in tears, before storming out and slamming the door, but I bet she caused it. That one loves creating a fuss.'

'What do you know about the Dark Skies Festival?'

'Alex planned to build an observatory here. Steve loved the idea too; he was thrilled about the festival. Anything that attracts tourists helps our business. This place is already booked solid for that weekend, it's awful that Alex won't be around to enjoy it.'

A tear trails down her cheek and I reach over to touch her hand just as her husband appears in the doorway. Steve assesses our body language, his expression murderous.

I pull back slowly to prove that my gesture was intended as comfort. 'Ella was telling me about Alex Rogan,' I say.

'My wife's sensitive; his death's upset her badly. We left a food parcel for Sally today to pay our respects.' The landlord's tone is polite, even though anger still burns in his eyes. His arm is braced around Ella's shoulders, but her vacant stare has returned.

'I'd better go up. Thanks again for your hospitality.'

I'm so sleep-deprived that the landlord's jealousy slips from my mind before I reach my room. The window has a direct view of the sea, merging with the dark sky. A text has arrived from Zoe telling me that Shadow is behaving himself and she's coming over tomorrow to support Sally Rogan. The news is a relief but not a surprise – she's always quick to help a friend in need. Zoe has returned at the worst possible time, just as a vicious murder case kicks off, limiting our time together. The sound of waves beating the shore is as relentless as a metronome. I peel off my clothes then climb into bed, my muscles slow to relax. My last thought is for the killer, drifting into sleep like me, certain he'll never be found.

9

Sunday 7 November

My head is still fuzzy with dreams when I wake up on Sunday morning to find the pub silent. It should be my day off, but all leave is cancelled until the killer's found. Daylight filters through thin curtains, drawing attention to the room's stylish furniture, including a flat-screen TV, plush grey carpet and a seascape on the wall that fizzes with colour. I assume that the décor has been a labour of love for Ella Tregarron, to offset the tedium of winter when the same tiny band of regulars visits the pub every night. The couple must love the place to plough so much of their profits back into it.

I force myself through a brutal twenty-minute floor routine until my muscles burn from lunges, squats and press-ups, sweat dripping down my back when I get into the shower. I hate all forms of exercise apart from sea swimming, but it's a necessary evil with a build like mine, to prevent muscle from running to seed, and it keeps my thoughts clear as the pressures of a case intensify.

My first port of call is the lighthouse keepers' cottages, to check whether Jimmy Curwen has returned. The door to his bedsit still hangs open, and it looks like his birds will soon go hungry: the seed tray is almost empty, their water supply running out. I can only think of two possible explanations for Jimmy's continued absence: either he killed Rogan and he's lying low, or he clashed with the killer and has come to harm.

There's no one around when I head for the quay to catch the ferry back to Bryher for a fresh set of clothes. Arthur Penwithick is as shy as ever during the half-hour ride home. The ferryman has known me since childhood, yet remains silent as the boat scuds over water that's as flat as a mill pond, so I stand by the bow, watching the wake unfurl. There's no wind today, but it's bitterly cold, the sky only one shade lighter than the anthracite-grey sea.

My dog bounds towards me as I step onto the jetty at Bryher, almost toppling me by planting his paws on my chest. One of Shadow's best qualities is his inability to hold grudges. He's still dancing at my feet when my uncle, Ray Kitto, steps through the doors of his boat-yard. Ray's shock of hair may have turned silver, but he's still straight-backed with a lean build, his face so hard-boned it looks like it's been carved from granite. Facing him is uncannily like confronting myself in thirty years' time.

'Zoe left Shadow here. One of the fishermen took her over to St Agnes earlier,' he calls out. 'Have you had breakfast?'

'I can always eat.'

Ray disappears inside and I step through the doors of the boatyard. His latest commission is an oak-framed dinghy, upturned on trestles, its lapping neatly dovetailed. I run my fingertip along one perfectly smooth seam. Ray has been a boatbuilder for thirty years; he can construct a fifteen-foot dinghy using instinct alone, never consulting a template, cutting and measuring every strake by eye. I used to fantasise about working with him when I spent my school holidays in his yard, but patience has never been my strong point. The smell of the place turns the clock back to my childhood, the air redolent with varnish, white spirit and decking wax.

'Are you coming or not?' Ray calls down the stairs.

'Extra bacon for me, I'm starving.'

I watch my uncle cooking the meal, aware that this is my second free breakfast in as many days, but Ray's kitchen is minute compared to the industrial space at the Turk's Head. My uncle has fashioned every surface from leftover wood, including the square-topped stools and work surface. He hums to himself while he turns rashers of bacon, as if he's modelling the pleasures of bachelordom.

We sit side by side to eat breakfast, on a bench I helped him build when I was nine years old, looking out at a colony of gulls hovering over New Grimsby Sound. Ray isn't opposed to conversation, but he appreciates silence. If I keep my mouth shut, our meal will pass without a single word. He pours coffee from a battered metal pot, but I hesitate before accepting it: Ray always serves it black and thick as tar, the flavour bitter enough to corrode your taste buds.

'That stuff smells toxic,' I say.

'If you make it weak you lose the flavour.' He takes a long swig from his mug.

I attempt a few cautious sips before turning to him again. 'I need you to build me a boat, Ray. Nothing fancy, just a skiff with two berths, for travelling between the islands.'

His expression remains neutral. 'What's your budget?'

'Two grand, maximum.'

'You're dreaming, boy. That won't even cover the materials. Build it with me next spring if you want to save on hired labour.'

I consider his offer for moment. 'I'll book a fortnight's leave in March.'

'I thought you might go back to London.'

'Why?'

He takes another swig of coffee. 'Missing the bright lights, aren't you?'

'No more than usual. I need a boat, like I said.'

'Let's schedule it when you've got firm dates.' His shrewd eyes assess me again. 'Borrow the lapstrake for now.'

'Can you spare it for a while? I'm staying on St Agnes until I find out what happened to Alex Rogan.'

'Take care on the water. There's a storm over the Atlantic, a hundred miles west. If it tracks this way it'll do damage.' He keep his eyes trained on the grey expanse of sea outside his window. 'I heard what happened on Guy Fawkes Night; I imagine it ruined your evening.'

'Better for me than him. The poor sod had a bad death.'

'You'll have your work cut out on St Agnes.' He wraps his hands tighter around his mug. 'They're decent folk, but old loyalties run deep.'

'How do you mean?'

'Most families have lived there centuries; God-fearing people, wary of outsiders. I can't see them telling tales on each other.'

'I'm not looking for gossip, Ray. I just need to know why a man with a kid on the way was brutally murdered on Bonfire Night. What have you heard about Alex Rogan?'

'Only that Sally's dad wasn't best pleased about their whirlwind romance.' My uncle turns to face me again. 'Be careful, that's all. The islanders won't like being questioned; some will see it as meddling.'

'What would you do in my shoes?'

'Talk to Stan Eden at the lighthouse. People respect him; if you win his support, you're halfway there.'

Ray rises to his feet in silence to collect our plates.

He stands at the sink, humming again as he rinses them under the tap, bringing our conversation to an end. I thought I'd kept my restlessness well-hidden, but my uncle is so observant, nothing escapes him. The dog is whining for exercise so I head back outdoors. While Shadow bounds across the shingle beach in a state of euphoria, I follow behind at a slower pace. Ray has issued a warning and a solution, but I'm no closer to understanding why a man of my age met such an agonising death.

I process the information while walking home. My house stands at the southern tip of Hell Bay, a one-storey granite cottage that my grandfather built when he was younger than I am now. It's in need of repairs, but there's no time to fret about DIY; I must get back to St Agnes before anyone else gets hurt. Shadow bounds across the threshold in high spirits, clearly anticipating food, pausing only to sniff at the post lying on the doormat. A small padded envelope bears my full title, and a slice of granite drops into my palm when I upend it. Letters have been scratched into the stone's surface in a spiral, like the markings on a snail shell, but all I see is a whirling alphabet, failing to form words. I peer at the object again, then compare it to the photo on my phone from Burnt Island. The letters have been inscribed in the same neat style. The postmark on the envelope shows that it was posted second class from St Mary's – to arrive after the body was found.

I drop the stone into my coat pocket without caring about fingerprint evidence. If the killer is smart enough to discover my address, he's got enough nous to sterilise his materials before sending me a package. He probably found the stone on a local beach, but I'll have to wait until I get back to St Agnes to decipher it. It's too soon to tell whether the coded message is intended as a warning or a threat.

10

Jimmy's body aches when winter sunlight spills across his face, waking him from a night of fitful sleep. Panic overtakes him as he drifts back into consciousness and finds himself in unfamiliar surroundings. He's lying on a pew in the island's only church. Wooden eaves soar above him, long fingers of oak spliced together two hundred years ago. He remembers his mother explaining how the church was built from the remains of a shipwreck, its bell salvaged from a clipper that foundered near Tolgillian. The place has provided Jimmy with shelter from the cold, but he misses his own four walls and the prized possessions he has spent years gathering. It feels like the first strong wind could carry him away, his bones as fragile as a bird's, but he must honour his promise to the burning man before the police put him in jail. His feet still ache from searching the island the night before, peering through windows, trying to work out who would set a man alight.

The Birdman gazes through one of the arched windows at grassland rolling away to the sea. The earth is studded with ancient gravestones, grey and uneven as broken teeth. The sight makes him shudder. The man in the fire had no head-stone to bear his name, only a bed of flames to lie on, and soon the church's comforting silence will be out of bounds. Worshippers will arrive to sing hymns and whisper the prayers his mother loved.

He can't visit his birds again until nightfall, but wandering the island's shores since childhood has revealed all of its secrets. If he listens hard enough, the fields and hedgerows will explain why the man died. Jimmy can hear the raw keening of a tern summoning him outside. He gathers his bag then hurries from the church, leaving no trace of himself behind.

11

I arrive back on St Agnes at 11 a.m. with Shadow chasing towards the boathouse. I won't be able to return home until the killer's found, but the island's beauty is fair compensation. The wide sweep of sand on Blanket Bay would tempt me to take a dip – if the weather were ten degrees warmer. When I step inside the building, Mike Walbert has installed paraffin heaters, which blast out heat as I climb the stairs. Eddie is hunched over his notepad by the window. The young sergeant has abandoned his uniform for once, dressed in jeans, boots and a thick jumper, but his excitable expression remains. When I show him what the killer sent me, he gazes at the stone, as if ancient secrets lie below its dry surface.

'What do you think it means, boss?'

'It's written in Cornish, but some of it doesn't translate on the language website. We need to find an islander who's fluent.' I sit down opposite him. 'It's okay to use my first name, you know. I answer to Ben or Benesek, whichever you prefer.'

He looks embarrassed. 'DCI Madron says junior officers should always treat their seniors with respect.'

'We've worked together all year. Why not drop the formalities when he's not around?'

'It feels weird. I was in the sea cadets for years and they made us address officers by rank.' He looks at the chip of stone again. 'Do you think the killer's targeting you?'

'He sent the package before the body was found, so he was smart enough to figure out I'd be running the investigation. The gift's meant to keep me on my toes. We don't know if he'll strike again, that's what worries me.' I put the piece of granite back into my pocket. 'There was no sign of Curwen at his bedsit last night. Have you had any sightings?'

'Not a whisper, but Jimmy wouldn't go on the attack. He's so timid he runs away if you try to speak to him.'

'What about those kids he chased? He almost got arrested for threatening behaviour.'

'The little sods were raiding gulls' nests on the cliffs.' He puts down his notebook. 'Jimmy must have a reason to hide from us.'

'You haven't seen him lose control?'

'Never. He'll be terrified if he found Alex's body.' Eddie looks uncomfortable when he speaks again. 'Jimmy was the first person to welcome me and Michelle to our flat. He left shells and wildflowers on our doorstep; I can't believe he'd do something like this.'

'The report says those children were terrified. People agree he's got a nasty temper, but we'll find him soon enough with everyone keeping watch. Have you found out who Alex spent time with, apart from Sally?'

Eddie still seems concerned, as if he wants to continue defending the Birdman's corner. 'I often saw him on the quay last summer, fishing with Stan Eden and Liam Poldean.'

'We need to speak to them, but let's visit Sally again first. If we search the place thoroughly we might find out why Alex was targeted.'

I make a vain attempt to lock Shadow inside, but he's wise to all my tricks, sprinting through the fire escape before the door's closed. Our walk takes us past St Agnes's church, where a handful of worshippers are filing inside, dressed in sombre winter clothes as if their God disapproved of brightness. The slim figure at the back of the line is Martin Tolman, the architect, his wife Deborah standing beside him as they follow the other members of the congregation into the building. Seeing the couple reminds me to interview Tolman soon. Our brief conversation in the boathouse raised as many questions as it answered, but I envy him his faith. I'd love to be able to rely on a greater power, even though I'm a natural sceptic. My belief system doesn't extend far beyond the here and now.

Sally's home lies at the edge of Middle Town, fifty metres from her shop. It's a typical Scillonian building; two storeys high, crafted from local stone, with slate roof tiles and a deep porch to provide shelter from bad weather. The entire island appears to have visited before us. Cards, bunches of flowers and containers of food have been left by her front door. I can see the two women huddled together on the sofa through the front window. Zoe is clutching Sally's hand while she cries, which doesn't surprise me. Her kindness is bone-deep, but I can tell she's shaken when she greets us. She leads Eddie and me through to the kitchen, dressed in faded jeans and an old blue jumper, still managing to look gorgeous, even though her eyes are glossy with tears.

'How's she doing?' Eddie asks.

Zoe shakes her head. 'She's ranting and raving, which beats keeping it all inside. Her GP came over from St Mary's to check she's okay. He's left sedatives to help her sleep, but it's hard keeping her indoors. Sal keeps taking walks by herself. I think it's her way of staying sane.'

'Has she had many visitors?'

'I've sent most of them away.'

'Keep a list of names and times, please. Can you stay here for the next few days?'

Zoe looks confused but nods her agreement. Murderers enjoy watching the pain they've caused, often remaining close to the victim's family; I'll need to keep a close eye on Sally's most frequent callers.

'I'll keep her company for as long as she needs, but Sal's desperate for news. Will you speak to her, Ben?'

'If she's strong enough to talk. Stay here, Eddie. It's best if I see her alone.'

Shadow lingers in the kitchen, clearly hoping for food. I can hear Sally murmuring through the closed door of her living room, but I raise my hand to knock regardless. Her appearance has changed dramatically since yesterday. There's no sign of the outgoing, chatty woman who greeted me and Eddie in her shop, or the rebellious girl I knew at school. My old friend is slumped on the sofa, her dark blue top stretched tight across the mound of her belly, eyes swollen from crying.

I glance round her living room while she blots her face with a tissue. I've been here often, but have never studied her possessions with forensic interest before – now I'm searching for anything to explain Alex Rogan's brutal murder. A wedding photo taken outside the Turk's Head stands on the mantelpiece, with Ella and Steve Tregarron smiling in the background and most of the island community surrounding them with glasses raised. Despite the man's public profile, the couple chose a modest ceremony, followed by a party at the local pub. Rogan is a slim, dark-haired man with a good-natured grin, clearly relaxed in front of the camera, but all I know for certain is that he was an expert in his field, writing books and presenting occasional TV programmes about the night skies. I feel a stab of regret about spending so little time in his company. I should have visited him and Sally more often, then he'd have confided in me if something was bothering him.

'Try to say what you remember, Sal. It could help us find Alex's killer.'

'It won't bring him back.' Her voice is a flat drone.

'I'm sorry you're suffering like this.'

Her head snaps in my direction, her cheeks reddening. 'People keep saying how fucking sorry they are. Do you think I care? My son will never meet his dad.'

'I promise to find out what happened.'

'I'll kill whoever did it.' Sally's stare is fierce enough to burn. 'You don't know how it feels, Ben. You've never lost someone you love.'

I could recite a litany of names, starting with my parents, then my old work partner Clare who took her own life, but none of that's relevant. Her grief is still so raw, she can't see or hear anything else. I've never been much good at comforting people, but this time there's no choice. When I put my arm round Sally's shoulders she collapses immediately, her face pressed against my collarbone. I rest my hand on her back, waiting for her emotions to flood out, some of my own tension releasing as her tears flow.

I scan the room again while she weeps. The couple's shelves are filled with books, on topics ranging from meteorites to the history of jazz. Rogan may have been a committed stargazer, but the couple's home is earthy and unpretentious, the well-worn furniture proving that they kept their feet on the ground. After several minutes, Sally pulls back, her breathing unsteady. When her gaze catches mine again there's shame as well as grief in her expression.

'You don't need this, I'm sorry,' she mutters. 'I've messed up your shirt.'

'It doesn't matter.'

She notices the marks on my neck. 'Did I leave those scratches?'

'Don't worry, Sal. They'll soon heal.'

'I'm turning into a monster. Thank God it was you that told me, not some stranger who'd never met Alex.' She leans forwards to clutch my wrist. 'Find out why he died, Ben, please. I can't sleep till his killer's in jail.'

'It's only a matter of time. Are you up to answering questions?'

She dabs her eyes again. 'I can try.'

'Did Alex have his laptop with him the morning he left?'

'He takes it everywhere. It's his lifeline.'

'How do you mean?

'All his contacts are on there, and everything he's written.'

She slumps forwards suddenly, covering her face with her hands. I want to press harder, but it would be unwise to rush a pregnant woman whose world has just fallen apart. When Sally reaches for my hand again her eyes are so reddened by tears it looks like she's got conjunctivitis.

'I want every detail.' Her voice quakes with a fresh

wave of tears. 'Promise not to hold anything back; give me an update every day.'

'If it helps, of course. Has your father been in contact?'

Her frown deepens. 'Dad can't forgive me for being a difficult teenager; he thinks it made Mum ill.'

'You're a businesswoman now. Why can't he move on?'

'He was never around when I needed him. It's got to the point where we can't even listen to each other.' She shakes her head wearily. 'That doesn't matter anymore; I have to focus on Alex.'

'How did he spend the night before he left?'

'He went to the pub for a quick pint. He was home by ten.'

'Can you think of anyone Alex had argued with?'

'Only Dad, but I stayed out of it. Getting him to change his mind is like trying to shift Everest. Alex wanted the rift healed before the baby comes.'

'What about Naomi Vine?'

'It pissed him off that she fought his application to turn the lifeboat house into an observatory, but we don't know her personally. She's not the sociable type.' Sally wipes her hand across her face, clearly exhausted. 'Sorry, my brain's stopped working, I can't think anymore.'

'We can talk again tomorrow. Is it okay to search Alex's office?'

'Just find out what happened, please. It's killing me not knowing.'

'Have you got his email address and password?'

Tears ooze from her eyes again. 'There's a notebook in his desk drawer. Alex could hold all those huge theories in his head, but forgot anything practical.'

There's no point in telling her to keep calm for the baby's sake; grief isn't an emotion you can suppress. I sit with her for a few more minutes, relieved when Zoe arrives. Sally's vulnerability makes me even more determined to find the truth, but it's frustrating that she's still too upset to describe the run-up to her husband's death in detail.

Rogan's office is an annexe downstairs. It contains a battered leather sofa and shelves stacked with papers, files scattered across his desk. A book still lies open, as if he might return at any minute: *The Universe in Your Hand: A Journey through Space, Time and Beyond*. I glance at the opening paragraph, but lose the thread before the first description of quantum physics ends. Eddie scans Rogan's documents while I inspect the rest of the room. There's a large sheet of black paper pinned to the wall, which turns out to be a star map, with galaxies and nebulae circled with white pencil marks. His stargazing equipment is stacked by the wall, ranging from an antique telescope that's barely a foot long to one that must weigh 150 pounds, attached to a trolley that can be dragged over rough terrain. The man's love for his subject hits me for the first time. He threw all of his energy into organising a festival for stargazers, purely to share his passion for astronomy with like-minded souls under some of the darkest skies in Europe.

Rogan's notes confirm that he was establishing an international reputation, working at Harvard before gaining a research fellowship at Oxford. Recently he had been visiting the Roseland Observatory on the mainland before coming home to write up his research; I find his articles about distant planetary systems in copies of the *Journal of Cosmology*, but nothing to explain why he was targeted. His emails reveal that he was making friends on St Agnes, arranging a fishing trip with Mike Walbert and trips to the pub with Liam Poldean.

It's only when I rummage through his desk that an envelope just like the one I received slips into my hands. Rogan's name is neatly printed on the front, the postmark showing that it was sent – again from St Mary's – a week ago. It contains a strip of wood bark, with some Cornish words inscribed in small black capitals. When I check the image on my phone, the words are identical to those left at Rogan's murder scene. The killer sent his victim a warning, then repeated the message when he died, which means I may be next on his list.

I'm about to leave Rogan's office when some scorch marks on the window frame catch my eye, confirming Martin Tolman's claims about a previous murder attempt. The killer planned to start his blaze here, meaning Rogan's telescopes would be consumed first.

There may be little evidence of his attempt to set the house alight, but it's worth asking Liz Gannick to complete a detailed search. Eddie's phone rings while I'm still gazing down at the burned paintwork, his brow furrowed with concentration until the conversation ends.

'A dog walker from Middle Town says they saw Alex the night before he went missing. He was visiting Naomi Vine's house.'

'That's interesting. He told Sally he was going to the pub, and those two didn't see eye to eye. What do you know about Vine?'

He shakes his head, frowning. 'Not much, she stays in her big old house most of the time. I haven't seen her since the bonfire party.'

My interest lifts, because Vine was one of the few people to miss our meeting after Rogan's body was found. 'Let's pay her a visit.'

It feels good to exchange the grief trapped inside Sally's home for a practical task. We head south, the landscape revealing that the only reliable form of work on St Agnes is farming; dozens of small fields are full of sheep grazing, or green shoots of winter barley. It's only when we reach the edge of Wingletang Down that the natural order fragments. Nothing can be built on the half-mile of rocky heathland that extends to the southern coast because it's a designated Site of Special Scientific Interest. Walkers can wander freely, provided they stick to the paths, but all other activities are illegal. Last summer I had to shift a gang of teenagers who pitched tents there, hoping to avoid camping fees. The land may once have been tended by Neolithic farmers, but no one has cultivated it for thousands of years.

'Spooky, isn't it?' Eddie mutters. 'My dad says the down is like a rabbit warren, with Bronze Age graves connected by access tunnels. Most are blocked off in case they collapse.'

The landscape is beautiful but barren. The down looks particularly austere in winter, descending to the dunes at Horse Point, with few interruptions except oddly shaped outcrops of rock. Cairns mark the sites of ancient graves, their peaked outlines too numerous to count, the dead outnumbering the living on St Agnes by a significant majority. Suddenly the wind feels colder than before, making me long for shelter.

Naomi Vine's place stands at the edge of the down, the final building before the land reverts to wildness. I've never been inside, but my brother and I were fascinated by it as kids. The mansion is easily the grandest building on the island. It's ringed by high walls, ironwork gates protect the entrance, with only its top storey and slate roof visible from outside the compound. I don't know much about the woman who lives there, apart from her success as a sculptor. The papers called her an *enfant terrible* when she won the Turner Prize two decades ago: she used to appear regularly on TV shows about art, her style witty but combative. Her house looks like a fairy-tale castle, barricaded from reality, but it's more likely that the walls were built decades ago to protect it from winter's vicious winds.

My curiosity increases as we reach the gates, their embossed ironwork yielding to rust. Overgrown tamarisk and elder bushes almost block our path, but the gardens must once have been impressive. There's a marble fountain at the centre, surrounded by gnarled rose bushes and a terrace spanning the width of the property. The swimming pool is empty, apart from a silt of dark brown mud and a residue of leaves. Dozens of lead-paned windows gaze down at us, but there's no sign of the sculptor's presence, apart from a pair of ten-foot-high steel obelisks guarding her front door. Eddie gives a low whistle, impressed by so much grandeur.

'This place must be worth a mint,' I say, pushing the doorbell.

'A million for the land alone,' Eddie replies.

When no one responds, I peer through the letterbox and see no sign of life, only a row of paint cans dumped by the wall.

Suddenly the dog releases a frenzy of barks. He stands on his hind legs, scratching at the door handle, and my concerns for Naomi Vine rise. She could have met the same fate as Alex Rogan in such an isolated place.

'Stop fussing, Shadow. I'll find a way in, Eddie. You search the grounds.'

We walk in opposite directions, circling the building,

but it looks impenetrable, with most of its shutters bolted. It's only when I reach the back that I manage to prise open a sash window. The dog whimpers pitifully as I force my hand through the opening.

'Calm down, drama queen,' I say, but his whining intensifies when I boost myself over the window ledge.

I land on an expanse of parquet, my boots clattering on the slick surface. Naomi Vine's drawing room must have been grand decades ago, with an ornate marble fireplace and a candelabra hanging from the ceiling. The place looks like a work in progress, with too little furniture to fill the space, the pervasive silence convincing me that no one's home. Shadow is still barking frantically outside, as if he's afraid of being abandoned.

My eyes scan the woman's furnishings, looking for clues to explain her absence. The state of Naomi Vine's living room suggests that she's not interested in comfort, despite owning the island's most valuable property. There are few luxuries, apart from sculptures in the woman's own distinctive style. An elegant steel column stands in the corner, almost touching the ceiling, and half a dozen bronze sculptures grace her mantelpiece, showing an abstracted female form slowly rising from a crouching position, until her arms greet the sky. An old-fashioned phone stands on a coffee table, and a few colourful but threadbare rugs cover the parquet.

There's a sudden clattering when I reach the back of the house. It comes from behind heavy oak doors, but once I barge through, breaking into the property seems like a big mistake. Naomi Vine stands in front of me, aiming a blowtorch at my chest, a stink of molten iron filling my airways. The sculptor is wearing black jeans and an emerald green vest, the headphones over her ears explaining why she didn't hear my footsteps. She looks like a grown-up version of the warrior girls in video games who I fancied as a kid: ugly-beautiful, with sinews straining in her arms as she angles the torch in my direction, the tattoo snaking from her shoulder to her wrist undeniably sexy. Her auburn hair is cropped shorter than mine, and although her stance is combative, her skin is milk-pale. The expression on her face looks more like fear than fury.

'Who the fuck are you?' Vine spits out the words.

'DI Ben Kitto.' I hold out my badge at eye level.

She lets out a shaky laugh, but fear still shows on her face. 'You almost gave me a heart attack.'

'Switch off the flamethrower, please. Why aren't you answering your phone?'

'I never pick up when I'm working.'

It looks like she ignores basic physical needs like eating and sleeping, too. There are blue-black circles under her eyes, her cheekbones are hollow and her mouth is too large for her delicate bone structure. Vine's studio reveals how hard she's been working: light spills from a skylight window onto a huge aluminium sculpture, with metal leaves spiking out from its core. Ghostly white plaster heads peer down from

103

shelves high above us and welding gear litters the floor. The sculptor's frown returns when she catches me assessing her studio with interest, but at least she's turned off her blowtorch.

'Can we talk, please, Ms Vine? I'm investigating Alex Rogan's death.'

A look of sadness crosses her face. 'Come and sit down, but watch out for solder; it'll damage the soles of your shoes.'

I walk past the huge tree-like sculpture to a sitting area at the back of the studio, noticing broken floor tiles. Naomi Vine seems comfortable with her property's shabby grandeur, even though she moved in a year ago. She keeps her back to the wall while she gestures for me to sit on a battered wooden chair, arms folded tight across her chest. It looks like the first loud noise could shatter her nerves, although the cause of her anxiety is unexplained. She reaches for a cigarette before meeting my eyes again.

'I was upset about Alex. I didn't know him well, but he called by recently.'

'He was seen here the night before he died. Can you say why?'

'The pair of us were vying for the same building. It seems ridiculous now, but we'd had a row in the pub about the relative value of art and science. He gave a charming apology, so I forgave him. Alex asked if guests could stay here during his festival. There aren't enough hotel rooms on the islands to accommodate them all.'

'Did you agree?'

She nods her head. 'I felt obliged to say yes, but regretted it straight away. I hate having my privacy invaded. We had a glass of wine to be neighbourly, then he went home.'

'How long did he stay?'

Vine shrugs her shoulders. 'Less than an hour.'

'Had he ever called round before?'

'Never.'

'He didn't tell his wife he was coming here.'

She stubs out her cigarette, keeping her gaze averted. 'That's odd, it must have been a spur of the moment thing.'

'Do you get many visitors, Ms Vine?'

'Naomi, please.' She hesitates before answering. 'I don't seek out company. I left London to escape social obligations and focus on my work, but Rachel Carlyon calls, and the Birdman occasionally.'

'Jimmy Curwen comes here?'

'I always call him Birdman. The name fits him perfectly; he never settles anywhere for long. The guy's face is extraordinary, I'll have to sculpt him sometime.'

'He's hidden from us since Alex was killed. If you spot him, please call me immediately, and don't let him inside.' I'd like to press for more details about Rogan, but the woman still looks as fragile as spun glass. 'No one's seen you since the bonfire.'

'I'm preparing for a big show in Paris.'

'How did you hear about Alex's death?'

'Rachel phoned. The poor thing's terribly upset about his wife being widowed; I did my best to console her.'

'Forgive me for saying this, but you seem tense, Naomi.'

She folds her arms tighter across her chest. 'I left London because I was attacked. A mugger assaulted me near my house at night; I managed to fight him off, but the shock affected me for months. I thought the islands would be a safe place to stay.'

'They are, most of the time.' I let my gaze wander round her studio again. 'This is a great house, but it needs work, doesn't it?'

'The views sold it to me.' She offers her first full smile since I arrived. 'I'll give it an overhaul this spring, if I can find a decent builder. It's a perfect creative retreat.'

'Unless policemen disturb your peace.'

She gives me a wry look. 'I'll keep my windows locked in future.'

'You shouldn't be here alone, until the killer's found. He might be targeting newcomers to St Agnes. Why not take a room at the pub or let someone stay with you?'

'That wouldn't work.' The fear in her eyes remains, even while she defends her solitude.

'Why not?'

'I grew up in care. Sharing a crowded dormitory cured my need for company on a permanent basis.'

'At least keep your phone switched on.'

'I can't change the habits of a lifetime. I need silence to concentrate.' She pauses before addressing me again.

'There's something else you should know, Inspector.'

'What's that?'

Her gaze fiercens again. 'I can protect myself. It's tragic that Alex died, but it won't drive me from a place I love.'

'Promise to keep your property secure, Naomi.'

She gives a grudging nod. I'm not convinced by her explanation for Alex Rogan's visit, but her contradictory manner is fascinating to observe; she can oscillate between toughness and vulnerability in the blink of an eye. I have to remind myself to stay focused. In a place this small, outsiders can seem exotic, and Naomi's energy is pulling at me.

'I saw your show at the Tate in St Ives last year,' I say. 'Books normally appeal to me more than art, but your work fitted the space perfectly. The exhibition was impressive.'

'I've never met a cop with artistic interests before.' Finally the woman has relaxed enough to mock me. 'Come back, if you're interested. You can see my new pieces.'

'You wouldn't mind?'

'My store room's full to bursting, and it would give me a break from hard labour. Drop by – when you're less busy.'

I pass her my card. 'I'll call first to check you're free. Can I search your gardens before I leave?'

'Go ahead.' Her eyes narrow again as the conversation ends.

107

Vine's tension returns as we walk to her back door, as if she's dwelling on Alex Rogan's death, or her previous attack. Her wariness remains when she says goodbye, and I'm glad to hear the bolt slide shut behind me, proving that my security advice is being taken seriously.

Shadow's barking reaches fever pitch when I walk back along the path that circles Vine's property. Eddie is coming towards me from the opposite direction, but the dog stays glued to my side while I look for evidence Rogan may have left behind. The overcast sky makes the mansion look ghost-ridden, its tall roofline haunted by a flurry of gulls. The dog barks again as we reach a ginnel stacked high with firewood, but all I see is a neglected garden with trees planted so close together they seem to advance like predators, gnarled rosebushes blocking out the light.

Eddie joins me a few minutes later. 'Did you find Naomi Vine?'

'Something's spooked her. The most likely scenario is that she and Alex were having a flirtation. Why else would he lie to Sally about paying her a visit? She's been attacked before. My guess is that she's afraid to leave the house in case the killer's targeting her too. Let's check the grounds and outbuildings again.'

There's no need to mention that Vine's intense manner and creativity intrigued me. All traces of Rogan's final visit appear to have vanished, but my main concern is that the sculptress could be facing the same threat. Shadow is still on edge, snapping at my heels as I search the overgrown gardens. I find two unlocked sheds and an outbuilding packed to the rafters with rusting metal, but no sign of damage. The dog's barking continues until the ironwork gates finally clang shut behind us.

12

Shadow's calmness is restored once we leave the old mansion house, but I'm still processing why Naomi Vine reacted defensively to questions about Alex Rogan's visit. She claims it was a one-off, but her property is so isolated he may have visited many times without anyone noticing.

Eddie returns to the lifeboat house alone while I set off to interview Martin Tolman again, hoping for more details about the killer's attempt to torch Rogan's house two weeks earlier. Tolman lives above St Warna's Cove in a house he designed himself. It's a pristine white box with double-height windows, the front door steel grey. The ultra-modern structure looks more suitable for upstate New York than a cliffside at the edge of the world, its outline too sharp-edged for its ancient surroundings, with the fields behind unrolling like a length of bottle-green velvet.

Tolman's appearance is as austere as his home when he answers the door. The man's dark suit, hollow cheekbones and well-cut grey hair remind me again of an old-school film star. His wife hovers in the background, dressed in the same sombre clothes. Deborah has an elegant tennis player's build and jaw-length silver hair that hangs in a neat curtain. She used to be a medic, but her manner would unnerve most patients; there's little warmth in her smile when she shakes my hand.

'Can you leave your dog outside, please? We prefer not to have animals in the house.' Deborah Tolman delivers her request with polite firmness.

I turn to Shadow then fling my arms wide, giving him freedom to roam. The dog bounds away without a backwards glance.

My opinion of the couple's home changes once I see the interior. I was expecting minimalism, but the walls are drenched in rich greens and blues, a few stylish paintings adding interest to their living room. I spot a small cast-iron sculpture of a woman saluting the sky on one of their shelves, similar to the ones in Naomi Vine's home, suggesting that the couple are on close terms with their celebrity neighbour from across the bay.

'It's good to see you, Ben.' Tolman gestures for me to sit by the window. 'Is it okay if Deborah stays? She may be able to help.'

'Of course, I was hoping to see you both. I'd like to hear about your conversations with Alex. How well did you know him?'

111

'I'm afraid I only chatted to him at church,' Deborah Tolman replies. 'I'm not much of a pub-goer.'

The architect frowns as if he's recalling precise details. 'He attended evensong for a few months last autumn; I sensed that he was troubled.'

'How do you mean?'

'Spiritual questions seemed to bother him. He was allowing logic to cloud his beliefs. I took him to the pub one night to see if I could help. Alex said he loved it here, but believed some islanders resented incomers.'

'Did he name anyone?'

'He didn't elaborate. I told him to tell the police about the arson attempt, then he admitted that he was still adapting to the smallness of the place. He asked if I'd ever regretted coming back to St Agnes.'

'You lived here before?'

'I was born in Middle Town like Deborah, but my parents moved away for better job opportunities.' Tolman's face is solemn. 'I told Alex that my decision to come back has improved my life immeasurably. Deborah and I met when I travelled here from my home in France. How could anyone feel hemmed in when we're surrounded by endless sea and sky?'

His statement pulls me up short because it echoes the message left by the killer at the murder scene, but that could just be a coincidence. When I glance out of the window, Tolman's question makes sense. The couple's view must change constantly; granite boulders on the beach below are catching the light, while the Atlantic pales into the distance.

'I hear you're giving Jimmy Curwen a free place to stay.'

He replies with a casual nod. 'We bought the cottage to renovate, but it feels wrong to leave it empty when someone's in need. It's divided into two flats; Jimmy's using the smaller one.'

'Do you know where he is at the moment?'

'I'm afraid not. Jimmy's secretive at the best of times. I've been encouraging him to come to church, but shyness keeps him away.'

'One more thing, please, before I go. I'm trying to build up a picture of Alex's last twenty-four hours. We know he spent time with Naomi Vine before he died, but I need more details.'

'Are you suggesting they were having an affair?' Tolman's movements freeze. 'He never mentioned being unhappy at home.'

'Alex wouldn't be the first to stray, even in a place this small.'

He rises slowly to his feet. 'I'm sorry, that's all I know. Come back any time if you have more questions.'

The Tolmans seem eager for me to leave, and I'd like to know why the architect looked surprised when I told him who Rogan visited. The man seems too worldly to be shocked by an extramarital fling. The couple lead me along the hallway before I spot a book of Cornish phrases lying on a table.

'Which one of you is learning the language?' I ask.

'Both of us, but Martin's far more fluent. He's been studying longer than me,' Deborah replies. 'There's little chance of improving when so few people here know the language.'

'Let us know if we can help further,' her husband says, steering me towards the door.

The architect has retreated into himself by the time I say goodbye. Deborah Tolman soon vanishes inside, but he remains in the doorway when I look back, a funereal figure, dwarfed by the grandeur of his home.

Shadow bounds across the grass to greet me once I get outside. The lighthouse is the first thing I see when I turn inland, reminding me of my uncle's advice to speak to Stan Eden. I don't know whether to be daunted or impressed that my dog is already racing towards the building, his telepathic skills growing stronger all the time.

There's a slow tapping of footsteps when I knock on the lighthouse's door. Eden's face is impassive when he greets me, clumps of white hair protruding from his scalp, his matching beard in need of a trim. He must be in his seventies, but looks in good health, his pale blue eyes inspecting me closely. I still remember Eden visiting my secondary school to speak about his long career as a lighthouse keeper. The job struck me as romantic back then, but his way of life had already vanished.

'Come for a tour have you, young man?'

'I was hoping for a chat about Alex Rogan.'

'I don't have much to say.' Eden's wariness fades by a few degrees when he spots Shadow. 'Is that a police dog?'

'He'd never pass the training. If I leave him at home he wrecks the place.'

The old man scrutinises my face again. 'Ray Kitto's nephew, aren't you?'

'That's right, I moved back to Bryher earlier this year.'

'Help me check the building if you like. The volunteers always miss things.'

He's already climbing the spiral staircase so I follow in his wake. The building's history clings to its walls: the air smells of sea salt, brass polish and the keepers' tobacco. We're climbing higher now, and the ascent would be cruel for anyone with vertigo. The steps are made of perforated metal, giving a clear view down to the concrete floor, a hundred feet below. Our boots send echoes ringing around the lighthouse's circular core, like coins dropping through a grate. Despite his age, Stan Eden has enough stamina to describe the building's history as the steps wind upwards.

'The first lighthouse stood here in the sixteenth century, but keeping was hard work back then. They lit fires in the brazier each night, hoping mariners would see the flames. Gaslight didn't take over until the nineteenth century. It was still being used when I worked here.'

'That sounds dangerous.'

'Only if staff were badly trained. One of my colleagues got second degree burns from releasing too much fuel into the canopy before lighting the flame.'

'Were you always stationed here?'

'Trinity House could send us anywhere. The hardest light was Bishop's Rock, five miles west of here. Sometimes the seas were so high we'd be stranded for weeks with little food. I preferred working here, while my wife was alive.'

By now we've reached the gallery with its high glass walls. I can see the ring of metal where the beacon once rotated, but the circular room is empty, apart from winter light flooding through the windows.

'The building's had its guts ripped out. I'm campaigning for the lantern to be replaced, but it won't happen in my lifetime.' There's a frown on his face when he turns in my direction. 'We worked long hours in those days and the discipline was brutal. If you missed a minute of your shift, the head keeper could get you sacked.'

I spot a chair with pillows and a blanket draped over it, facing out to sea. 'Do you sleep here sometimes?'

He replies with a fierce stare. 'Old habits die hard, young man. I've spent hundreds of nights here over the years.'

'You must have saved a lot of lives.'

Eden's wizened features relax suddenly. 'Many ships would have foundered on the western rocks without this light.'

I'd like to ask about Alex Rogan but the man slips into a reverie as we circle the glass-walled room. I can see the entire island from the gallery, all the way down to Wingletang Bay. Eden must enjoy keeping watch over familiar terrain during his long vigils. He peers out at the Atlantic, as if it's still his responsibility to protect mariners from harm. The man's expression is calm as he surveys the ocean and I understand why his opinion carries so much weight on St Agnes. His work has given him a long view, letting him see past every obstacle. I'd like to request his support, but sense that a direct appeal would be rejected.

'What is it you want to know?' he asks.

'Why Alex Rogan's body was found on Bonfire Night. You understand the island better than anyone.'

'That's a terrible business. It makes no sense at all.'

'You fished with Alex sometimes, didn't you?'

'He joined me some evenings last summer, if the water was high.'

'Did he seem afraid of anything?'

'Only fatherhood. He was nervous, but excited . . .' Eden's voice quietens. 'I'll fish with anyone who wants to drop bait off the quay, but Alex interested me more than most. He never bragged about his achievements; I liked his dry sense of humour.'

'People aren't giving much away. I need to interview Jimmy Curwen, but he's nowhere to be seen.'

'The Birdman was at his flat last night.'

'Are you sure?'

'I saw him from up here, outside the keepers' cottages. Jimmy's a neighbour of mine. He always feeds his birds just before bedtime.'

'Call me if he comes back, please. It would help the investigation.'

He studies me again. 'You went to Naomi Vine's house earlier today, didn't you?'

'You don't miss a trick, Mr Eden.'

'Call me Stan, but you should know, that woman's not popular here. Most people wish she'd pack up and leave.'

The boldness of his statement shocks me. 'Why's that?'

'We welcome incomers who respect our ways, but Naomi Vine only thinks of herself. I don't want her sculptures littering our beaches. She'll be trying to buy the lighthouse next.' His voice is filled with disgust. 'She's almost persuaded the council to let her dump her rusting bits of metal all over Blanket Bay.'

It interests me that the island's most respected citizen has taken such a strong dislike to its most creative newcomer, as if he's terrified of change. 'Alex visited her the night before he died.'

'Maybe that was his mistake. I should go now, it's time to lock up.'

'Thanks for your help,' I say, pressing my card into his hand.

'Give my regards to your uncle. That man builds the finest boats in the Scillies.'

'He'll be glad you think so; he sends you his best

wishes.' I take the piece of granite from my pocket, then hand it him. 'Before I go, could you translate these words for me, Stan?'

'Someone's not keen on you.' Eden speaks in a lilting Cornish accent: '*Gas kres dhe Sen Agnes na gaffo tan dha enev.*'

'What does it mean?'

He seems in a hurry to pass back the stone. '*Leave St Agnes in peace, or fire will claim your soul.*'

13

Jimmy is hiding in a thicket of alder trees at the edge of Wingletang Down. He saw the police leave the old mansion empty-handed; they must be looking for whoever set the man on fire, so he's following in their footsteps, determined to complete his promise. Jimmy wishes he could visit Naomi Vine too, but he's afraid the policemen will return. He tips his head back to inspect the sky. Shearwaters are winging down to the island's south coast in search of a fresh shoal, reminding Jimmy that his own hunger is growing, his food supply almost exhausted.

He waits at the edge of the down, keeping watch over the grand house. Before it fell into disrepair, its windows gleamed, but he won't be safe to steal through the gates until nightfall, even though the woman who owns it has always been kind. Curiosity made him peer through her windows months ago until she beckoned him inside: Vine let him stand in her studio, watching her work, then gave him a food parcel to take home. He's returned often since then, and she never sends him away.

Gusts of wind blast his face with cold and Jimmy knows he must find better shelter. Fear hits him as he emerges from the thicket, but the landscape is deserted. The other islanders will be eating Sunday lunch at home, the drizzle heavier than before. His mother used to take him rambling over the rough grass, but the shapes that jut from the scrubby soil seem too human to be rock formations. Jimmy recites their names as he passes: Saddle Rock and Carn Adnis, then the Devil's Punch Bowl. Its towering form looks like a giant's cup carved from granite, balancing on the land's wide palm, yet it has always stood there.

Jimmy's throat is tight with anxiety, until he spots a cormorant's feather on the grass, as sleek and glossy as black satin. He tests its softness with his palm then places it in his pocket to add to his collection. The find gives him enough courage to go on as the rain thickens, until the back of his neck prickles with anxiety. Jimmy senses that he's being watched, but when he spins round, there's only open land descending to the shore. The sensation could just be electricity from the gathering storm. He hurries on at his quickest pace, feet slipping on the mud while he heads for a cave in the middle of the down.

14

I stand by the boathouse window, watching bands of rain mark the sky with hard black lines. Right now I'd happily swap places with the lifeboat crew that worked here years ago, despite the storm warning that's currently in place. I love my job most of the time, but at this point in the investigation, nothing is certain, apart from the killer's desire to rid the island of outsiders. Madron's voice is terse when I call to give him an update. The DCI waits at the end of a crackling line while I explain about the new message written in Cornish.

'It sounds like the killer wants the island all to himself. He's watching you, so don't spend time alone, Kitto. Do you hear?'

'Loud and clear, sir.'

'Any risky behaviour and I'll take over.'

DCI Madron hangs up abruptly. The man always reacts badly to pressure, and there's nothing more chaotic than a murder investigation – until it starts to make sense. I'd love to discuss strategies with him, but his knee-jerk reactions to every new threat make each case harder to manage.

I push my resentment aside to focus on Alex Rogan's death. It's already 3 p.m. and the vital forty-eight-hour period since discovering his body has almost passed; so far no unusual behaviour has been reported among the islanders. Rogan seems to have been accepted by the local community, but I haven't seen him and Sally recently enough to judge if their marriage was happy; it's possible that he was neglecting his pregnant wife to enjoy a fling with Naomi Vine, complete with lovers' tiffs. The only person he had a serious dispute with was Keith Pendennis, yet I've found no hard proof against Sally's father. And the elusive Birdman is still out of reach, even though he was seen tending his rescued gulls last night. No one has come forward with information about potential suspects yet. It's starting to feel like the islanders have signed an oath of secrecy.

The Helston family are next on my list. The last time I visited their home was during the summer, after Adam completed his community service for starting the fire that destroyed the Walberts' hay barn. I doubt that a seventeen-year-old boy could commit such a violent, well-organised crime, but it would be remiss not to interview the island's only confirmed arsonist. Shadow shows some good sense for once when I head for the door. He remains curled up on an old blanket under the table, unwilling to face the elements. I set off alone to the island's sheltered eastern side, with rain spitting at my face.

The Helstons supplement their income as farmers by running a bulb shop each summer so tourists can grow St Agnes's famous plants in their own gardens. There's nothing celebratory about the bulb shop today: a closed sign hangs in the window, but someone must be inside the dilapidated farmhouse next door, because a light glows in the hallway.

Julie Helston offers me a cautious smile of greeting. She's carrying a few extra stone, her skin puffy with tiredness, and even though she's around forty-five, she's dressed like a pensioner: her blouse is a drab shade of brown, buttoned up to her throat, mousy hair pinned into a bun. She ushers me into her kitchen, then gestures towards a table loaded with baskets of fabric and cotton reels. I notice that one of the containers is packed with tiny leather shoes.

'Let me clear this mess away,' she says.

'Don't worry, I've got plenty of room. Have you been sewing?'

'I make rag dolls for a mail order company each winter, while the shop's closed.'

My gaze falls on rows of two-inch-wide faces, with lips and eyes neatly stitched into place. It doesn't surprise me that Julie Helston needs a second income, but such repetitive work would send most people mad.

'How many can you sew each day?'

'Twenty, if I start early.' She picks up a half-finished doll, and I can tell she would rather continue than deal with my intrusion, her shoulders rigid with tension.

'I'm investigating Alex Rogan's death. Have you heard about it, Julie?'

Her gaze is glued to the doll's crimson smile. 'Sam was at your meeting; he told me what happened. It's tragic that Sally's been widowed so young.'

'Are your husband and son here today?'

'They're in the fields, but they'll be back soon.'

'How's Adam doing?'

'Fine, thanks. Sam keeps a close eye on him; he'll never do something that stupid again.'

'Did you ever find out why he started that fire?'

Her defences slip by a fraction. 'I wish to God he'd say. He still claims he had nothing to do with it, but he'd been in so much trouble at school it fit the pattern. I felt awful for Mike and Louise, even though their insurance covered the damage. The Walberts have been friends all our lives.'

'What was Adam doing, in the run-up to Bonfire Night?'

Her expression hardens. 'So that's why you're here. My son's been in trouble before, so you're coming after him again.'

'I have to check everyone's alibi for the fourth and fifth of November.'

'He was working with his dad.'

'Are you sure Adam never left the farm?'

'The pair of them stayed in the flower shed till late. We've only let Adam see his mates at the weekend since his arrest.'

My gaze drops to a deep crack in the wall opposite, just above the skirting, with a smear of mud beside it. Someone must have kicked it hard to cause so much damage.

'Did Adam put that hole in your wall?'

Her eyes blink shut. 'My son's easily upset, like most teenagers. He'd never do anyone serious harm.'

I glance around the cottage-style kitchen while she blusters; a framed photo above the range reveals a family that no longer exists, preserved in celluloid. Sam and Julie Helston are an attractive couple smiling for the camera, with their only child giving an impish smile. Adam looks around twelve years old: a handsome, fresh-faced lad, already morphing into adulthood, but not yet renowned at Five Islands School for truancy and bouts of fighting. When I look up again, Julie Helston's scowl has deepened.

'You can't really believe our boy killed someone. He's seventeen, for God's sake.'

'The murderer's still here, Julie. I'm checking everyone's movements.'

She rises to her feet in a hurry. 'Search his room, you won't find anything there.'

'That's not necessary at this stage.'

'Do it now, please. Then you won't bother us again.'

I feel uncomfortable following her upstairs, the

woman's footsteps heavier than before. Adam Helston's bedroom is typical of any teenage boy. The air reeks of cheap tobacco; there's a Plymouth Argyle FC poster on the wall and pictures of Paloma Faith pouting into the camera, crumpled T-shirts thrown across his unmade bed. I search the drawers of his bedside cabinet and under the furniture, with Julie watching my every move, guarding her son's reputation like a security officer outside a mausoleum.

I point to a stack of boxes on top of his wardrobe. 'Can I see those please, Julie?'

'Stay there, I'll get them down,' she snaps.

She places half a dozen cardboard containers on the bed. The first holds old football programmes, tickets and certificates, the next a brand new pair of Adidas trainers, but it's the largest one that draws a dull squeal from the boy's mother. It contains strips of rag, a box of matches and dozens of firelighters, individually wrapped in cellophane, releasing a sharp tang of chemicals.

'He promised us he wasn't involved,' she whispers.

Before I can ask another question, footsteps thunder up the stairs. Sam Helston looks shocked to see me when he bursts into the room, his face soon clouding with suspicion. He appears older than a man in his mid-forties; his son's exploits have painted deep lines on his face. Adam lingers behind. The boy's dark hair is cut into an arrogant rock star's quiff, but he's refusing to meet my eye. If he's surprised to see his fire-starting kit on display, he's wise enough to keep his mouth shut. Sam Helston positions his stocky frame to block my exit, while Julie cowers in the corner.

'What are you doing here?' Helston asks, his voice gritty with anger.

'Investigating Alex Rogan's murder.'

'Get on and find Jimmy Curwen then. The bloke's a fucking freak.' He steps closer, his gaze boring holes in my skin.

'We're searching for him, don't worry.'

'Leave now before I chuck you out. Julie's had more than she can take from your lot.'

'Stop it, Sam, please,' she murmurs. 'I asked him to search Adam's room; I thought it would get them off our backs.'

Helston's anger changes direction when he sees the contents of the box. He shoves his son's shoulder so hard that the boy bounces off the wall. 'What have you done? You stupid little shit.'

'It's not mine,' Adam blurts out. 'I've never seen it before.'

'Bloody liar.' His father spits the words into his face.

I lay a hand on the man's arm before he can throw a punch. 'Let me speak to Adam alone, please, Mr Helston. You can wait downstairs.'

Julie scuttles out of the room immediately. Her husband raises a warning finger to his boy then trudges away, leaving an ominous silence hanging over the room. Adam Helston's body language is more defensive than ever, just like when I arrested him for starting the fire in August. The boy's behaviour struck me as odd at the time. Mike Walbert found him standing at the edge of the field, transfixed by the blaze, making no effort to escape. I insisted on a blood test, but toxicology results came back clean. The lad must have been stone-cold sober when he threw the match. His arms are folded tight across his chest, as if he's expecting a sudden attack.

'Where did this box come from, Adam?'

'How would I know? I never put it there. I didn't start the barn fire either.'

'Why doesn't that convince me?'

'I watched, that's all. The fire had already caught when I got there; that building was past saving.' The boy shoots a furious look, his hands bunching at his sides, and it occurs to me that his teenage rage could easily translate into murder.

'You've got six months left on your suspended sentence. One wrong step and you'll serve it in a juvenile detention centre. Do you understand?'

'Loud and clear, but I've done nothing wrong.'

'Come on, Adam. This box holds enough firelighters to burn a castle down to the ground.'

'Someone planted them, like last time. Can't you see?' Words fly from the boy's mouth at high velocity. 'Why would I risk buying that stuff? Even my parents don't believe me. They want me to stay here shovelling shit all day long. Dad says I've blown my chances of getting a decent job.'

'You want to leave St Agnes?'

'I hate farming. Liam Poldean offered me an apprenticeship, but Dad won't listen.'

Something about the boy's clear eye contact persuades me he's telling the truth, but I wait for him to calm down before speaking again. 'A criminal record won't stop you trying another career. The army would take you, or even the police, if you pass the entry course. Everyone makes stupid mistakes at your age.'

The boy's face lightens by a few degrees, but he doesn't reply.

'Who could get in here without being seen?' I ask.

'I'm in the fields all day, but Mum would know. She hardly ever goes out.'

Adam's parents are still too tense with anger to answer questions when I go back downstairs with the box of firelighters under my arm. I tell them to keep watch over their son, day and night, until I come back. The rain is heavier once I leave their property, yet it's a relief to breathe air untainted by misery. Adam seemed to be telling the truth, but I can't prove he's not connected to Alex Rogan's death; his parents' alibi is his only defence. The boy seems trapped in a toxic situation, his father determined to keep him on the family farm. Maybe I'd go on the attack too, in his situation. I'm reminded of my own youthful belief that bigger adventures lay over the horizon.

My phone buzzes in my pocket when I get back to the incident room. The clipped voice at the end of the line belongs to Dr Keillor, his statements so brief he seems unwilling to waste a syllable.

'The lab results are back, Ben. Shall I email you the results?'

'Give me an outline now, please.'

'Alex Rogan died roughly fifteen to eighteen hours after leaving home, which places his death before dawn on the fifth of November. Tissue samples show high levels of cortisol in the surviving muscle mass.'

'What does that mean?'

'Stress hormones are released into the bloodstream when someone experiences pain. It means he was conscious when he was set alight. The killer probably smashed his skull to stop him screaming.'

'You can tell all that even though he was burned?'

'Cortisol's a powerful chemical. That's why abattoirs keep livestock calm before they die; it taints the flavour of meat when it's cooked.'

'Are you saying that Rogan was tortured before he died?'

'Your killer wanted to see him burn, the head wound was an afterthought. The only saving grace is that toxicology shows he'd been given a dose of flunitra-zepam – better known as Rohypnol.'

'The date rape drug?'

'There was enough in his system to make him slug-gish and easier to control. It might have numbed some of the pain.'

'Whoever did it must have hated his guts.'

'Psychology's not my forte, I'm afraid.'

'Sorry, I was thinking aloud.'

'That's my worst failing, Ben; it's a feature of my grand old age. Without meaning to sound rude, I hope we don't meet again soon – unless it's at the pub. I'm happier on the golf course than conducting autopsies these days.'

I mull over the pathologist's findings after our conversation. I need a forensic analysis of Alex Rogan's house, but travel restrictions are in place until the storm warning lifts. My only chance of expert help is from Liz Gannick, who is still with her relatives on St Mary's, unable to travel back to the mainland. There's curiosity in her tone when I make the call. I can tell how badly she wants the killer found, not only to add gloss to her reputation.

'The harbour's in lockdown,' she says. 'I'll come over tomorrow, when the ferries are running again.'

I feel a pang of envy for Gannick's job after she hangs up. She has to confront the results of violence every day, but chasing down the perpetrator rests on my shoulders alone. It crosses my mind that I could pick her up in Ray's lapstrake, but Madron would remove me from the case if he knew she'd been subjected to rough seas.

Eddie arrives at the lifeboat house as I'm shoving my phone back into my pocket, so I tell him about the arsonist's toolkit in Adam Helston's room. I still find it hard to believe that a teenage boy would plan such a well-coordinated murder campaign. The killer's use of the Cornish language is relevant too. He appears to resent outsiders' interference in his tiny kingdom, but so far the only islanders with a proven interest in the language are Deborah and Martin Tolman, even though neither have a clear reason to harm Alex Rogan. Eddie keeps his gaze trained on my face as I pass on the details. Ever since we started working together he has tracked my movements closely, as if my behaviour provides better guidance than the policing manual. But right now it feels like the blind leading the blind. He shakes his head in disbelief, the news ending his usual stream of chatter, until he gazes down at the piece of paper still clutched in his hands.

'I've called all the local boat owners and ferrymen. No one's given Jimmy Curwen a lift off the island.'

'Good work, Eddie, now all we have to do is find him. He's still our chief suspect.'

'I don't agree, sir.' He looks awkward, his gaze fixed on the table. 'Like I said, the bloke seems gentle. Most of the time he keeps out of people's way. I think we should be pursuing other leads.'

'Anyone can flip out, Eddie, and Curwen's got more reason than most. He fits the psychological profile of most violent criminals perfectly. He's isolated, with time on his hands, and ostracised by his community since scaring those kids. Let's organise a search party tonight. If he's lying low, he'll only move around after nightfall.'

'Can you do me a favour first? Michelle's been in

a state since Rogan died. She respects you; there's a chance you can calm her down.'

I give a rapid nod. 'Let's go now, then set up the search.'

We must be making progress because Eddie has never invited me to his home before, our talk centring on the case as we walk back to Lower Town.

The Nickells' rented apartment is over an old granary, with a fine view uphill to the lighthouse. Eddie looks embarrassed as we climb the fire escape to the second floor, as if he's regretting his invitation.

The couple's living room gives an insight into his home life: the young sergeant prides himself on being organised at work, but the cramped space is chaotic, with clothes drying on racks and a play mat on the floor heaped with toys. The furniture looks like it was donated by a variety of well-meaning relatives, with armchairs in different styles and colours. Michelle hurries from the kitchen as soon as we arrive. She's holding their daughter Lottie over her shoulder, the infant bawling at the top of her lungs.

'Thank God you're home,' she tells Eddie. 'She's been crying for hours. Can you take her?'

'Hang on,' he replies. 'Let me get my coat off first.'

Michelle dumps their baby in my arms before I can protest, then disappears back into the kitchen. I can count the number of infants I've held on one hand. It feels unnatural to be left with the howling creature while Eddie follows his fiancée; the baby's face is scarlet with fury, tiny hands curled into fists as she releases her frustrations.

'That's a horrible noise,' I tell her. 'What's your problem?'

Eddie leaves me alone for an uncomfortably long time. I try every method going to quiet the baby, from rocking and jiggling, to pulling faces, until humming a Coldplay song in her ear finally does the trick. After two choruses she's limp in my arms, gurgling with contentment. She may have old-fashioned musical tastes, but at least she's behaving. The kid keeps burrowing closer to my chest, making quiet snuffling sounds. Michelle looks astonished when she and Eddie finally reappear.

'You're a miracle worker, Ben. She's been bawling for hours.'

'Try playing her Radio Two,' I reply. 'Eddie tells me the news about Alex Rogan's been getting to you.'

Her eyes moisten suddenly. 'I keep having nightmares about Eddie getting hurt.'

'He can handle himself. Why not go round to a friend's house while he's at work, just for a while? You'll worry less if you're with people.'

I spend the next twenty minutes reassuring her, and by the time I pass Lottie back, the baby is out for the count, barely stirring when she reaches her father's arms. The look on Eddie's face is a revelation. I often think of him as a schoolkid, but his expression combines pride with responsibility. I'm about to tell him to stay at home until the search for Jimmy Curwen begins, but there's no chance of leaving. He's standing straight-backed, blocking my exit.

'We've got a favour to ask,' he says.

'Go ahead.'

His voice falters when he speaks again. 'We're having a naming ceremony for Lottie next spring. Would you consider being her godfather?'

'Are you serious?' The question is so left-field it takes a while to register.

I could point out that I've never let people get close, spending ten years undercover with the Murder Squad, learning how to vanish. I prevent connections from running too deep, except with relatives and friends I've known for a lifetime. Even the dog arrived in my life by default. If I agree to Eddie's request, the connection would be one more factor anchoring me to these islands permanently, when I'd rather believe that nothing ties me down.

Michelle studies my face intently. 'We want the best guardian to look after Lottie, in case anything happens to us.'

'You're not expecting a plane crash, are you?'

'I hope not.' Eddie gives a shaky laugh.

'How about your old schoolfriends?'

He shakes his head vehemently. 'They can't even look after themselves. We need someone responsible.'

I glance down at the sleeping child; her face is smaller than the palm of my hand, long eyelashes splayed across her cheek. 'Let me think about it.'

Whether I say yes or no, it's clear from the way the couple handle their daughter like a crystal ornament that she's transformed their world. Michelle plants a kiss on my cheek before I leave, although the conversation has put me on edge. Eddie has placed me on a pedestal and sooner or later I'll tumble back down to earth.

I can still feel the baby's weight against the crook of my arm when I get back to the boathouse, wishing I could give the islanders better protection. In an ideal world I'd flood St Agnes with officers, searching under every stone, but a sudden influx of strangers would send the community into a blind panic. I'll have to rely on brains instead of manpower. My thoughts are working overtime as I sketch out a profile of the killer. Whoever murdered the astronomer loves the medium of fire, trying to set Rogan's house alight before abducting him. He must be a sadist, too, because he subjected Rogan to the worst kind of savagery, keeping him drugged and bound on an exposed hilltop until nightfall.

If the Birdman's the culprit, Alex Rogan must have done something to cause his hatred. But what crime did the astronomer commit to warrant such violence? Could the Dark Skies festival have triggered the killing? The Cornish messages suggest that hatred of outsiders lies behind the crime, but they don't lead me any closer to Jimmy Curwen. Anyone could use a dictionary to translate simple phrases into a dead language.

I find it hard to believe that a seventeen-year-old boy would commit such a violent act, sending out messages in advance, but Adam Helston's previous crime rings my alarm bells. Keith Pendennis enjoys his reputation as a tough guy, and his feud with his daughter has lasted years, but there's no proof that he killed her husband, despite the anger bubbling underneath his skin. The Birdman is still my main suspect, despite Eddie's protests. He could be sheltering in one of a hundred barns, outbuildings or caves, but I'm determined to find him before daybreak. When I look outside, the dark is impenetrable, only a thin scattering of stars illuminating the night sky.

15

Jimmy sees the search party arrive from the mouth of a cave on Wingletang Down. The tall policeman is leading a dozen islanders across rough grassland, the group keeping their heads bowed while torch beams trail across plants and boulders. Jimmy slips from the cave's entrance and vanishes through the trees. If he moves fast, he can circle back and stay out of their reach.

Voices carry on the still air. Jimmy hears everything the crowd says, but most of it is too complex to make sense. All he knows for certain is that they are looking for him, using walking sticks to push back weeds and peer under brambles. It crosses Jimmy's mind to step into the light and give himself up. He's exhausted and hungry, but can't forget his promise to avenge the man in the fire.

Suddenly, one of the searchers heads straight towards him, forcing Jimmy to duck under a gorse bush, its dry thorns tearing his skin. He waits until the torch beams fade before emerging back into the open, but a new kind of discomfort is making his skin crawl. Someone is watching him again, tracking his movements like a hawk suspended above its prey. If he moves a muscle, he will be at their mercy. He stays motionless in the shadows until the search party vanishes across the down.

16

It's nine o'clock when I finally return to the Turk's Head without having glimpsed the Birdman. Curwen spends his days roaming the island, so he must know every nook and cranny, his invisibility testing my patience. I leave Shadow tethered to a railing behind the pub, with only a slight twinge of guilt. His fur will protect him from the night-time cold and he would only damage the pub's pristine interior.

Ella is alone behind the bar again tonight, the fire burning low in the inglenook. My head is too full for conversation, even though she gives me an expectant look when I order food to take up to my room. Ella's smile is wistful when she offers to feed Shadow as well. The woman's mysterious behaviour makes me wonder again about the source of her unhappiness, but her kind gesture tempts me to lean across the bar and plant a kiss on her cheek, even though her husband would be outraged if he caught me near his wife.

I stand with my back to the radiator once I get

upstairs, thawing away the night's cold, too wired to sit down. I ought to do something recreational to switch off my thoughts, which are still buzzing from the fruitless search. The internet is working again when I open my laptop to check my email, but it's operating at a snail's pace, as if the connection could soon expire. When I glance out of the window, the Atlantic is a solid expanse of black. The air still feels ominously calm, the storm keeping its distance for now. The Skype symbol flashes when my gaze returns to the computer screen and my brother's face appears, transmitted all the way from upstate New York. Ian is a year older than me, our relationship built on a lifetime of jokes and brutal teasing. His face is so similar to mine it's like confronting a tidier, clean-shaven version of myself, dressed in a doctor's white coat.

'Why are you bothering me? Haven't you got patients to harm?'

'Even successful orthopaedic consultants take breaks.' He never fails to remind me that his job outclasses mine. 'What's with the hair? You look like Poldark.'

'Just give me a tin mine and a stallion to ride across the fields.'

He sniggers like a twelve-year-old. 'Pity you don't have his luck with the ladies.'

'I get my share.'

'When's the last time you had a sexual experience with a living, breathing female, instead of Pornhub?'

'None of your business.'

'Lower your standards, mate. Some lonely spinster might take pity.'

'I'm too busy. There was a murder here on Bonfire Night.'

'Jesus, what happened?'

My brother's face grows serious. Underneath the banter, I know he's been checking on my welfare ever since my return to the islands. He listens carefully as I give him the bare details, then updates me on his family. His wife's tired of her high level career in medical admin, but his six-year-old daughter is having the time of her life singing in the school choir.

'You should hear her let rip. She's like a mini Adele.'

'Does the world need another?'

His face looms closer to the screen. 'Are you okay? You've been moping since that girl ditched you. Nina, wasn't it?'

'Thanks for reminding me.'

'Get back in the game, bro, before you forget how.'

'Thanks for your heartfelt concern.' I'm about to say goodbye when he throws a sudden curveball.

'We're thinking of coming back to the Scillies next year. I want Christy to know her roots.'

I stare at him in amazement. 'You'd trade New York for a few lumps of rock in the middle of the Atlantic?'

'In a heartbeat.' The raw homesickness in his voice takes me by surprise.

'Do it, then. There's room at mine till you get settled.'

I'm still reeling when our conversation ends. Ian has always seemed happy with his sophisticated lifestyle, but the same urge to escape city life for clean air, familiar faces and ocean views dragged me back here too. I didn't wallow after he left for the States, but it took me a while to accept his absence. It felt like one of the few people who knows exactly how I tick had disappeared from view.

The prospect of my brother coming home is enough to boost my spirits as I run an internet search on Alex Rogan. Wikipedia offers a detailed profile, describing him as a 'charismatic astronomer, adept at sharing his knowledge with the masses.' On the surface the man's life was a glittering success, but someone hated his presence on the island, even though he appeared happy with Sally. Maybe the murderer resented his attempt to bring more people to St Agnes. His celebrity status was affecting the island's delicate chemistry, breaking down the isolation that has preserved local customs for centuries.

Curiosity makes me check Naomi Vine's profile, too. Her biography confirms that she grew up in care; her tough start in life makes her achievements even more impressive. There's a picture of her from two decades ago outside the Tate Modern, the art world falling at her feet. She had just finished at art college when she became an overnight success. Her looks were distinctive even then: vivid auburn hair cut into a short fringe, highlighting a pale-skinned face, her over-sized features compelling rather than beautiful. Her determination to succeed shows in the set of her jaw, as if she intends to win every battle without yielding ground. Another image shows her outside the Royal Academy beside a prize-winning sculpture. The artwork towers over her, made up of hundreds of broken mirrors, each reflecting a different vision of the city. Vine's career has waned since that first stellar success, but it kept her on the world stage for several years. The article makes me keen to visit her studio again. The connection between us felt more like friendship than attraction, but I'd still like to get to know her once the killer's found. Until then, I need to understand why Alex Rogan beat a path to her door without telling his wife.

My final task is to check Adam Helston's notes from his juvenile court hearing. He only got into trouble at school during the six months before he set the barn alight, his behaviour warranting three exclusions for fighting with classmates. Sam Helston's anger makes more sense as I scan the report: he and his wife have spent the past year hoping their son will turn a corner. Julie seems to be paying a heavy price for Adam's misdeeds, stuck indoors embroidering dolls so that each day ends with a row of perfect children lined up on her kitchen table.

My eyes are burning when I finally stop working, a headache brewing at the base of my skull. I ought to rest, but sleep seems like a distant prize tonight, so I text Zoe instead. When no reply comes back I pull a battered copy of *The Great Gatsby* from my holdall. Books have been my biggest obsession since I was a kid, particularly classic American fiction, but I've only read one chapter when Zoe taps on the door. Her new image as an elegant brunette makes her seem more grown-up than before. She can still light up the room, even though her day with Sally has muted her smile.

'I brought refreshments, big man.' She brandishes a bottle of vodka.

'In that case, you are truly welcome.'

'This is pretty swanky.' She scans the stylish room with interest, but when she looks up at me again her distress is obvious.

'How's Sally doing?'

'She should be in hospital till the shock wears off – stress is making her claustrophobic. My biggest challenge is keeping her indoors. All she wants to do is walk, but I keep telling her it's not safe to go out at night. She's so fragile, I'm afraid she'll crack up.'

'What's she been saying?'

'Sal's got it into her head that Alex was having an affair, but when she emailed me in India a few weeks ago everything was fine.'

'Why did she suspect him?'

'She's got no proof. Sal thinks the woman's husband may have found out and killed Alex, but that's just guesswork. The poor thing's driving herself crazy.'

'Hopefully I'll have some answers soon. Are many people visiting the house?'

'Loads.'

She pulls a crumpled piece of paper from her pocket. Her list shows that almost every family on St Agnes has paid their respects, but Sally's most frequent caller is Liam Poldean. The builder has gone to her home each day since Alex's body was found, yet her father has failed to put in a single appearance.

'How come Liam's called by so often?'

'He was mates with Alex, and he and Sal had a thing back in the day.'

'They were together?'

'For about a year, when you were living in London.'

My thoughts take time to adjust to this new information. Poldean may still be harbouring feelings for his ex, the friendship with her husband no more than a cover. I'll have to take a closer look at his alibi, even though he claims to have been caring for his boys when Alex Rogan met his death.

Zoe pours vodka into a couple of mugs. 'You've got a tough job on your hands.'

'Tell me about it. Everyone's keeping their mouths shut.'

'They'll only talk if they've got something to say.'

We sit together on the window seat, her expression calm despite the day's concerns.

'There's something different about you, Zoe.'

'My life's easy compared to this. I'll soon be back in Mumbai doing a job I love.'

'You're extending your contract?'

'I'm considering it. I miss everyone here, but the school's a brilliant place to work.'

'It's your decision.' The words sound sour as they slip from my mouth, but it's too late to recall them.

'What's bothering you, Ben. It's not just the case, is it?'

'You're worse than Ian. Everyone's nagging me.'

'Why do you lock yourself away? You've done it since you lost your dad.'

'That's ridiculous, he died when I was fourteen.'

'It started then. You found it hard, not getting to say goodbye.'

'He drowned at sea, that was never going to happen.'

'You hid in those books of yours.' She's holding my gaze so firmly, it's impossible to look away. 'Nina Jackson texted me last week. Do you ever hear from her?'

I try not to react, but hearing her name for the second time tonight makes me flinch. Since Nina moved home to Bristol, my romantic life has consisted of a few pointless one-night stands. 'Why would I? She left me high and dry the best part of a year ago.'

'She asked about you. I'm surprised she hasn't made contact.'

'Give it a rest, Zoe.'

'You're lonely, big man.' She leans closer, scrutinising me just like my brother did, making me back away. 'Why not give her a call?'

'Time's moved on, Zoe.'

'God, you're a stubborn bugger.' She prods me in the ribs hard enough to make my eyes water.

148

'What do you know about Naomi Vine?' I ask, steering the subject away from my personal life.

'You're not interested, are you? She's a tricky one.'

'She's unusual, that's all.'

Zoe rolls her eyes. 'I considered buying one of her pieces for the hotel last year, but they cost a fortune.'

'Has she got a partner?'

'She's more of a loner. Naomi likes controversy. Some people love the idea of her sculptures on the beaches, and others hate it. I think a row of women on Blanket Bay beckoning sailors home would look great. It would attract more visitors to St Agnes.'

'But the old-timers prefer their privacy.'

Zoe nods in agreement. 'That's where the conflict lies.'

I still believe that Rogan's visit to Vine's house is linked to his brutal killing, but it would be wrong to share any more professional concerns. It's only when I've drained my vodka that I notice Zoe's expression grow thoughtful.

'I've got some big news, but I won't share it till you lose that terrible beard.'

'It's not going anywhere.'

'You're too tired to listen properly anyway. Let's talk again tomorrow; I should get back to Sally.' She hesitates before speaking again. 'Do you think she could have hurt Alex? I feel awful saying it, but some of her reactions seem off to me.'

'She's pregnant, Zoe. Like you said, shock and hormones are making her act weird, that's all.'

She rubs her hand across her face. 'It's been such a shock. Maybe I'm imagining things.'

'People saw her open the shop that morning, her alibi's pretty solid.'

'Yesterday she walked out in the middle of the night. It's like she can't sit still. I thought guilt might be getting to her.'

'She's grieving for her husband. Can you stay there till you fly back?'

'You don't have to ask. I should go and check she's okay.'

'Can you do me a favour first?'

'What?'

'I need a haircut. My boss keeps nagging, but I can't get over to the barber's on St Mary's.'

'You haven't let me touch your hair since I gave you the world's worst mullet.'

'I'm praying you've improved.'

Zoe has had many incarnations in her short life. She trained as a hairdresser before following her heart and studying music at university, her dreams of a professional singing career stalling when her parents' retirement required her to run the family hotel.

'That raven black hair of yours deserves better care. I'll see if Ella's got any decent scissors.'

I sit in front of the mirror with a towel round my shoulders, watching two-inch locks of hair fall into my lap. Shadow is whining outside, clearly unhappy about being excluded from the party, but I'm not complaining. It's been months since a woman touched me, and Zoe smells just as good as I remembered. Our friendship places her off limits, but it's still a pleasure to inhale her scent of jasmine, lemon soap, and something earthy and appealing that's all her own. When I open my eyes, she's assessing my reflection with a critical gaze.

'Not bad.' She runs her fingers through my hair again, lifting it, then letting it fall. 'If you smartened up, women might actually fancy you.'

'Only if they go for sleep-deprived giants.'

'You've always been a big, handsome thug. Your new haircut makes you look like a movie star.'

'Bollocks.'

I can't see any signs of Hollywood glory myself. The mirror shows a heavyweight boxer, rising awkwardly to his feet to avoid confronting his reflection. There are dark smudges under my mud-green eyes, black hair cropped shorter than seems natural. But at least part of Madron's edict has been fulfilled: whatever happens now, he can't accuse me of insubordination.

I check my phone before walking Zoe back to Sally's house. A text from Naomi Vine arrived two hours before, inviting me round to see her work. I wish I'd seen it earlier. She must get lonely in that big, neglected mansion, and the invitation would have allowed me to kill two birds with one stone: I could have discovered the secrets she's hiding and seen her new work at the same time. I fire off a quick reply, asking to drop by another evening, then release the tether on Shadow's collar. The creature howls with pleasure before bounding through the cool night air.

My restlessness lingers after Zoe hugs me goodnight, so I take the dog for a longer stroll. The wind is finally rising after days of stillness. It follows me along the shoreline, like a hand between my shoulder blades, shoving me onwards. Clues swirl around my head with the same wild energy as the breeze. So far I'm the only person other than Alex Rogan to receive an angry Cornish curse from the killer. He died three days ago, leaving me to discover who's singling us out, and why the murderer is trying to frame a troubled seventeen-year-old boy. I follow the shingle beach to Porth Killier, but the island is sleeping peacefully, lights out in every cottage. The killer may be combing the beaches, like me.

17

Monday 8 November

The wind tugs at Jimmy's outsized jumper, sending chills down the back of his neck. The only building in sight is the old mansion house, with dawn's first light reflecting off its perimeter wall. Exhaustion and the need for shelter carry Jimmy through its gates, taking cautious steps along the path. Naomi Vine sometimes leaves small food parcels for him on her doorstep, but it's so early, she might hear him moving around and call the police. The shutters of the downstairs windows are all closed; it's impossible to see inside. No sound is coming from the house, so she must still be asleep. Jimmy's anxiety lingers when he finds the back door ajar, but it's a relief to escape from the wind's constant attack. A light shines at the end of the corridor, drawing him towards it. He feels certain his friend wouldn't mind him taking a piece of bread from her kitchen, but footsteps suddenly ring from the walls.

Panic makes Jimmy scrabble for a hiding place. He shelters in a cupboard just in time, the space so confined that his arms press tight against his sides. Footsteps have been replaced by china shattering, and the sound of metal beating against a solid surface. The door reduces the voice outside to a drone of angry words. He listens hard but can't tell whether the speaker is male or female. He recognises a few of the Cornish phrases his grandfather used, their Celtic intonation rising and falling. His body trembles when someone cries out in pain, fear rooting him to the spot. Jimmy closes his eyes and tries to picture swallows flying low over the island, twisting ribbons through the sky, but the scene refuses to take shape. All he can see is black air in front of his face while the vicious sounds continue.

PART 2

'There may be a great fire in our soul, yet no one ever comes to warm himself at it, and the passers-by see only a wisp of smoke.'

Vincent van Gogh

18

I hate shaving, but this morning I have no choice. My new haircut clashes with my overgrown beard, making me look like a Hell's Angel, which would horrify Madron. The *Shipping Forecast* is predicting gales in Plymouth, Fastnet, Sole and Lundy while I drag my razor over winter-pale skin. The storm is arriving at the worst possible time, isolating St Agnes from the rest of the world.

My mobile rings at seven thirty, just as I'm inspecting the breakfast tray that Ella has placed outside my room. The speaker introduces himself as Gavin Carlyon, then apologises for calling so early, his voice slow and halting. It takes me a moment to recall that he lives on Gugh, not far from Keith Pendennis's cottage. The man's voice is a thick Cornish drawl as he asks me to visit his home. I agree to see him later this morning, remembering that his wife Rachel is the only islander to form a close friendship with Naomi Vine. She may be able to explain Alex Rogan's last visit to the reclusive sculptor's house.

Shadow barks at top volume when I launch myself into the great outdoors, his behaviour only improving when I drop a handful of dog biscuits at his feet. There's a tang of salt in the air, the wind playing havoc with people's gardens as I walk between Middle Town's low cottages with the dog chasing my heels. I notice that Sally's curtains are closed, but the lights are on in every room, so I tap on the door to check she's okay. There's no sign of Zoe's thousand-watt smile when she answers, her voice a low murmur.

'Neither of us slept much last night. Sal went on another midnight ramble; she was hysterical when she got back. The poor thing cried for hours.'

'Do you need help?'

She's slow to reply and I sense that she still harbours suspicion towards her close friend. 'Sal won't let anyone else stay over. I'll give you a call later,' she says, before closing the door.

My spirits have lowered when I head for the boat-house. Zoe is always observant; if she can see warning signs in Sally's behaviour, I may have missed something. People saw her opening the shop less than an hour after Alex left home for the last time. It strikes me as unlikely that a pregnant woman would lure her husband to Burnt Island, overpower him, then subject him to a terrible death, but experience has taught me that anything's possible. I'll have to ask Zoe to monitor Sally's behaviour closely until I'm certain she's innocent.

Eddie is in an upbeat mood when I climb the stairs of the boathouse, his voice excitable. 'Liz Gannick called,' he says. 'She's stuck on St Mary's; the ferries are still cancelled.'

'Bloody marvellous,' I mutter under my breath.

The investigation has faced constant obstacles. The island's elusive Birdman is roaming free, and the weather is slowing our progress to a snail's pace. It takes effort not to vent my frustration when Madron calls for an update. The DCI's voice is cool when he tells me to dress appropriately for tomorrow's press briefing, as if a suit and tie could solve a murder case. The conversation leaves a sour taste in my mouth, so it's a relief when Mike and Louise Walbert appear on the slipway outside; helping them will provide a useful distraction.

Louise is wearing her usual primary colours: a scarlet coat with an emerald green scarf and yellow wellingtons, brightening the wintry day. She hands me a biscuit tin when I go out to greet them.

'I made you and Eddie some sandwiches.'

'That's a kind thought, Louise.'

Her husband lumbers closer, the collar of his coat raised against the wind. 'Can we talk to you, Ben?'

'Of course. Why not come upstairs?'

Walbert shakes his head. 'No need, it won't take long.'

We huddle together in the empty hangar, our voices bouncing back from the walls.

'Go on, Mike,' Louise says. 'Get it off your chest.'

'It may be nothing, but I've seen Steve Tregarron going over to Burnt Island a few times. There's a direct view across Blanket Bay from our farm. He's the only person I've seen up there lately ... apart from Alex Rogan, that is.'

'Maybe he's taking exercise.'

The farmer shakes his head. 'Steve's an indoor man, but he's been out in all weathers, late in the evening when I'm checking the sheep. He was carrying a holdall last time I saw him crossing the causeway.'

'When was that?'

'Last Wednesday night, about ten o'clock.'

Louise meets my eye. 'Mike hates telling tales. I had to persuade him to come here.'

'You're just reporting facts. I wish everyone would do the same.'

Walbert looks relieved when they walk away, like a weight has been lifted from his shoulders, his wife's hand tucked in the crook of his arm. I try to imagine the pub's affable landlord setting out to commit murder, then taking elaborate steps to cover his tracks. It's possible that he orchestrated the events on Bonfire Night, leading me to Rogan's body to make himself look innocent, but interviewing the publican again must wait until I've visited Gavin Carlyon.

'Fancy making a house call, Eddie?'

My deputy jumps to his feet immediately, making me feel like a jaded old hand. He releases a stream of chatter as we cross the island, our route winding between rain-soaked fields, but thankfully he avoids repeating his request for me to become Lottie's godfather.

I can see why locals call the tidal causeway that connects the two islands the Bar: a ridge of yellow sand stands a few feet above water, with unpredictable currents boiling on either side. The lifeline will connect the tiny islet to St Agnes until late tonight, before being consumed by rising waves. Apart from Keith Pendennis's austere cottage, the only properties on Gugh are the Carlyons' home, a holiday cottage and some empty barns. During the hours when the islet is cut off by the tides, the residents can circle their tiny kingdom on foot in less than ten minutes.

Eddie turns to me again once we've made the crossing. 'Could you handle this much isolation?'

'No way, but it gives the residents peace and quiet.'

Keith Pendennis is standing by the window as we pass his cottage; the man looks so preoccupied I'm not even sure he's seen us climbing Kittern Hill. The Carlyons' property is smaller than Naomi Vine's, but still imposing; a detached Victorian villa peering down at the ocean. My guess is that a merchant chose the plot a hundred and fifty years ago for its fine view of St Mary's. The man who appears in the porch seems to have time-travelled back to the days when his home was built. Gavin Carlyon's waistcoat and white shirt would suit a Victorian gentleman, his thinning brown hair tucked behind his ears, half-moon glasses resting on the tip of his nose. When he steps closer, the light reveals deep burns across his jaw and neck, the skin a livid red.

'Thanks for coming,' he says. The man's eye contact is so intense he appears unwilling to blink. 'You just missed my wife; she's working at the shop this morning. People are keeping the place open to support Sally.'

Carlyon's home is the opposite of Naomi Vine's ramshackle mansion, with period details lovingly preserved, from cast iron fireplaces to ornate plasterwork. The man's office has a table loaded with books, a vase of dried flowers on the mantelpiece gathering dust, and a grandfather clock ticking loudly in the corner. The three of us remain standing while Carlyon's gaze flits from Eddie's face to mine.

'I've got some ideas about your case, but it will take me a moment to explain.' The man's speech is slow and portentous. 'St Agnes was a traditional community when I was a boy; most of the population were employed locally in farming or fishing. We've coped with all sorts of threats since then.'

'How do you mean?'

'Water shortages, for a start. It's a big problem not having a fresh supply. We paid to have boreholes dug, but we'll soon need a desalination plant.'

'I was talking about criminal threats.'

'Let me come to that, Inspector. We value our unique culture here. Don't get me wrong, everyone welcomes the summer tourists. They boost our economy and keep the place lively, but it's a blessing when the season ends; I'm happy when life slows down again. The race for modernity hasn't brought the rest of the world much happiness, has it?'

'Is this connected to Alex Rogan's death?'

'I hardly knew him, apart from occasional chats in the pub. He seemed unassuming and likeable. It's people like Naomi Vine who cause unrest. The place was peaceful until she started chucking her money around.' The man's composure has vanished, his stare maniacal. 'My wife won't hear a word against that woman. Rachel finds her inspiring, believe it or not.'

'You think Naomi Vine's linked to the murder?'

Carlyon gives a slow nod. 'Woe betide anyone that gets in her way. I clashed with her last month at a planning meeting with the council and she followed me back here, calling me every name under the sun. If you ask me, she's got mental problems. She can't stand being opposed. I think she targeted Alex for some reason.'

'Are you suggesting she killed him?'

'Only two people on St Agnes have the temperament for murder, in my view: Jimmy Curwen and Naomi Vine. But she's the most likely candidate. The woman's got a vicious streak.'

His description clashes with my impression of Vine during our meeting. The sculptor's tough upbringing could explain why she fights her corner a little too hard. 'Claims that serious have to be based on proof, Mr Carlyon.'

He puffs out his jowls. 'Pursue my theory, Inspector, and you'll see I'm right. I believe her influence here has been evil.'

'That's a strong word to use about a newcomer.'

'She's tearing our island apart. I only wish that my wife could see it.'

'I'll speak to Rachel separately about this.'

'You'll find her scrubbing the shop from top to bottom. My wife thinks all of life's problems can be removed with bleach.' His anger suddenly dissolves. 'Before you go, can I ask a question? Your family's been on Bryher over a hundred years, hasn't it, DI Kitto?'

'That's right, five generations of fishermen on my father's side.'

'Can I interview you after the investigation? I'm creating an archive of the longest-established island families.'

'My uncle's your best bet. Ray's got plenty of family photos and birth certificates.'

Carlyon offers an unctuous smile. 'I'll give him a call.'

'Can you remind me how you spent the fourth of November?'

'Working here, alone with my books. My wife caught the first ferry over to St Mary's to see friends. I barely left the house.'

It would have been easy for him to walk across to St Agnes and attack Alex Rogan for bringing an unwelcome taste of modernity to the island he guards so jealously. I glance at the genealogical charts on the wall on my way out, bloodlines picked out in contrasting colours. It doesn't surprise me that Carlyon makes a living from history, so obsessed by the past that every newcomer threatens his lifestyle, but it's odd that he has shown so little interest in the recent murder until now. When he escorts us to the door, daylight exposes the depth of his scar. The wound is outlined with puncture marks from stitches that must have kept a skin graft in place. I'd like to ask how he acquired such a serious injury, but Carlyon seems the type to resent personal questions.

Eddie whistles under his breath as we walk away. 'That place gives me the creeps; it's like a time machine. And the bloke's not the full ticket, is he?' His look of wonder proves that my deputy needs to learn that everyone has peculiarities, still so new to murder investigation that every key decision is mine alone. Carlyon's unblinking stare made me uncomfortable too, but he may have reasons for his suspicions.

I study the Carlyons' property again from the foot of Kittern Hill. It didn't take long for him to reveal his dislike of Naomi Vine. He couldn't find one positive word to say about the sculptor, but his accusation that she's connected to Rogan's death appears to be based on a single argument. The woman I saw in her studio seemed afraid to set foot outside, despite her show of independence. Carlyon's criticisms may have more to do with resentment of the sculptor's influence over his wife.

'When did Carlyon get those burns, Eddie?'

The question makes my deputy wince. 'Bonfire Night, last year. The guy needed an operation to reconstruct his jaw.'

The man's pain must have been agonising, but his injuries don't explain his eagerness to blame a man's death on an incomer. We're about to walk back across the Bar when Keith Pendennis emerges from his cottage with his Jack Russell at his side. Shadow is delighted to see his canine companion again, the two dogs haring across the beach, but the fitness coach barely raises a smile. He's dressed in a thick winter coat and boots, his scarf shielding his face. Pendennis comes to a halt a few metres away, his manner less aggressive than last time.

'How's the investigation going?' My old coach's direct communication is welcome after Gavin Carlyon's pompous lectures.

'We're making progress, Keith.'

'Let me know if I can help.'

'Sally still needs your support. She's struggling to cope.'

'The ball's in her court.' Pendennis's face suddenly clouds over. 'If she makes the first move, I'll consider going round.'

The man calls his dog then sets off across the Bar at a rapid march. His departure leaves me wondering why he's unwilling to bend, despite his daughter's suffering.

19

Jimmy's bones ache from hunching inside the narrow cupboard since dawn. The noises ended over an hour ago, but he's been too scared to leave his hiding place, terrified of being found. His legs tremble when he takes his first tentative steps outside, careful not to make a sound. Jimmy's nerves steady as he absorbs the silence. All he can hear is the wind rattling shutters and whistling through chimneys. When his panic finally subsides, he walks down the corridor, searching for his friend.

An open doorway leads him to Naomi Vine's studio. The place looks like a bombsite, with tools scattered among shards of broken glass. Plaster figurines lie broken at his feet. He touches a metal sculpture of a woman's face, but deep scratches have been grooved through its eyes. Jimmy sets an upturned stool back on its legs, the rest of the damage too great to fix. He's still staring at the ruins when a guttural sound comes from the other side of the room.

A chair stands at the centre of the huge inglenook fireplace, surrounded by firewood, a reek of paraffin hitting his airways

167

as he draws closer. Naomi sits with her head bowed, arms chained to the seat, her ankles fettered. His gait falters when he remembers the burning man, but he forces himself closer. Naomi's bright green top is stained with blood that oozes from her temple in a steady trickle, one of her eyes puffed shut by bruising, but at least she's alive. He peels away the black tape from her mouth, allowing her words to spill out in a dry whisper.

'Thank God. Help me, please.'

He tries to free her, but panic makes his hands clumsy, the chains refusing to budge. He manages to drag the chair from the fireplace and the woman's voice is steadier when she speaks again, even though her eyes are glossy with fear.

'Fetch help, quick, before he comes back. He'll kill me next time.'

Jimmy flounders back down the corridor, where Vine's phone lies smashed on the floor. He rushes to the nearest exit with panic rising in his chest, but the door handle refuses to give. He hurries along the corridor, hunting for another escape route. Every window is sealed and all the doors locked. Jimmy stands in the corridor, frozen in panic until an idea comes to him. He hurls a chair at the nearest window, then clambers through the opening. Shards of glass tear the palms of his hands but he barely notices the pain as he escapes down the path.

20

The wind is rising when Eddie goes back to the boat-house to phone some of the islanders and check on their welfare, leaving me to walk alone to Middle Town. Shadow attempts to follow me, whining pitifully when I send him after my deputy, but I can forecast that Rachel Carlyon wouldn't appreciate the dog's presence while I ask questions about Alex Rogan. There's no sign of her as I enter the shop, until I spot her kneeling in the corner, mending a broken light fitting. The air smells of disinfectant, as if she's been scouring the place like her husband predicted. Rachel must be inches taller than Gavin, her slim figure slowly unbending as she rises to her feet. Her grey hair is cut into a mannish crop, navy blue jumper rolled at the sleeves, thick glasses obscuring her eyes.

'Could we talk please, Mrs Carlyon?'

She gives a cautious nod. 'Not for long I'm afraid; I have to finish this then collect stock from the quay. The delivery boat's bringing supplies from St Mary's.'

'The ferries aren't running, but feel free to carry on working while we talk.' I take a seat on a stool by the door. 'It's good of you to support Sally.'

Rachel Carlyon's expression remains wary as she applies her screwdriver to the back of the light. 'This place isn't just a shop. It's our pharmacy and post office, too; we all need it to stay open.'

'I'm asking people about Alex Rogan's death. Someone must have an idea why it happened.'

'It's tragic for poor Sally. Alex was so enthusiastic about the night sky, it made me want to learn more about the stars.'

'Can you think of anyone he'd argued with, Mrs Carlyon?'

'Call me Rachel, please.' She keeps her gaze fixed on her task. 'I never heard Alex say a harsh word to anyone. You'd have to be mad to hurt a man like that; he was such a gentle soul.'

'Your husband agrees, but he's not keen on Naomi Vine, is he?'

Her screwdriver hovers in the air. 'I keep telling him it doesn't matter if she holds different opinions from everyone here, newcomers deserve a warm welcome.'

'How did you two become friends?'

'I took some flowers round when she arrived. We got chatting and made each other laugh. She can't believe I've never been abroad, but travel's never tempted me; the islands give me everything I need. She keeps trying to persuade me to go over to Paris for her next show.'

'Why does your husband dislike her so much?'

'Gavin prefers the past, but Naomi's forward-looking.' Her face lightens again. 'She's a breath of fresh air.'

'You seem fond of her.'

She gives a cautious nod. 'It's about time someone dragged us into the twenty-first century. Gavin was born in the house where we live now; he believes it's his duty to preserve every brick. My husband wants to protect the whole island.' She reattaches the light to the wall then flicks the switch to check it works. When she turns to face me again, her shyness returns.

'Does your cleaning work keep you busy, Rachel?'

'Only in summer; the holiday properties here and on St Mary's are all empty now.'

'Thanks for your help. If you remember anything about Alex, please give me a ring.' I pass her my card. 'I meant to thank you for joining the search party last night.'

She twists a duster in her hands. 'Gavin would have come too, but he had one of his migraines.'

I leave her applying beeswax to the counter, as if elbow grease could solve all of the island's problems. The only time the woman's face became animated was when she spoke of her new friend, her husband's passion for the past clearly grating on her.

By the time I return to the boathouse it's mid-morning; rain is pummelling the roof, the storm finally announcing its presence. My frustration mounts as

I study the mile-wide sound that separates St Agnes from St Mary's. The waters are a blur of disordered waves, ruining my chances of sailing the lapstrake over to collect Liz Gannick. There's still no news of Jimmy Curwen, even though Eddie has called every household on St Agnes. It surprises me that anyone could stay hidden for three days on an island barely two miles long, but the Birdman has lived here all his life. When I check the list of islanders we've interviewed about Rogan's death, my eyes light on another name.

'I know you've seen Liam Poldean already, but let's pay him another visit. I've been told that he and Sally had a relationship years ago.'

Eddie looks surprised. 'The bloke's got a solid alibi for Thursday; neighbours saw him playing with his kids at home then down on the beach.'

'He may have information about Alex. Those two were close, weren't they?'

My deputy keeps his thoughts to himself when we leave the lifeboat house with Shadow in tow, but I can tell he thinks the visit's pointless. Despite his intelligence, Eddie is too quick to assume innocence. It's taken me a decade of murder investigation to realise that anyone can turn violent if they're pushed hard enough. He relaxes again once I ask for more details about Liam Poldean, explaining that the builder has established a good reputation locally. He's spent the past five years renovating the old cottages on St Agnes.

'Liam's a decent carpenter, too,' he says. 'The bloke's a jack of all trades.'

Poldean's house lies at the heart of Middle Town, a modest terraced property with a front garden choked with weeds. Shadow gallops away at a sprint when I ring the doorbell, clearly unwilling to stay cooped up indoors. The builder's expression is long-suffering when he greets us, probably because a three-year-old boy sits astride his shoulders, arms locked tight around his father's neck. Poldean looks like a typical dad, dressed in ill-fitting jeans and an ancient Snow Patrol T-shirt, his tow-coloured hair in need of a comb. He rolls his eyes in mock despair by way of greeting.

'Come in, but be warned – my kids are having a mad half hour.'

He leaves the door hanging open as we follow him inside. A slightly older boy appears at the top of the stairs and releases a blood-curdling scream to attract his brother's attention. The younger child slithers from his father's shoulders and races upstairs, a door slamming loudly in his wake.

'Thank God, now they can torment each other instead of me,' Poldean sighs as he shows us into his living room. 'Val's at her mum's on St Mary's till the end of the week. It's taught me that looking after pre-school kids makes my job look easy.' The man is wide-eyed with exhaustion and his lounge resembles a bombsite, with model cars, Lego and playing cards littering the floor.

'I know how you feel,' Eddie replies. 'Lottie wakes us up every morning at three a.m.'

Poldean's face grows sober. 'Is something wrong? I wasn't expecting to be interviewed again.'

'We just need some background on Alex Rogan. We're struggling to get a clear picture and I know you were friends.'

He clears toys from the sofa before sitting down. 'I expected him to be some stuck-up boffin, but he was a decent bloke. He had this fantasy about building a house one day, so we traded information in the pub. I told him about brickwork and laying foundations, and he explained how the solar system works.' He releases a despairing laugh. 'It sounds mad, but we could talk for hours. Listening to him made me wish I'd knuckled down at school instead of chasing girls; he made big, complex ideas easy enough for an idiot like me to understand.' The man's voice sounds choked when his speech finally ends.

'Sorry if this is hard for you.'

He looks away. 'Sally's suffering the most. Her baby won't have a dad.'

'I hear you've been round to see her. I'm sure she appreciates it.'

'She's still in shock. I don't think she knows which way to turn.'

'Didn't you two go out together once?'

'In our twenties.' His gaze locks onto mine. 'We stayed friends. She's like a sister to me and Val now; she babysits for us all the time.'

The man's speech is too defensive for my liking. It takes bravery to attempt a relationship with a fellow islander in a place this small. If things go wrong you only have two choices: you can bear a grudge, or accept the fact that you'll bump into your ex every day for the rest of your lives.

'What did you and Alex talk about last time you met?' I ask.

'The Dark Skies Festival. He wanted to make it a success, so it could run every year. I agreed to help guests set up their telescopes on Covean Beach.'

'Did he seem worried at all?'

'A bit preoccupied, but nothing to write home about.'

'Alex visited Naomi Vine the night before he died. Do you know why?'

'He never said,' Poldean replies, frowning. 'Naomi's not my favourite person, to be honest. A few months back, she wanted a quote for all the building work needed at her place. I sweated blood over the costings, but she never got back to me.' He hesitates before continuing. 'Alex had better manners. He was the smartest person here, but he had too much class to put anyone down.'

'Naomi must have some redeeming features.'

'Her sculptures are great, but that contract would have come in handy. I could have booked a holiday for my kids. Val's desperate to take them to Disney World.'

'You seem pretty busy. Everyone knows you do good work.'

He acknowledges the compliment with a shrug. 'I rely on word of mouth; I can't afford mistakes.'

'Adam Helston said you'd offered him an apprenticeship.'

'It won't happen. The lad's keen, but his dad keeps him on a short lead.'

I'm about to ask another question when a crash comes from upstairs, followed by an anguished howl. 'Jesus,' he mutters. 'That'll be another trip to casualty.'

'We'll leave you to it, Liam. Thanks for your time.'

'Can't you just handcuff them to their beds till Val gets back?' Poldean gives another tired smile before heading upstairs.

I almost trip over a mountain of Lego as we let ourselves out, still none the wiser about why Alex Rogan died.

21

St Mary's Sound looks unnaturally calm when I reach the quay at midday, even though a red alert is still in place for all shipping from here to the Solent. With luck, I can ferry Liz Gannick back to St Agnes before the next storm system hits. I take the police launch, which has twice the motor power of Ray's lapstrake. Shadow tries to leap aboard, but I point inland, letting him know that he's a free agent. Madron would climb the walls if he knew that an unauthorised dog had been allowed on a police boat. The crossing takes less than half an hour over the smooth channel, but local fishermen have heeded the weather warnings and moored their boats in Porth Mellon Harbour, protected from the swell by Hugh Town's long breakwater. The marina is filled to capacity, with skiffs and trawlers packed side by side like a shoal of colourful fish. It's only as I moor the boat that my lucky escape registers. A band of clouds has chased me across the sound. The storm is starting to feel real, its endless rotations finally reaching land.

The waves grow taller as I hurry along the quayside. Most of the time I love living in the Scillies, until circumstances remind me that our geography makes us vulnerable: we're forty-five kilometres from the mainland, forced to solve emergencies with no outside help. On any other day I'd pull up my hood and watch the storm gather, but Liz Gannick is waiting for me again at the Mermaid Inn. The chief of forensic services still looks like an angry sprite when I arrive, her bleached hair slicked back, petite frame hunched over a table in the corner. Her clothes are more suitable for a rock concert than a murder investigation: tight jeans, Doc Martens and an electric blue coat folded on the seat beside her.

'Late again, Inspector.' Gannick takes in my new haircut and freshly shaved jaw. 'You chose an odd time for an image makeover.'

'The DCI insisted.' I point at the waves outside, smashing against the quay. 'We could be here a while. What are you drinking?'

'Black coffee, no sugar.'

Gannick is still stony-faced when I return from the bar, but I won't apologise for inevitable delays. She carries on brooding while I down my cappuccino, but curiosity eventually cancels her disapproval.

'I need a full team for site analysis. Working alone will slow my progress considerably. Are you ready for that?'

'One's better than none, and I hear you're top dog.'

She gives me an arch look. 'If you're going to mock, my offer's withdrawn.'

'I'm serious. You're tipped to run the national forensic service in a few years' time, aren't you?'

'The seniors would block it. I've already broken too many glass ceilings.'

I expect another flash of temper, but Gannick appears calmer when she peers out at the waves lashing the breakwater, fishing boats bobbing higher with each new surge.

'We're not going anywhere, so why not give me a progress report?' she says.

It takes us an hour to discuss details, and I'm glad the pub is almost empty, with no one close enough to eavesdrop. Gannick's pale brown gaze assesses me while I describe each stage of the investigation, from interviewing islanders, to the calling cards written in Cornish. Her interest sharpens when I explain that Jimmy Curwen still hasn't been found.

'The guy sounds vulnerable. He'll have walked into the sea by now, if he were involved.'

I shake my head. 'Curwen may have exaggerated his difficulties. If he's smart enough to stay out of our reach for so long, it's likely he could have sent those messages, planned the abduction, and set Rogan on fire. There has to be a reason why his coat was at the murder scene, but there are other suspects, too. The pub's landlord, Steve Tregarron, was seen on Burnt Island just before the murder.'

'That doesn't make him a killer.' Gannick's voice sours. 'I prefer evidence to guesswork, which is another reason why I left the force. If you start talking about mindsets and *modus operandi*, you'll piss me off.'

'I bet that doesn't take much.'

'Do you want my view?' Her cool gaze levels with mine. 'Sexual jealousy is the trigger for most violent crimes, like acid attacks or ritualised burnings.'

'You think someone was stalking him?'

'I can extract physical evidence from any crime scene, but you'll have to figure out why he died for yourself, Inspector. Witness statements always bored me to tears.'

'Why not use my name? It's bad enough that my deputy insists on calling me "Sir".'

'That's the least of your worries.' She pushes her coffee cup away. 'I just want to know why Rogan was burned alive. His phone and laptop were thrown onto the funeral pyre too; the lab found metal hinges and traces of silica in the ashes.'

'I got a transcript of the last six months' calls from his mobile phone company, but all it proves is that he loved his wife. Rogan rang her six times on one day when he was working away. His email record's clean, too.' The sea still looks too forbidding to make the return crossing so I risk a personal question. 'How are you enjoying your new job?'

'It's got its challenges.'

'I still don't get why you left a senior police job for

a sideways move into a different field. You seem tough enough to deal with the old boys' network.'

'It's everywhere you look.' She stares at the tabletop as if she's committing the beermats' designs to memory. 'The institutional bullying got too much. Colleagues would be polite to my face, then call me a sad little cripple behind my back. The prejudice is too engrained to tackle head-on.'

'You expect that from me as well?'

'The jury's out. So far your team's been respectful.'

'Have your duties got easier since you moved to Cornwall?'

'Death's not selective, it treats everyone the same, no matter where you live. I should know, I've cheated it enough times. Medics tell me I'm the luckiest woman alive.'

'How do you mean?'

'I was born with spina bifida, plus a heart defect that required major surgery. I've had more operations than you've had hot dinners. I died twice on the operating table, yet I'm still here.'

'Just as well, your expertise could be crucial to this case.'

I'd like to press for more details, but Gannick flips open her laptop and begins typing at a furious pace, ending our conversation abruptly. I should feel grateful that a senior forensic scientist is working alongside me, yet her spiky manner turns communication into a mine-field. It must stem from her old colleagues' disrespect, but she'll have to trust me for our work to be effective. She barely looks up from her computer screen until the squall subsides an hour later.

Gannick maintains her silence as we make the crossing to St Agnes, letting me focus on steering the launch to safety. The water swells with unseen currents while the storm gathers pace for another attack. My respect for the forensics chief increases as waves batter the prow of the boat; she doesn't flinch, even when the craft rocks violently from side to side. The only sign that she's happy to reach St Agnes is the width of her smile when she levers herself onto the jetty. Despite the rough journey she shows no sign of flagging.

'Shall we go straight to Alex Rogan's house?' she asks.

It's only 4 p.m. and I'd like to take her to the property straight away, but I'm mindful of Zoe's warning about Sally's fragile state of mind. A forensics officer combing through her belongings might be more than she can stand. 'Early tomorrow's the best plan, when it's light. I've booked a room for you at the pub.'

'I'll say goodnight, then.'

Gannick disappears towards the Turk's Head, the building coming into view as we walk up the quay, her crutches tapping across the concrete at breakneck speed, leaving me to cart her equipment indoors. Dusk is gathering already, and I'm about to follow her when Shadow appears out of the gloom, giving a bark of greeting. He seems to have enjoyed his hours of freedom and it's obvious that he's been fed because he makes no complaint about being tethered outside the pub again.

'Behave,' I tell him. 'No barking until I get back.'

The dog's pale eyes give me a pitying stare, as if he resents my lack of faith. He stations himself in the pub's courtyard, ears pricked like he's expecting company. He gives a low whine of disapproval when I heft Liz Gannick's kit over the threshold, but the establishment's carpets wouldn't survive long with him indoors.

The bar is virtually empty when I enter, just a few late-afternoon regulars gathered for a drink before dinner. The old lighthouse keeper, Stan Eden, is relaxing in an armchair by the hearth, chatting to Louise Walbert. Steve Tregarron is alone behind the bar, restocking shelves with bottles of beer, his wife absent for once. The landlord appears to have recovered from seeing Ella chatting to me, but the man's pallor reflects years of hard drinking and smoking. He takes a beat too long to produce a professional smile.

'Are you staying here for the duration, Ben?' he asks.

'That would be great, if possible.' I drop onto a stool opposite him.

He nods at the empty room. 'We're not exactly heaving, so it's no problem. Keep the same room, a few doors down from your colleague. You can come and go as you please by the back door.'

'That's ideal, thanks.' I hesitate before asking my next question. 'You know the islanders better than anyone, Steve. What was your view of Alex?'

Tregarron hesitates before placing more bottles on the shelf. 'He fell for Sally hard, and he seemed thrilled about their baby. One thing keeps nagging at me though: a film crew were planning to make a documentary about his festival next summer. He knew that would rattle some cages.'

'Why?'

'It'll attract more visitors and some islanders prefer a quiet life. I think he was hoping the problem would go away.'

'A pity it didn't,' I reply. 'You've been seen walking out to Burnt Island a few times recently. Can you explain why?'

His shoulders flinch before he replies. 'I've got a new hobby.'

'What's that?'

'Stargazing, believe it or not. Alex leant me a telescope.' Tregarron points at a narrow case on the counter behind the bar, but his expression's wary, as if he's waiting to be caught out. 'He said Burnt Island was the best place to go, because it's furthest from any light pollution. I've been teaching myself about the constellations.'

'Did you see anyone on your travels?'

'Not a soul; some nights it feels like I've got the universe all to myself.' The dreamy look soon slips from his face. 'I can't imagine going back up there any time soon.'

I rise to my feet. 'The force will pay for my room,

Steve. Give me an invoice whenever you like; I'll make sure it's paid on time.'

'Your stay's on the house; Ella and I just want the killer found.' His face is solemn when he presses a key for the back door into my hand.

I thank him for his hospitality then lug Gannick's crate of equipment upstairs. The man's explanation should reassure me, because it would have been hard to fake his shocked reaction when he led me to Alex Rogan's body, yet his latest response struck the wrong note. It's possible Tregarron's wife may have flirted with Alex Rogan, sending him into a fit of jealousy, but I've got nothing to prove it.

I dump the box outside Gannick's door then retreat to my room to gather my thoughts. Outside my window, clouds race across the darkening sky. The water is black enough to make me wish the lighthouse was still operating; I've never felt more in need of illumination as the case flounders. I run through a mental list of people who'd listen to my frustration, but the obvious choice is Zoe. Her smile is running at half-strength when she answers my Skype call after three rings.

'I came looking for you earlier, big man. Are you avoiding me?'

'Not by choice. How's Sally doing?'

'She's outside again. I tried to keep her here, but she wants to visit all the places Alex loved on her own. I worry for the baby when she's so upset.'

'I'll be coming by tomorrow with the forensics officer.'

'That should help, she's desperate for answers.' The signal's poor, her image fraying at the edges. 'Are you ready for my news?'

'Depends if it's good or bad.'

'It might cheer you up. I think it's the best ever.'

'Hit me with it then.'

'I'm engaged.'

The screen blanks for a second, giving me time to resurrect my smile. 'What did you say?'

'We're getting married in July. Dev runs the school's music department, but we can't decide whether to stay in Mumbai or live here. He's amazing, Ben. You're going to love him.'

'How come I've never heard about him before?'

'It's been a whirlwind, but the timing's perfect for both of us. His parents are traditional Sikhs and he's got a huge family; it should be quite a party. You'll have to come over.'

'Congratulations, Zoe, I'm glad you're happy.' Emotions curdle in my stomach, like milk turning sour. 'I'd better get back to work. We can talk tomorrow.'

I hit the off button then let the news register. Zoe has been part of my landscape for so long, it's impossible to imagine a future without her living just across the bay. The selfish part of me wants her to stay single, so the friendship we've built since childhood won't have to change. I always believed I'd get the chance to vet whoever she chose to marry, but she's made the decision without even checking my opinion.

22

Jimmy is alone on the down as dusk arrives. He hasn't followed Naomi's request even though her plea for help this morning is still ringing in his ears. He set off for Middle Town and almost reached the settlement before panic drove him back. How could he explain to anyone that she's in danger, when he can't even speak? Naomi said that the killer might return; it would be his fault if the man hurt her. He's been patrolling the area around her house all day, too afraid to leave it unguarded. He can't face another death on his conscience, so he watches the front entrance, from inside a thicket of elm trees, with an old branch gripped in his hand as a weapon. He has stared at the old mansion's gates for so long his vision is blurred. The night birds are beginning their evening chorus, but their song is hard to interpret. Are they telling him to keep watch, or run for help? He dithers for another minute before deciding. He must find someone trustworthy, who will understand what's wrong.

When he looks up again, the Tolmans' house is lit up like a beacon across the bay. Jimmy gives the old mansion a final glance before floundering through the bushes. He's out of breath when he reaches the Tolmans' property, where lights blaze from the ground floor windows, but when he raps on the door, the architect's wife answers. Deborah stands there waiting for him to speak, but all that emerges from his mouth is a rush of garbled sounds.

'Leave that stick in the porch then come inside, Jimmy.'

He points across the bay, trying to make himself understood, but Deborah just smiles and opens the door wider.

'Martin's at the pub, but he'll be back soon. Come through to the kitchen; you look hungry.'

Deborah leads him to the kitchen then places a cup of milk and a wedge of cake in front of him. His hunger is so great that he gobbles it down, without noticing that she's left the room, but once the food is finished, her quiet voice echoes through the wall. She's calling the police, her tone low and insistent, filling him with panic. He rises to his feet so fast the chair clatters to the floor. If the police take him, Naomi will never escape. Mrs Tolman calls out his name as he runs down the hallway, but it's too late. He yanks the front door open then runs back through the clearing.

23

I'm alone at the lifeboat house, sifting through witness statements, when Deborah Tolman calls me at 8 p.m. She sounds troubled, saying that the Birdman came to her home earlier in an agitated state, only to disappear again. When I put down the phone, I regret sending Eddie home, but don't want to summon him back. He's done hours of overtime since the case started, and the Birdman has an uncanny ability to hide from us. It's likely that he's sheltering in one of the island's caves or barns, always staying one step ahead. I pull on my waterproof to carry out a quick search around the Tolman's property, even though it may not yield a result.

The weather has stopped its assault on the island when I get outside, but I can tell the reprieve is only temporary. The atmosphere feels too still, as if the storm is just holding its breath. Shadow seems happy to join in the search, chasing after my torch beam when I scan the fields. It takes less than ten minutes to reach the Tolman's house, where Deborah is waiting for me.

'Jimmy ran down the path inland,' she says. 'Shall I come with you?'

'No need, stay indoors and keep safe. Did you work out why Jimmy came here?'

'Martin's one of the few people he trusts. I think he was hoping to see him, but he was out walking.'

'I'll look for Jimmy now, don't worry.'

Despite my advice, Deborah Tolman still looks anguished as I back away. It's frustrating that the Birdman has come within touching distance, but there's no sign of him as I comb the paths along the clifftop, then spiral inland, checking every outbuilding I pass. After a fruitless hour of walking, I call it quits, resigning myself to look again tomorrow, but Shadow's behaviour deteriorates as we reach Middle Town. He's barking at full volume, the sound so anguished that I lean down to grab his collar. My dog is straining to escape, releasing high-pitched howls, his movements frantic. I glance around to see what's spooked him, but find no obvious cause.

'Shut up,' I hiss, yet he carries on baying at the clouds. 'You're a bloody liability.'

He slips from my grasp, sprinting down the lane through Middle Town. It crosses my mind to let him run, but there's every chance he'll circle back and continue his infernal howling in the small hours, just for the fun of it. I've only been chasing after him for a few minutes when the air sours, my mouth filling with the taste of smoke.

Shadow is leading me towards Naomi Vine's house, where flames are spearing through a hole in the roof. Adrenaline makes me run faster. If I don't act soon, she'll be burned alive, just like Alex Rogan. The front door is unlocked when I push it open and it's clear that I'll have to act fast. The choking air is growing hotter all the time.

'Stay back,' I yell at the dog, who's still at my heels, barking frantically.

I make a quick call to Eddie but he doesn't pick up, so I leave a voicemail telling him to alert the volunteer fire officers, before plunging into the smoke. Even with the collar of my coat pressed over my face, the fumes attack my airways in seconds, my eyes streaming. I try to recall the layout of the house, groping along the hallway to the staircase. If Vine hasn't escaped, she's likely to be in her bedroom.

Flames are climbing the wall when I reach the top storey, the air pungent with chemicals. I kick open a bedroom door but there's no sign of her. The rooms are all empty, but the fire is gaining hold, smoke drifting through cracks between the floorboards. Flames billow through the central stairwell, so I take the back stairs, where I'm greeted by a fresh pall of smoke. There's a crackling sound as the wooden panelling catches, then a roaring noise, like a cry rising to a shout, but I flail through the dark until I reach a pocket of clear air in the cavernous living room. It dawns on me suddenly that Naomi will be trying to save her work, but flames are bursting through the doors of her studio. Heat and smoke prevent me from going further until I spot a figure on the floor.

The Birdman is lying on his side, his ragged clothes filthy with soot. Fierce heat sears my skin as I lift his dead weight over my shoulder then make for the exit, but a line of flames spears from the floor, blocking our way out. I take a deep breath before running through the fire. It seems to take forever before we spill out onto the lawn, my lungs heaving for air with smoke billowing from my blackened clothes. I'm lucky not to have sustained injuries, but Jimmy is still semi-conscious when I lay him on the grass, smears of soot marking his narrow face. The oddness of his appearance hits home, now that I see him up close. His grey hair stands out in uneven clumps, so ragged he must cut it himself; bundles of feathers protrude from the pockets of trousers that are inches too short and riddled with holes. I'm still coughing myself hoarse when it occurs to me that Naomi Vine could still be inside.

Yellow flames leap through the attic windows with greater intensity than before, the core of the mansion crumbling. Roof slats are dropping to the ground behind us, but my strength is fading. It requires stamina to haul the unconscious man towards the gates while lumps of brick rain down on us. A section of lead guttering smashes to the ground, missing us by less than a metre as I carry him to safety.

'Are you all right?' Eddie is running along the path, his torchlight shining in my face.

I double over, coughing smoke from my lungs. I'm almost certain that Jimmy Curwen started the fire, but I'll need to check how the island's teenage arsonist spent the last few hours.

'Check on Adam Helston, Eddie, quick as you can.'

Eddie sets off at a rapid jog. Curwen is coming round at last, his gaze sharpening. The man's breathing sounds hoarse but at least he'll be fit to interview. If he's the arsonist, he must have a vicious nature: Naomi welcomed him and this is how he repays her. It looks like he set light to the building then got trapped inside.

'Were you alone in there, Jimmy? Or did someone help you?'

The man shuts his eyes, too cowardly to return my gaze. I can feel the flames' heat from twenty metres and there's still no sign of the fire officers, removing my only hope of searching for Naomi. The noise is deafening as window panes fracture and more of the roof collapses. The Birdman doesn't speak as the blaze takes hold, but tears leak from his closed eyes. The damage he's caused seems to give him little pleasure.

When I look back down the lane, a stout figure is heading towards us, his white beard visible against the dark. Stan Eden must have seen the blaze from the lighthouse and hurried down to help. His gaze skims the Birdman's face before he turns in my direction.

'I can take him to mine, if you want. He'll catch cold out here.'

'Thanks, Stan. Keep him locked indoors till I can join you.'

Curwen's face is as blank as a sleepwalker's when he stumbles to his feet. The man's clothes look ready to fall apart; his worn-out boots are filthy with mud and his jumper is covered in scorch marks, hands wounded by cuts and burns. He's shaking so violently that I drape my coat round his shoulders then watch Stan Eden lead him towards his home, a ten-minute walk away in Middle Town. The Birdman seems oblivious to the drama he's caused. He keeps his head tipped back as he walks, his gaze fixed on the sky.

Fire officers are arriving at last. A tractor is dragging the hydrant towards the blaze, with half a dozen volunteers running ahead. I have to yell to make my instructions heard, above the sound of the roof collapsing, but the thin stream of water has little effect. I leave Mike Walbert in charge until I can return. My biggest concern is to find out what Jimmy Curwen was doing inside Naomi Vine's home.

There's no sign of Shadow until his bark echoes in the distance, letting me know he's safe. I stare back at the building when we near the village; the old mansion house looks like a giant Catherine wheel, with fire spewing from upstairs windows and yellow flames searing the brickwork. I have no way of knowing whether Naomi Vine is still trapped inside.

24

Stan Eden's home is the last lighthouse keepers' cottage in the terrace, and I arrive there at 11 p.m. From the outside it looks unremarkable, with a drab green front door, but the décor proves that the old man's lighthouse obsession runs deep. Pictures of an extinct lifestyle line his hallway, their monochrome ink turning sepia. They show uniformed men being winched from dinghies onto landing platforms, and playing chess in minute kitchens, while waves batter the windows. I feel a pang of envy for a profession with such clear rewards. The keepers endured hardships, but knew they were saving lives, while some murder investigations never get a result. Adrenaline is still pumping through my system, even though the immediate danger has passed; soot is making my skin itch, flakes of burned paint falling from my hands.

Jimmy Curwen is sitting at the kitchen table with a blanket round his shoulders, his eyes glassy. His nickname seems even more fitting when I study his features again. There's an avian quality to his sharp nose and his gaze that never fixes on anything for long. Eden has provided a basin of hot water and a flannel, but Curwen hasn't bothered to wipe the dirt from his skin; the man's expression is so blank the fire seems to have cauterised his emotions. I need to get inside his head, but he won't even make eye contact.

'Why did you visit the mansion house tonight, Jimmy?' I ask.

The Birdman's hands tremble in his lap. He only responds when Eden puts a glass of water in front of him, gulping down the liquid in rapid swallows.

'Can't you interview him tomorrow, when he's rested?' Eden asks. 'He's welcome to sleep here.'

'Jimmy may have started the fire, Stan. He should be in a holding cell till we know what happened.'

The old man gives me a stern look. 'There's a lock on the bedroom door, but he'd never harm me. I've known him since he was born. He's a boy, trapped inside a man's body.'

When I look at the Birdman again his lips contort into odd shapes, fists clenching in his lap while he tries to speak.

'Tied up . . . in the fire.' His words are a hoarse whisper.

'Is that how you left Naomi, Jimmy?'

The Birdman's face bows over his lap, tears landing on the backs of his hands. It's obvious that he's too exhausted to talk again so I lead him upstairs to Eden's spare room. I make him take off his boots before he curls up on the single bed, like an exhausted child. I pity him, no matter what evils he's committed. His clothes stink of smoke, his face gaunt with tiredness, matted grey hair plastered against his skull. He looks ill-prepared for the media spotlight that will glare down on him if he's the killer.

Once I get back downstairs, my eyes scan more photos of lighthouses. I'm still studying the images when Eden returns with arms full of firewood, chuntering under his breath. He drops down on the stool opposite, fingers tugging at his white beard.

'You can't prove that Jimmy started that fire, can you?' he asks.

'He was in the building, Stan. I have to know why.'

'Jimmy would never harm anyone. He's faced enough tragedy in his lifetime.'

'What do you mean?'

'The lad saw his sister fall from the Bar at high tide. Her body washed up on Covean Beach three days later; that's when he stopped talking. Jimmy was ten years old. He's only been interested in saving his birds ever since.'

'That's a sad story, but Naomi Vine may have been burned alive in her own home. He's been on the run for days. It looks like he started the blaze then got trapped inside.'

Eden scowls at me. 'People scapegoat him for being different, and you're no better.'

'I have to base my judgements on evidence.'

'Jimmy wouldn't harm that woman. Plenty of people want her gone, but he'd never hurt a soul. He'll crack up if you lock him indoors.'

'Keep him here till tomorrow, please, Stan. He should be in secure accommodation until I've interviewed him.'

'The lighthouse has got beds in the living quarters and locks on the doors.'

'We'll take him there tomorrow. Thanks for your help.'

I return to the fire, where Eddie is keeping watch. The emergency water tank is being refilled, but at last the flames are dwindling. Plumes of smoke funnel through the hole in the roof, an orange glow pulsing behind the upstairs windows.

'Not a pretty sight, is it?' Eddie says.

'Seeing someone's home destroyed never is. What's the news on Adam Helston?'

'His room's below his mum and dad's. He could have sneaked out then run back there before I arrived.'

'We'll do a full search tomorrow. At least Curwen's under lock and key.'

The sergeant throws me a questioning look, but has enough sense to keep his views about the Birdman to himself. Guilty or innocent, I need to find out why he was present at both fires and has been on the run for days. We stand side by side, powerless to do anything except watch the property smoulder. I remember a specialist fire investigator telling me once that arsonists love watching the misery they cause. I scan the grounds of Naomi Vine's house then spin round to look back down the lane, aware that the killer may already have us in his sights.

25

Tuesday 9 November

Pain wakes Jimmy at dawn, the wounds on his hands pulsing with heat. He peers through the curtains towards Wingletang Down: the old mansion has stood on the skyline since before he was born, but now smoke is billowing from its roof. He remembers Naomi Vine's low voice pleading for help. If she lies at the heart of the blaze, he's to blame. Tears course down his cheeks, for the man in the fire, and the woman he failed to set free.

Ben Kitto will ask more questions when morning comes. The tall policeman puts him on edge, his build so huge he looks like a giant from a child's storybook. Jimmy wants to explain everything he's seen, but the detective's dark green stare silences him. He thinks of the pain on Naomi Vine's face and longs to run back to her house, praying she's still alive.

Jimmy runs his fingers along the window frame, managing to lever it open. It crosses his mind to swing his legs over the sill and let himself drop, but the distance to the concrete patio is too great. He'd break his legs if he tried to jump. Cold air caresses his face, but there's no birdsong to comfort Jimmy tonight. Even the owls have deserted him.

26

I leave Shadow by the back entrance of the Turk's Head as the morning light intensifies, determined to reward him for alerting me to the fire. Without his help, Jimmy Curwen would have died at the scene. I peer through the window of the pub's kitchen where a light shines above steel-topped work tables, but there's no one around, so I help myself to a handful of sausages from the fridge. Shadow gives a bark of appreciation when I reappear with his unexpected feast.

'How did you know people were in danger?'

The dog is too busy wolfing down his reward to listen, but I wish he could answer. His acute sense of smell would make him an ideal sniffer dog, if only his wayward behaviour could be corrected.

Once I get back to my room, I peel off my clothes then step under the shower. The water that swirls down the plughole is tinged grey as I shampoo soot from my scalp. Lack of sleep hasn't caught up with me yet, my brain spinning with information. The Birdman only gave a single reply, saying that Vine was tied up in the fire. There must be a link between Rogan's brutal killing and the destruction of the sculptor's home. It's possible that someone started the latest blaze then trapped Jimmy Curwen inside the building, intending to let him burn, leaving Vine's body lying in the wreckage too, but the Birdman's odd behaviour still makes him my chief suspect.

The storm has strengthened when I dress in the half-light. Trees and bushes are being pummelled by the wind, glass vibrating inside the window frame with each new gust, while rain falls in solid sheets. The elements seem determined to slow the investigation, and any forensic evidence at Vine's house will be diluted. My phone pulses in my pocket just as I'm preparing to leave my room, DCI Madron's name appearing on the screen. His sole focus is on today's press conference. The weather conditions mean that the journalists must question me by Skype, rather than face-to-face.

'At least the killer's under arrest, Kitto.'

'I need to question Curwen before charging him. We don't have any clear evidence.'

His tone cools. 'I imagine Liz Gannick will find plenty of proof that he torched Naomi Vine's house.'

'When she does I'll let you know.'

'I hope you're keeping her sweet. If she files a negative report we'll all suffer.'

'I realise that.'

'Don't show any doubt to those journalists, they'll eat you alive.'

'I have dealt with the press before, sir.'

'It's a pity I can't get over to run the event.' Madron sounds disappointed, but for me it's a lucky escape. The storm may have cut St Agnes adrift from the outside world, but I'm free to complete my work without interference. The only downside is that Eddie and I will have to enlist volunteers to get the job done. One of our first tasks will be to take Jimmy Curwen to the lighthouse, then recruit islanders to stand guard.

I leave my room before 8 a.m., lack of sleep making me desperate for coffee. Ella Tregarron is in the pub's kitchen already, unloading plates from the dishwasher, her expression tense as she pours me a coffee from the percolator. The investigation needs to make progress fast, to stop unknown threats putting the islanders on edge.

Liz Gannick appears in the doorway as I finish my drink. She looks ready for business, her petite frame clad in waterproofs when she follows me into the bar. She listens in silence when I explain about the fire.

'I'm surprised you slept through the commotion,' I say. 'A dozen people turned out to help, but the fire investigator can't fly here in this weather.'

Gannick nods at the breakers racing across the shore. 'The forecast says the storm could last two more days. You may as well show me the ruins, before I check Rogan's house.'

She doesn't complain when scouring wind attacks us during our walk, using her sticks to swing between puddles, while Shadow chases away to find shelter.

The damage to Vine's house looks worse by daylight. A pall of smoke still hangs over the building, despite the rain, and it's clear that the property has been comprehensively destroyed when we enter the overgrown garden. My expertise lies in murder investigation, not arson, but even I can see that someone worked hard to create such a powerful blaze.

It hits me for the first time that if her remains lie inside the building, Naomi Vine's death would have been just as agonising as Alex Rogan's, making me wish I'd defended her better. Window frames are scorched and splintering, revealing the house's blackened interior, parquet singed from the floor. Gannick remains silent as we circle the grounds, pausing to take photos on her phone.

'The fire started inside,' she comments.

'How do you know?'

'You'd see trails on the external brickwork if flammable liquid had been poured through windows or doors.' She turns to face me. 'I imagine they set a chain of fires through the core of the house, for a quick result. A wooden-framed building like this would go up in minutes.'

I remember the panelling inside the living room and the lime-washed beams in Vine's hallway. The place didn't stand a chance once fire started. Rain is falling harder than before, but it's too late to save the property now the damage is done. Gannick picks her way along the path at a rapid pace, swinging her legs over pieces of fallen masonry, like an athlete shifting her weight between parallel bars. Many people would rely on a wheelchair in her situation, but her independence is admirable; if I were in her situation, I might be tempted by the easier option. The woman is paler than before when we return to the front entrance, and I'm not surprised. There's something horrifying about seeing the mansion in its ruined state, especially when it may also be a murder scene. I'm about to climb the steps when Gannick gives me a sharp look.

'Never enter a crime scene without overalls; you should know that by now.' Her tone is brisk when she passes me a bag containing a white Tyvek suit and overshoes.

'The structure's unsafe, Liz. Stay here while I check the hallway.'

'You asked *me* for help, remember?' Gannick's features are hard with irritation. 'I'm not police anymore; I run my own operation.'

The set look on her face proves that resistance is futile. When we approach the front entrance the lock is still intact. Naomi Vine must have welcomed the killer inside, unless he already had a key.

'I told her to keep the place secure.'

'She didn't listen,' Gannick mutters. 'Or it was someone she trusted.'

She falls silent as we enter the hallway, debris crunching underfoot.

The air reeks of smoke, and blackened plaster is falling from the stairwell where the mahogany balustrade has been reduced to spent matchsticks. Gannick motions for me to remain by the entrance before unrolling silver fabric across the floor. Her face is shiny with concentration as she assesses every detail, running her torch beam over the worst fire damage.

Naomi Vine's living room is a blackened shell; only her largest sculptures are intact, the metal covered by a patina of soot. Part of the ceiling has collapsed in the kitchen, units burned from the walls, but the worst devastation is in Vine's studio. I can't tell whether fire or vandalism has caused greater damage. There's a crater in the floor where boards have collapsed, holes gouged from the walls, many of her sculptures defaced.

'The roof may come down,' I tell Gannick. 'Don't spend long in here.'

'I can't rush my work.'

'Those beams could collapse any minute.'

'For God's sake,' she snaps. 'Let me do my job. If she died here, we need to find her body.'

It crosses my mind to haul her outside, but her help may be essential, and I owe it to Naomi to find out exactly what happened. 'I'll put a guard in the hallway until you're ready to leave.'

It only takes Eddie ten minutes to report for guard duty. The young sergeant looks astonished when I explain that the killer may have been hiding here for hours, keeping Naomi Vine captive, just like Alex Rogan.

'I didn't search this place yesterday. I thought it was secure,' he murmurs.

'So did I. It's not your fault, Eddie.'

His expression lightens by a fraction. 'Shall I check the grounds again?'

'Keep watch here until Liz finishes her search.'

My deputy stations himself in the ruined hallway while I scan the grounds. Some of the trees nearest the house have charred branches from flames that spilled through the windows last night, when the blaze was at its height. The rest of the overgrown gardens look undisturbed, until I see that the largest outbuilding has been left open, and a telltale stench of paraffin catches the back of my throat. The killer probably made several trips here, storing the flammable liquid he needed to start a fire until the deed was done. I peer through the entrance, unwilling to destroy evidence he may have left inside, but rags and tins of turps lie on the work bench. Either the killer has tried not to leave fingerprint evidence or he doesn't care about being found.

Once I've searched the grounds thoroughly, I return to the gates, which provide the only entrance to the property, unless he scaled the ten-foot-high brick wall. I curse under my breath when I spot something hanging from the ironwork gate, suspended from a wire. It's an oyster shell, its edges softened by the sea's pounding. The killer has followed the same pattern as before,

leaving another taunt for me to find; a stream of capital
letters have been written on the shell's smooth lining.
He must have a cool head to leave his calling card then
saunter away from a burning building. I'm dropping
the shell into an evidence bag when Eddie runs along
the path, his face pink with excitement.

'Gannick's found something, boss.'

The forensics chief is on all fours in the studio, examining the inglenook fireplace. The muscles on the back
of my neck tense as I crouch beside her, certain that
she's discovered Naomi's corpse.

'It looks like someone was held here,' she says.
'There's a length of chain and a padlock, but no sign
of a body.'

I study the blackened metal in silence, a flicker
of hope rising in my chest. The find supports the
Birdman's claim that Naomi Vine was tied up in the
fire. The sculptor struck me as a tough customer, and
she's already fought off one attacker, but she can't have
escaped her fetters like a modern day Houdini unless
she was released. I need to understand the common
denominator between her and Rogan, to find out why
they were both targeted, but above all I want to know
whether she's still alive. If she was having an affair
with the astronomer, someone could have been jealous
enough to attack them both, but I've got no definite
proof. The two victims are both talented incomers,
well-known in their field. Everyone warmed to Alex
Rogan, but Naomi Vine has made enemies ever since

she arrived. Someone on the island may have resented her presence enough to want her dead. If it's Curwen, there will be no more violence while he's locked away, but I'm not fully committed to the idea. The killer appears to be enjoying himself, his latest blaze more flamboyant than the bonfire that claimed Alex Rogan's life. My thoughts are racing too fast, aware that the campaign could escalate. The most likely outcome is that Naomi's body lies in another room of her ruined mansion, but if she didn't die in the fire, she's still in danger. There's an outside chance that the killer has dragged her to another location, preparing to start his next blaze.

27

A man's tall figure is waiting on the path when I leave Naomi Vine's house, his face obscured by his coat collar. Martin Tolman must have an important question if he's willing to endure a wind forceful enough to hurl fallen branches across the open land. The architect's distinguished features already appear blanched by the cold. Shadow normally treats strangers like long-lost friends, but today he releases a growl before snapping his teeth at Tolman, forcing me to grab his collar.

'He won't hurt you, Martin. It's just the wind making him edgy.'

Tolman keeps his distance when he nods at the house. 'I saw the smoke from across the bay. Can I help at all?'

'I need guards at the lighthouse this afternoon; people are taking it in turns. Can you be there by three?'

'That's no problem. Is Naomi safe?' His expression sobers as he says her name.

'We're searching the building now. Did you know each other before she moved here? I saw one of her sculptures in your lounge.'

'We're just neighbours, but I admire her work. Was she caught in the fire?'

'I hope she escaped. She may be sheltering somewhere nearby.'

'Do you want me to search the down?'

'That's a good place to start.'

Shadow reacts badly to Tolman raising his hand in a farewell gesture. He lunges forward again, jaws snapping, until I hiss at him to behave. The architect makes slow progress crossing the exposed ground, his black coat splayed by the wind. He seems far tenser than the last time we met, but for no obvious reason. It makes me question whether his link with Naomi goes beyond simple neighbourliness, but my immediate concern is for Liz Gannick, who is still scouring the ground floor of the torched mansion, despite hazards posed by falling timbers. After dodging the grim reaper twice, she seems certain that her life is charmed.

Eddie looks upset when he finally joins me on the path. I've known him long enough to understand that he hates unfinished business; if we don't find Naomi Vine soon his frustrations will slow him down. The young sergeant keeps his head down as we walk away, his features obscured by his scarf as we face the battering wind. Our next duty is to collect the Birdman from

Stan Eden's home, but my deputy comes to a halt as we reach Middle Town.

'Can I say something, sir?'

'Go ahead, Eddie.'

'We're going in the wrong direction. The Birdman couldn't have planned that fire; he lacks the intellect. Why not let me interview him, to find out why he was at Vine's property? You could carry on looking for her body.' The sergeant looks astonished by his act of rebellion when his speech ends, but concerns about the case have blunted my ability to listen.

'People keep saying Curwen's innocent, but his coat was thrown over Alex Rogan's body. He was in Naomi's house when it burned down – and he's given us the runaround for days. Jimmy Curwen is still our chief suspect. You can go back and help Liz Gannick if that bothers you, but let me get on with it.'

Eddie gives an embarrassed nod. 'Okay, boss, I'll leave you to it. I've said my piece.'

He hurries away, leaving me to complete my walk in silence. It's the first time my deputy has ever questioned my judgement, but it's too late to back down.

Jimmy Curwen is wearing fresh clothes when I collect him from Eden's house. The lighthouse keeper has kitted him out in old-fashioned jeans, a padded jacket and lace-up shoes. Last night's soot has been washed from his skin, but he's still carrying his prized possessions: bundles of feathers protrude from the pocket of the jacket as I lead him towards the lighthouse. Curwen keeps his face averted during the short journey, but a chorus of birdsong rises overhead, a row of black-headed gulls calling from the roofline of the house opposite, while a kittiwake hovers above us. The birds appear to be serenading him. The creatures are so used to sharing his food, they're expecting a free meal. Jimmy's behaviour becomes panicky when he sees Louise Walbert standing by the lighthouse. The island's solicitor has agreed to be his advocate, and for once her vivid wardrobe has been replaced by business clothes. She looks like a typical lawyer in her smart navy coat, clutching a briefcase in her hand, proving that she has more than one identity.

Curwen's thin face looks strained when we coax him inside, using a pincer movement to propel him up the spiral staircase, through the building's narrow core. The keepers' former kitchen is equipped with custom-built cupboards that line its curved wall. The melamine table has been scrubbed clean, but its surface is so scarred it must have stood there since the light was active.

'Take a seat please, Jimmy.'

The man's hands tremble while I read him his rights, his gaze flitting towards the door as if he's longing for freedom.

'Your coat was found at the scene of Alex Rogan's murder. The binoculars in the pocket were yours too. Was it you who laid your sheepskin over his body or someone else?'

His odd, beakish face is impassive when I repeat the question, but the look in his eyes proves that he understands every word.

'Try to say yes or no to each question, Jimmy,' Louise whispers.

The man studies the surface of the table, his hands clutched in his lap. My only option is to use another method. My old partner in London taught me that interviewing is about give and take; if you offer something, you get something in return.

I lower my voice to a quieter register. 'Ella's been feeding your birds. She's got a soft spot for you, hasn't she?' I pause before continuing. 'All you have to do is explain why you ran away after Alex died.'

The man's expression relaxes slightly, his mouth forming shapes, but only a hiss of air emerges when he tries to speak.

'I need to know about Naomi Vine, too. What happened at her house last night?'

Curwen's head is bowed, a few tears splashing onto the lino at his feet. Louise and I sit in uncomfortable silence while he weeps; there's no point in hurling questions at a man in no state to answer.

'Help us out, Jimmy. Tell me what happened. Then, if you've done nothing wrong, you can go.'

'He can only be held for thirty-six hours from point of arrest.' Louise looks apologetic, as if she regrets having to remind me of the custody law.

I address Curwen again. 'I'll leave you a pen and

paper then come back later. Write down what you remember about the last few days. The door will be locked, but you're not alone; people are taking turns to sit outside.'

I glance at the wall and notice that the clock's hands aren't moving. Maybe the last lighthouse keeper removed the battery on his way out, leaving time at a standstill. Frustration makes me feel like punching a wall, but professional courtesy prompts me to thank Louise Walbert before she retreats down the metal stairs.

Ella Tregarron is already waiting on the landing to begin her guard duty. She's swaddled in scarves and a padded coat, long black hair snaking across her shoulders, her skin clear of make-up. The landlady looks more vulnerable without her painted smile. I explain that another islander will take over soon, but to call me if the Birdman becomes agitated.

'I've brought Jimmy some food,' she says.

'That's a kind thought.'

I carry the Tupperware box through to Curwen, before locking him inside the small room. Ella has already begun her vigil. She's placed a stool opposite one of the windows, facing north across the island, while gusts of wind rattle the glass. She seems happy to watch the storm savage the island, until the next guard arrives.

28

Jimmy relaxes once the room empties. He stares down at the sheets of paper the policeman left behind, wishing he'd tried harder at school. But the letters danced across the page, impossible to pin down. When other boys taunted his silence, his mother let him stay at home, putting a stop to his education. The only words etched on his memory are the Cornish phrases his grandfather taught him decades ago.

He pushes the paper aside then peers into the food box. It contains sausage rolls, sandwiches and a couple of bananas. He puts the bread aside then stands with his back against the wall to eat, still hungry after days without proper meals. Then he opens the narrow window and peers outside. The ocean is unrolling to the west, with no interruption until it laps the horizon, gale-force wind roughening its grey surface. Sea birds hover above the island, hoping for shelter.

Gulls descend when Jimmy extends his hand from the window, scooping bread from his palm, his spirits lifting for the first time in days.

'I missed you,' he whispers.

Birds circle the window long after all the food has gone, pecking at the glass. Jimmy's mood plummets once the last one flies away. He sits at the table with shoulders hunched and nothing to distract him until the police return. But soon a woman's voice addresses him through the door. Ella's soft tone makes him smile: the landlady has been kind since his mother died, making sure he doesn't go hungry. She seems to understand that he would prefer to work for his living than beg scraps from neighbours, often leaving food parcels outside his flat.

He presses his ear to the door, to listen more easily.

'Are you okay, Jimmy? Tap if you can hear me.'

Jimmy raps his knuckles on the wood, hoping she will carry on talking. Ella's thick Cornish accent reminds him of home, her sentences rolling like a slow tide.

'The police will ask if you killed Alex Rogan.' Her voice quietens, until he can barely hear it. 'They'll keep you locked up until you say you're guilty. Say yes to every question, Jimmy. It's the right thing to do. Tell them you hurt Alex and it was you who set fire to Naomi's house.'

Jimmy's thoughts are confused. His father told him never to lie, yet he feels sure Ella is giving good advice, because her voice is gentle, and she has always supported him. He presses his ear to the wood and pays attention to her words. She repeats the message until it lodges in his mind and his memory of the real events starts to blur.

29

It's almost 10 a.m. when I return to the Turk's Head. I've left little time to prepare for the video conference, and pandering to journalists seems like madness during a murder investigation. The interview with my chief suspect has proved inconclusive, but I'm starting to wonder whether Eddie might be right. I should be in the incident room checking every piece of evidence, while Liz Gannick completes her forensic search for Naomi's body. I curse under my breath as I put on my one smart jacket then position my computer in front of a blank wall, thankful that my ancient jeans and mud-spattered boots will be hidden from view.

Six faces appear on my screen when the conference begins: journalists from the BBC, Sky, the Press Association and a few tabloids, as well as the *Cornish Gazette*. By lunchtime, Alex Rogan's death will be common knowledge, his celebrity status making the media hungry for details. My own image will appear on news websites within hours, but that's not important.

I need to stop anyone gaining details of Rogan's agonising death, to protect Sally from press intrusion. I
also have no intention of releasing information about
last night's events, until I know what's happened to
Naomi Vine. The first questions are easy, like the
opening problems in an exam, getting tougher as the
interview progresses.

'Why have you banned journalists from the island?'
one of the reporters asks.

'No one can visit St Agnes until the investigation
ends. There will be plenty of time for questions once
the killer's caught.'

'Have you arrested any suspects?'

'We're pursuing some strong lines of inquiry. I'm
confident we'll soon be able to name the killer.'

'A local source says that Alex Rogan died in a fire,
Inspector Kitto. And I've heard that the sculptor Naomi
Vine's house went up in flames last night. Is that true?'

I keep my expression neutral. 'I can confirm that a
property was set alight, but my investigation's ongoing.
I can't release any further details at this time.'

The local reporter throws me an easier question. 'Is
the Dark Skies Festival going ahead?'

'The Cornish Tourist Board will make a decision soon. Details will be published on their website
next week.'

I close the interview once the fifteen-minute time
slot ends, relieved to slam my laptop shut. If I don't
find the killer soon, the press will send drones over

the island, scouring every cove for clues. An islander must be profiting from selling information to the press, despite my warnings, but I need to focus on finding the killer, not rooting out spies. They're lucky I don't know their identity or I'd throw them in the lighthouse with Jimmy Curwen.

My walk to Sally's house gives me time to gather my thoughts. The killer may have attacked Alex Rogan and Naomi Vine for planning to put St Agnes on the map: Rogan wanted to share the beauty of the islands' dark skies, and Vine believed that her reputation would attract visitors to see her sculptures. It's possible that the Birdman has been drawn into the violence, but he can't be acting alone. The Cornish clues left at each crime scene increase my certainty that the killer is defending his territory, signalling to outsiders that they're not welcome. He seems to view anyone from outside St Agnes as the enemy, including me, even though my birthplace lies just three miles north by sea.

I'm still digesting the facts when Zoe emerges from the Rogans' home. Her expression's strained, but I can tell she's battling to stay calm for her friend's sake. She steps into the porch, pulling the door shut behind her.

'Sally went out again last night. I found her, shivering with cold.'

'Where did she go?'

'She was watching the fire on the down, babbling

to herself. At least she's making sense now. I made her take one of the sedatives the doctor prescribed.' She looks uncomfortable when she speaks again, her voice reduced to a whisper. 'Sal could have set light to Naomi's place, Ben. Anyone can see she's disturbed.'

'I'll come in and talk to her.'

It crosses my mind that Zoe's suspicions may be correct. Sally could have torched Naomi Vine's house, believing that she was having an affair with Alex, but the idea sounds far-fetched. Whoever set the fire planned how to send the huge property up in flames in the shortest possible time. Sally would have to be a skilled actor to put on such a convincing show of grief while remaining calm enough to execute such a complex crime.

I find her slumped on the sofa in the living room, dressed in leggings and a loose T-shirt, hands braced over the mound of her belly as if defending her baby from another attack. The air carries a sickly odour of air freshener and distress. Sally doesn't react to my arrival: shock must be hitting home – or the effects of the sedative she took – a dazed look in her wide-set brown eyes. My old schoolmate seems to be falling apart right in front of my eyes.

'I hear you took a walk outside last night, Sal. That's not a good idea. Please stay indoors until we catch Alex's killer.'

Her response is slow to arrive. 'If you can't find him, I'll do it myself.'

'You need to keep safe.' I study her tense features again. 'What time did you go out last night?'

'I don't know. I couldn't sleep, so I went for a walk. It's the only thing that helps me think straight.' Sally's voice rises to a shout suddenly, her skin reddening. 'The bastard that killed Alex is out there somewhere. No one's hunting for him.'

'That's not true, Sally. We're working round the clock.'

'Is it Jimmy Curwen? I heard he's been arrested.'

'You'll be first to know.'

'Alex deserves better.' Anger cuts through her drug-induced monotone again, her hands balling into fists. 'Get out of here, Ben. Don't come back till his killer's locked away.'

Zoe gives me a quizzical look when I step back into the hall, as if she expects me to share her suspicions, but I've seen every kind of grief reaction in my time, from numb denial to psychotic fury. If the person I loved most had been taken, I'd be lashing out too, desperate for answers. The depth of Sally's misery makes me certain she's not the killer.

'She's changed,' Zoe whispers. 'It feels like she's out of reach.'

'Keep her company while time passes. That's what she needs.'

She looks me squarely in the eyes. 'Are you angry with me, Ben?'

'Of course not. There's a lot on my plate, that's all.'

'Why not let me help?'

Her hand skims my wrist, but I can't afford distractions; if another victim dies, it will be because I've missed vital clues. Instinct tells me to clear the air, but I offer a quick goodbye and march away.

I follow the path towards the lifeboat house, ignoring the wind that's threatening to blind me. Halfway along the route someone calls my name and Shadow gives a joyful bark of greeting. The approaching figure is Steve Tregarron. The landlord's grey hair is plastered flat by rain, his face drawn by the cold breeze.

'This came for you, Ben.' He holds out a manila envelope that's blotched by raindrops, the printed label immediately recognisable. 'It was delivered last night.'

'Where did you find it?'

'At the pub, inside the porch.'

My concern rises immediately; the killer must be gaining confidence, fearless enough to walk through the village at night, risking exposure. 'Thanks, Steve. I don't suppose you know any Cornish, do you?'

He shakes his head. 'My gran taught me the months of the year and how to count to ten, but that's my limit.'

'Same here.'

The killer must despise our ignorance. Cornish was declared extinct a decade ago, and despite attempted revivals, a beautiful Celtic tongue has been allowed to die out. Apart from a few schools and societies, only a few hundred people can still speak it fluently.

Shadow bounces up to lick Tregarron's hand until the man bends down to stroke him.

'What time did you get home after the fire last night, Steve?'

'Four a.m. Ella only found the envelope this morning.' He gives Shadow a final rub before straightening up again.

'So it was delivered after dawn.'

I thank him and say goodbye, but the dog lingers on the path, whimpering. He's a creature of easy loyalties and Tregarron must have fed him recently, so he chases him back towards Middle Town. I'm alone when I hurry to the boathouse with the killer's latest missive tucked inside my pocket.

30

The message is written on an oyster shell, like the one outside Naomi Vine's house, but when I inspect it under a strong light, the words are different. Someone used a steady hand to inscribe a whorl of letters. I type the messages from both shells into the translation website, which only takes seconds. The one left outside Naomi Vine's home is short and simple:

Ty a's kyv y'n tyller sans.

I recognise a few of the words written in the message Steve Tregarron just gave me, but its overall meaning is a mystery:

Fisten ma na garthons faglow hy enev kyns bora.

It's only when the translation site converts the statements into English that they link together:

You will find her at the holy place.
Act fast, or by sunrise, flames will cleanse her soul.

I feel a sharp burst of relief. I was afraid the sculptor had died in the fire, but there's a chance she's still alive. The killer's timespan is clear even though the location is designed to confuse me. He's claiming that Naomi Vine has until dawn tomorrow to live, yet he's sending us on a wild goose chase while he plans his next fire. The entire island is a holy site, according to historians: the Scillies were one land mass before sea levels rose, with early civilisations burying their dead on mountaintops, which are all that remain of the ancient landscape. The killer could be referring to one of the cairns or entrance graves that litter the island, or he may be lying through his teeth. I'll need to organise another search of the island with Eddie once he returns from the fire scene with Liz Gannick.

There's no sign of Shadow when I set off for the Helstons' farm, determined to keep my approach methodical. Naomi Vine's got a tough constitution; if she's alive, the killer will be getting a run for his money. All I need to do is follow the trail he's left behind. If Adam Helston is innocent, the killer entered his home by stealth and placed a box of fire-starting equipment in his bedroom. Whoever murdered Alex Rogan has few scruples. What kind of killer would use a troubled seventeen-year-old boy to camouflage their guilt?

227

I stand outside the farm's front door, with rain dripping down the back of my neck. When Julie finally answers, she wears the same closed look as before, hiding her thoughts behind a blank mask. The woman is wearing a plain black dress, grey hair hanging down in rats' tails, as if she's determined to hide any signs of attractiveness.

'Can I come in, please, Julie? I've got a warrant to search your property.' She takes a single step back, forcing me to edge past her into the hall. 'Do you often leave the house empty?'

'Hardly ever,' she replies, her expression still guarded. 'Only when Sam and Adam are working outside and I pop out to see a neighbour.'

'Do you lock the door?'

She shakes her head. 'We never bothered until Alex Rogan died.'

'How often do you visit friends?'

'Two or three times a week. I see Rachel Carlyon or Louise Walbert for a cup of tea.'

I take a breath before trying a different tack. 'I'm not doing this to cause trouble, Julie. We both need to know who broke into Adam's room; it could prove his innocence.'

She gives a grudging nod. 'I went to the harbour to collect a food delivery last Wednesday and ran into Stan Eden, so we chatted for a bit. But the only other time the place was empty was Guy Fawkes Night. We were all at the bonfire party till midnight and the door was open.'

The news doesn't surprise me. Theft hardly ever happens on the islands, and the majority of people leave their doors unlocked all year round.

'Is it okay to search the ground floor?'

She grumbles in protest, but soon leaves me alone in her front room. It's full of shabby furniture, their outsized TV the family's only concession to luxury. The contents of cupboards and drawers include a file of letters from their mortgage company. The farm has racked up debts over the years, offsetting each new expense against the land's value until they are barely breaking even. Sam Helston's tension makes more sense now; he must feel like he's running on empty, as well as caring for a wayward son.

I move through the house at speed, aware that there's little time to waste if the killer's threat to kill Naomi Vine tonight is real. The upstairs rooms are equally blameless, just as I expected. The couple have cleared away any evidence of their son's love of pyrotechnics. I stare out from the window on the landing, noticing a thick evergreen hedge that shelters their back garden. The killer could have hidden behind it until the family went out for the evening, then entered the house without being spotted. Julie gives me a thoughtful look when I thank her for cooperating, but doesn't bother to say goodbye.

When I get outside, Sam Helston and his son are working in their packing shed, building boxes from thin sheets of plywood. By February the place will be full of hired labourers, preparing daffodils to be shipped to London, but right now the hangar rings with emptiness. I can see nothing incriminating here, only stacks of empty pallets.

'Sniffing round again, are you?' Sam Helston swings in my direction, while his son keeps his head down.

'Just doing my job. Thanks for helping put out the fire last night.'

He gives a grudging nod. 'It wasn't for your sake. Anyone would do the same.'

Adam steps closer to hear our conversation, even though his eyes remain fixed on the ground.

'Has anyone been hanging around the farmhouse?' I ask. 'I need to know who left that box in your room, Adam.'

'My mates come over from St Mary's sometimes, but they don't leave stuff here,' the boy replies.

'Our friends wouldn't try to frame Adam,' his father adds. 'What are you driving at?'

'An islander's responsible for this, and there'll be more violence if we don't stop it. Call me if you remember anything.'

When I hand my card to Helston he shoves it into his back pocket, his sour expression proving that he'll bin it once my back's turned.

I call for Louise Walbert on my way to Middle Town. She seems reluctant to attend the Birdman's second interview, only following me out of a sense of duty. When we approach the lighthouse, Jimmy appears at the high window, his expression as innocent as a child's. He's watching kittiwakes tumbling on the wind, mesmerised by their acrobatics. Gavin Carlyon has taken over guard duties and is waiting for us on the landing. The man is immersed in a book called *The Cornish Historic Family*, lifting his head to observe our arrival, his unblinking stare grazing my face. It crosses my mind that he may be glad that Naomi Vine's missing, so that his precious island can remain unchanged. I have to remind myself to be polite.

'Thanks for your help, Gavin.'

Carlyon's smug smile grates on me. 'No problem, it's given me time for some research.'

'Can you stay while we interview Jimmy?'

'I'm in no hurry.' He returns to his local history book, with its drab brown cover.

Curwen is standing on the far side of the room when I unlock the door, shifting his weight from foot to foot while terns skim past the window. The paper I left behind hasn't been touched. The man's face is bone white, panic crossing his features when we sit down at the table, but there's no chance to ask my first question. Carlyon's voice calls out before the door flies open. When Sally Rogan bursts into the room, her cheeks are florid, her expression grim as she lunges at Jimmy.

'You little freak. You killed him, didn't you?' Her hands close around the Birdman's throat before I can pull her away. 'I pitied you, scuttling around, hiding from the world. You evil bastard. Why did you hurt him?'

Zoe arrives as the tirade ends. Sally lashes out one last time before the fight drains out of her, and she collapses into her friend's arms. It's the first time I've seen her lose control so completely, convincing me that it's not safe for Zoe to remain in her house alone. I call Eddie to arrange for another islander to stay there, so two people can keep guard over Sally until she recovers, but the drama has unsettled the Birdman.

Jimmy looks more vulnerable than before, his whole body shaking. He's cowering by the window, as if he'd like to fly into the clouds to join the creatures he loves, but his fear doesn't exonerate him. He may still be involved in one islander's brutal murder and the abduction of another.

31

Jimmy is too upset by Sally's attack to hear the detective's questions. He can still feel the imprint of her fingers around his throat while he choked for air. Louise Walbert is watching him closely, her cool expression scaring him almost as much as the policeman's calm voice. His thin hands jitter on the table when the next question comes.

'Forget what just happened, Jimmy. Try to stay focused. You need to tell us how you were involved in Alex Rogan's death,' the policeman says. 'If you keep quiet, Naomi Vine will suffer. We know she's still alive, but she hasn't got long. Do you understand?'

He gives a slow nod, but his reply sticks to the roof of his mouth, syllables coating his tongue like sand. Louise reminds him that he can say 'no comment', but he's longing to explain. He's dreamed of fluency every night since childhood, yet by morning speech always deserts him.

'Did you help someone kill Alex Rogan?' the detective asks.

Jimmy remembers the fire on Burnt Island, the man's hollow eyes begging for mercy, but Ella's voice is ringing in his ears.

She told him to agree with everything the policemen asked, and she's the islander he trusts most.

'Yes.' His reply is a soft whisper.

The solicitor gapes at him. 'Do you know what you're saying, Jimmy?'

He tries to repeat the word, but it lodges in his throat.

'I don't think he understood.' Louise's voice is firm, her face angled towards Kitto. 'The killer leaves written clues, doesn't he? Jimmy can't read. His mother told me he'd never learned.'

The detective's green eyes scour Jimmy's face for a full minute. 'I want you to stay with Stan Eden. Sleep in his spare room tonight. Don't go anywhere without his permission; I may need to question you again.'

Jimmy doesn't fully understand the man's instructions until the door opens and he's set free. A wave of gratitude rises in his chest. If Ella hadn't given him the right advice, he would still be locked inside that airless room. His feet clatter on the metal stairs as he races from the building.

32

'Sorry about the interruption, Inspector. Sally barged past me before I could stop her.' Gavin Carlyon is lurking by the doorway after Louise Walbert leaves.

'It's not your fault. Can I ask a few questions before you go?'

'By all means, I'm happy to help.'

'How did you spend yesterday?'

He peers over the top of his half-moon glasses. 'I walked down to the quay for some exercise, but the bad weather ruined my walk. I started work around ten a.m. I'm tracing a family tree for an American with Cornish roots. Most of my research is for international clients these days.'

'Did you leave the house again later?'

'I don't believe so,' Carlyon replies, frowning. 'What's this about, Inspector? My wife's expecting me home. She hates being alone since the violence started. Surely you don't believe I'm involved?'

'You called Naomi Vine evil then her house burned down. That's quite a coincidence, isn't it?'

'I was talking about her influence on the island. It wasn't a personal criticism.'

'Do you speak much Cornish?'

He's blustering now, face red with anxiety. 'I imagine everyone here knows a few words. But Stan Eden's the expert; he learned the language as a child, and a few others like Ella Tregarron and the Tolmans have an interest.'

'The person I'm looking for is obsessed by the past, like you. Speaking in Cornish is his way of honouring the island's history.'

'I can translate old marriage and birth certificates – using a dictionary – but that's my limit.'

'Do you have proof that you spent last night at home?'

The quake in his voice could stem from anger or guilt. 'Rachel was with me. We watched some awful film on TV.'

'What was it called?'

'I can't remember, but she will. It was a tedious American melodrama that she adored.'

Carlyon's smug manner has faded, like a balloon deflating, relief on his face when he finally scurries away. I enjoyed crossing swords with him, yet I'm no further forwards. The man's conflict with Naomi Vine is on public record, but there's no proof that he started the blaze, and when I call his wife, she barely hesitates before confirming that they watched *Pearl Harbour* before going to bed around midnight.

*

Shadow has returned to the boathouse before me; he's dozing on a blanket in the corner, probably sleeping off a heavy meal of scraps from the pub's kitchen. Eddie and Liz Gannick are both hunched over a laptop, studying pictures of Naomi Vine's ruined home. My deputy turns in my direction as I arrive, the atmosphere between us still awkward after our disagreement.

'I've asked extra people to help Zoe look after Sally. Is she okay?'

'She's calming down. What did you find at Naomi's place?'

'A lot of damage, but no human remains upstairs. The fire went through the stairwell to the top floor. Most of her furniture's been destroyed.'

'It's the same downstairs,' says Gannick. 'Vine's sculptures have been defaced too.'

'Someone set out to destroy what she values most,' I reply. 'Just like they wanted to damage Rogan's telescopes.'

'This was in the ashes, near the fireplace where we found the chains.' Gannick points at an evidence bag that contains a glass vial, with drops of colourless liquid inside. 'We'll need substance analysis to check it's Rohypnol, but I bet he's used it on Naomi Vine too. Plenty of websites sell it.'

I peer at the thumb-sized bottle, trying to imagine the killer handling it. 'He'll wait for nightfall to set his next bonfire.' I pull the oyster shells from my pocket. 'These are the only clues he's left us, saying she's being kept in a holy place. She'll be dead by dawn if we don't find her.'

Gannick is frowning with concentration as she studies the Cornish words inscribed on the shells' smooth linings. We pass the next ten minutes in a flurry of discussion. My deputy looks relieved when I explain that Jimmy Curwen has been released into Stan Eden's custody. He couldn't have left the latest message at the pub because he was locked inside the lighthouse, but someone may have brainwashed him into assisting them, which could be why he confessed to being involved in Alex Rogan's death. I may have been chasing a false lead for days, too influenced by the fact that he went on the run. But it was his coat we found at the scene, so I can't completely rule out Jimmy's involvement. Sally's reaction proves that he has been tolerated rather than accepted by most people on St Agnes. The possibility that I made a mistake fuels my urge to find Naomi Vine by nightfall, or the responsibility for her death will be mine alone.

'I need a list of islanders who know Cornish,' I tell Eddie. 'The killer could be using a translation website, but it might be someone with a deeper knowledge.'

He grabs his phone. 'I'll do some checking around.'

'Tell the islanders to stay indoors once it gets dark. If the killer's roaming around, I don't want anyone getting hurt.' I reach for my coat. 'We need to investigate shrines and graves on the island, too. I'll search the church first.'

Shadow's tail is wagging like a metronome, oblivious to external threats. The dog streaks through the boathouse door, overjoyed to greet the fresh air again. The church is visible from almost every part of the island, sitting at the top of an incline, an architectural prompt not to forget God's laws. I don't know how many of St Agnes's residents are active worshippers, but it's not surprising that they were a devout community in the days when most men fished the rough Atlantic Strait. The sea's proximity would have been a constant reminder of its dangers.

I glance around the churchyard, checking for signs that the killer has visited recently, but see only dozens of tombstones, listing at odd angles after centuries of hard weather. There are no recent graves because the council has declared all of the islands' cemeteries full, so Alex Rogan will have to be buried on the mainland. The church is typical of Scillonian architecture, with no airs and graces. It has granite walls, a low spire and a few stained glass windows depicting the island's lighthouse and fishermen toiling at sea. The interior is simple too, its white walls and narrow pews suitable for St Agnes's tiny population.

The church is unlocked when I twist the brass door handle. Vases of flowers stand on either side of the entrance, the air scented with incense. It's only when I cross the threshold that I notice a figure on one of the pews. The man is deep in prayer, face bowed over his lap, a murmur of disjointed words reaching me at the

239

back of the nave. My footsteps break the man's reverie, and when he swings round I see that it's Liam Poldean. His eyes are so bloodshot I can tell he's been crying.

'Sorry to disturb you. I just need to take a look around.'

'That's okay, Ben, I was just going.'

'Don't hurry on my account,' I say, dropping onto the pew next to him. 'I didn't know you were a believer.'

'I'm not a regular,' he replies, with a dry laugh. 'I've been so busy with my kids it's only just hit me that Alex has gone. Good friends are hard to find out here. You rub along with your neighbours, but people you really like don't come along often . . .' his voice peters into silence.

'I know what you mean.'

'Mike Walbert's letting my boys feed his sheep, so I came here to clear my head.'

'Did it help?'

'Not really.' He wipes his hand across his face, embarrassed by his show of emotion. 'It feels like I'm doing bugger all to support Sally. The frustration's screwing with my head.'

'You could tell me which islanders know the most Cornish.'

'Keith Pendennis understands a few words, and Stan Eden sings the old ballads in the pub, if he's drunk enough. You could hear a pin drop when he gets to his feet. I wish I understood the lyrics.'

Poldean's voice is so wistful that I study his face

again. Sadness for his lost friend seems to mingle with regret for the passing of a language that was spoken on the islands for generations by our ancestors.

'Would you mind doing something else, Liam?'

'Anything you need.'

'Bring everyone to the lifeboat house by two o'clock. Naomi Vine's missing; we need to find her fast.'

Poldean gets to his feet immediately, his stride purposeful when he clatters down the aisle. I'd like to spend longer in the church's peaceful atmosphere, but time is passing too quickly. I search the place thoroughly before I leave. The vestry is empty apart from choristers' challises hanging from hooks on the wall, and there's a mouldering smell of damp. I find no sign of the killer's presence in the nave either. If he plans to sacrifice Naomi Vine at a holy place on the island, he must have another location in mind, or he's waiting until darkness falls to move her.

Liz Gannick has made herself at home when I return to the boathouse, typing a report into her laptop at a hectic pace. Eddie hands me his mobile with an apologetic grimace and Madron's voice bleats out rebukes before it reaches my ear. The DCI wastes no time in criticising me for releasing Jimmy Curwen while no other suspects have been arrested. After a long verbal assault my patience wears thin.

'I have to go now, sir. We need to find Naomi Vine urgently.'

'Don't hang up, Kitto. Give me a full update.'

'I'll call back later.'

I curse under my breath after the conversation ends, but Liz Gannick offers a rare smile.

'You look ready to commit murder,' she says.

33

The islanders arrive in gaggles at 2 p.m., dressed in anoraks and wellingtons. I can see a broad range of facial expressions among the crowd: Rachel Carlyon looks anxious to find her friend, but Martin and Deborah Tolman are holding a private conversation at the back of the crowd, while Liam's two boys chase each other round the hangar. Keith Pendennis stands by the door, wearing the dead-eyed stare of a bouncer who's been on duty too long. I'll have to check the attendance list later, but some islanders are missing from the crowd. There's no sign of Ella and Steve Tregarron, and Gavin Carlyon must be sulking at home after our clash at the lighthouse.

Shadow whines loudly when I get to my feet; he seems keen to escape the packed building, despite the gale that's rattling the windowpanes.

'Thanks for coming back, everyone. I need your help to find Naomi Vine. We have to bring her home tonight, or she may not survive until tomorrow. We're getting a better picture of the man who killed Alex Rogan: he's fascinated by the Cornish language and might have been studying it recently. If any of you have information about who started the last fire, please speak to me or Eddie.'

The faces in front of me remain impassive.

'You'll be working in two groups, so we can cover the whole island, combing every beach, cave and property. We don't have time to get individual warrants to search your houses, so I'll take silence as assent. Speak up now if anyone has a problem.'

The smile slips from Martin Tolman's face when he hears that homes will be searched, but everyone else looks ready to start. The Helston family has turned out en masse, despite their low opinion of my investigation. I breathe more easily when Zoe slips through the door; at least I'll have one ally who's completely on my side. Eddie and I pore over a map of St Agnes, agreeing that he will search Middle Town and the northern section of the island, while my team covers the south. Liz Gannick volunteers to stay behind and answer the phone, which suits me fine; she's best placed to pacify Madron if he calls again.

My group includes Mike and Louise Walbert, Keith Pendennis and the Tolmans. Zoe falls into step beside me when we head across the down. I'm eager to get moving while it's still light, but the squall buffets us from all directions, sea air coating my lips with salt. Lumps of granite rear from the ground like pieces on a giant chessboard, their shapes resembling pawns and rooks. Liam Poldean is ahead of us on the path, his sons sprinting into the distance while he scans the open ground.

'It's bloody pissing down,' Zoe mutters. 'It feels like the Gods are against us.'

'How's Sally doing?'

'She can't sleep; it's making her pretty edgy.' She leans closer to make herself heard above the wind. 'Thanks for getting me more help; one of the neighbours is with her now.'

My previous mistake is still nagging at me when I reply. 'Keep a close eye on her, Zoe. If Sal leaves the house by herself, let me know.'

She nods in reply. 'Do you think Naomi's still alive?'

'It looks that way. At least she didn't die when her house was torched.'

'Let's find her then, for Christ's sake. The island's only two miles long.'

Zoe marches ahead, her attitude unchanged since we were in our teens; she's still unwilling to accept even a whiff of failure, pacing across the island with her Amazonian stride. Right now I don't care about her plans to leave, I'm just glad she's on my side. While Zoe races ahead, I fall into step beside Keith Pendennis. My old boxing coach acknowledges me without saying a word. The man seems too preoccupied for communication, but police work has taught me to hold my tongue to get a response. After five minutes of silence a question slips from his mouth.

'How's my daughter coping with all this?'

'It's more than most people could bear, Keith. She's angry as hell.'

'No change there,' he mutters. 'That's why we lost touch.'

'Sorry?'

'Things fell apart when Sal hit eighteen. She delayed going to uni and hung out with older blokes on St Mary's. There was bugger all we could do about her drinking and taking drugs. If we challenged her, she flew off the handle.' Pendennis stares at the ground as we walk. 'She attacked me in front of my wife, punching and kicking. I tried to calm her down, but nothing worked, so I told her to leave. Jeannie was ill by then; she needed peace to try to recover. We didn't hear from Sal for years afterwards, even when Jeannie's Parkinson's got bad.'

'That must have been tough on you all.'

'I never expected Sal to move back here. She rented the shop until she raised the cash to buy it.'

'But things didn't improve?'

'She let me give her away at her wedding, but she's still angry. I don't think she even knows I'm proud of her for turning her life around. She blames me for being a lousy dad.'

'Sal seemed happy enough when we were kids.'

'The depression started in her teens.' Pendennis's gaze is still fixed to the muddy path. 'She says I neglected her and Jeannie, spent more time at boxing matches than at home, and she's got a point. Training young champions gave me such a buzz, I forgot my responsibilities at home.'

'How long since the pair of you had a proper talk?'

He hunches his shoulders. 'It was just formalities at the wedding; we've barely spoken since.'

'It's never too late to build bridges, Keith.'

'Try telling her that. She's made it clear she's not interested.'

Pendennis shakes his head in denial, jaw clenched so tightly I can tell he's close to tears. I'd like to ask another question but he marches ahead. The man's statements have changed my view of him as a tough guy unwilling to bend. He's tried making amends, but Sally is unwilling to forgive and forget. I remember the way she flew at me when I broke the bad news about Alex, and her assault on the Birdman. While her father loves the discipline of physical sports, she struggles to control her passions. The conversation has increased my sympathy towards him, providing a different view of the lively, rebellious girl I knew at school.

We make slow progress across the fields at Garabeara in the centre of the island, but none of the team complains about the drenching rain as we traipse between fields edged by drystone walls. Small groups of islanders check each property when we reach Higher Town. Zoe and I search a vacant holiday home, with Deborah

Tolman's help. The former medic is so remote it's impossible to tell how she feels about the murder hunt, but she keeps busy, opening wardrobes and peering under beds. I search the outbuildings at the end of the hamlet, too, but find only crates of fertiliser and compost, releasing a dry smell of cut grass and decay. The team's faces are disappointed when we gather outside the bulb shop. Past disagreements with Naomi Vine have been abandoned during the crisis, everyone committed to preserving her life, forgetting the disputes she's caused. It's typical of island behaviour that the community is united against a common threat, but the killer could be hiding in plain sight, pretending to search for a woman he plans to kill.

Covean Beach opens before us after a few hundred yards. It's a perfect horseshoe, so sheltered that families flock here each summer, but today spikes of granite are poking from the sea, waiting to savage passing ships, the waves gunmetal grey. The black outline of Gugh is visible in the distance, but I need to prioritise searching the main island first, where most of the properties lie. I get the team to spread out in a horizontal line, to sweep Wingletang Down. Rain has made the grassland boggy, with pools of standing water collecting on its surface, mud clinging to our boots. Dozens of cairns punctuate the landscape, built from fist-sized rocks until they stand ten feet tall, marking the sites of forgotten graves. It's easy to recognise the down as an ancient cemetery. Huge shapes spring from the rolling landscape, Crooked Rock dominating the horizon like a giant bent double by the fierce breeze.

Many of the team look tired by the time we reach Beady Pool. The place was a favourite of mine when I was a kid, because beads that spilled from a seventeenth-century Dutch shipwreck can still be found in its rock pools at low tide. But there's no point in lingering today, so we carry on past Gull's Rock with the wind at our backs. Zoe is busy rallying people's spirits while I'm beginning to lose faith. The killer is a game player: he may only have sent his latest message to make me swerve in the wrong direction. We have peered into every cave and stone built grave on the down, clearing the bracken aside to look for Naomi Vine's body. I doubt he ever intended to leave her at one of the island's sacred sites. He may simply have cast her body into the sea, to avoid being caught.

After Horse Point we follow the coastline back up the western side of the island, where Porth Warna beach stands empty, its shingle scoured clean by the new gale riding in from the Atlantic. I walk ahead, with most of the searchers straggling behind, only Zoe and Mike Walbert keeping pace. The farmer's cheeks are ruddy from the wind's assault, but he seems oblivious after a lifetime facing the elements.

'We'll search St Warna's Well then send everyone home,' I tell him.

'The saint wouldn't appreciate this,' he says, with a

narrow smile. 'She came here in the fifth century for a life of quiet contemplation.'

'I could use some of that myself.'

I remember my school teacher explaining that religious zealots travelled to the Scillies from Ireland to live as hermits, sacrificing their souls to God. The well was built over a sacred spring and devotees of St Warna would crawl along a narrow tunnel to touch its source, but the site has fallen into disrepair. The sign beside the landmark is covered with rust, its entrance choked by knee-high grass. The well lies between two outcrops of stone and Mike Walbert is first to point his torch into the opening. He swings round to face me again immediately. His expression's excited, but all I can see is a shimmer of black polythene.

'There's something blocking the passage.'

'It could be rubbish blown in by the wind, Mike. The space is pretty narrow to drag someone inside.'

Liam Poldean peers through the opening. 'Want me to check? I'm smaller than you, it won't be such a squeeze.'

I shake my head. 'Stay here and watch your boys.'

Walbert ducks through the opening before I can stop him, so used to leading the island's campaigns that he's forgotten who's in charge. But his exploration won't slow us down for long; the chink in the rock only extends for a few metres. I wait in silence while the rest of the group straggles across the field, their faces pinched by the cold. I'm planning to send them home with their goodwill intact, until a noise like gunfire blasts from the opening.

Mike Walbert's yell makes me dive inside, inhaling smoke and sulphur. His form is slumped on the ground, a blur of orange flames dancing behind him. I call out, but there's no reply. When I pull Walbert's arm, his body is a dead weight and it's too dark to see the extent of his injuries, so I drag him out feet first, suppressing my panic. If the killer has rigged a second booby trap, it could detonate at any moment. Seconds tick by too slowly until I reach the open air without sparking another explosion. Liam Poldean's tense expression greets me when I haul the farmer onto the grass, then place him in the recovery position. Blood pours from a wound on Walbert's neck, his skin blackened by soot and mud, but at least he's breathing. My first reaction is fury: the killer told me to search the island's holy sites, leaving a booby trap where it was sure to be found. The bomb was meant for me – Mike Walbert was in the wrong place at the wrong time.

The searchers look shocked by the farmer's injuries, slow to comply with my request to stand back. Walbert's wife crouches over him, babbling words he can't hear while blood pours down his face. Deborah Tolman is lingering at the back of the crowd, but she's the only islander with full medical training so I call her forwards. Her face is ashen when she assesses the farmer's injuries, his body twitching as she checks his reflexes.

'He's been knocked unconscious, but his pulse is steady.' Deborah uses a handkerchief to staunch the blood then looks up at me. 'We need to carry him to my house.'

'Is it okay to lift him?'

'His back's not broken. I'm more concerned about head injuries; I want to monitor him and stitch those wounds.'

Liam Poldean and Keith Pendennis volunteer to carry Walbert the short distance to the architect's home, the farmer's heavy build making the task a challenge. He's already starting to come round, incoherent sounds spilling from his mouth, but his feet drag over the mud as they battle uphill. Louise Walbert paces behind while I stare into the mouth of the well, too angry to speak to anyone. If I'd acted faster, the man's injuries could have been prevented. I study the entrance again, trying to work out which islander could have rigged the homemade explosives. The rest of the search party look relieved to be sent home. Only Zoe stays behind, rain dripping from the hood of her waterproof, her expression outraged.

'The vicious bastard,' she says. 'A kid would have died if they'd gone in there.'

'I have to see what he's left behind.'

Zoe grabs my sleeve. 'Don't be stupid, you can't go in there again.'

'There's only one booby trap; I'd have triggered any others on my way out.'

I run my torch beam over the rough granite walls as I push through the opening again. I can imagine the early worshippers pressing their bodies between these rocks, crawling towards the holy source to cleanse their sins, but any purity the site once held has been defiled by the killer's violence. The dry heat of gunpowder fills my airways, even though the fire triggered by the explosion has died out from lack of oxygen. I collect the remains of the killer's bomb-making set for Gannick to analyse. Its design is simple; just a tripwire attached to a fuse, the device a few inches long, pegged into the rock at head height to cause maximum damage. If Walbert had been facing it when it detonated, he would have been blinded.

'What kind of bastard aims a firework at someone's eyes?' I hiss into the dark. But the answer hovers, just out of reach.

34

Jimmy has returned to the lighthouse with Stan Eden. The old man is doing maintenance tasks: oiling hinges and polishing door handles, but Jimmy knows he's being watched. Eden's keen eyes sear his face whenever he tries to back away, so he concentrates on a colony of Atlantic gulls winging inland to avoid the storm, as the sun slips towards the horizon. Jimmy sees a group of islanders gathering on the green below. He's too far away to read their faces, but their bodies look tired, the crowd only dispersing when a new band of rain pelts the ground. The lighthouse keeper stops working for a moment to stand by his side.

'Look at that bunch of hypocrites,' Eden says. 'Most of them can't stand Naomi Vine, but they're searching for her anyway. They're saying she survived that fire after all. If she's not found by morning, she'll go the same way as Alex Rogan.'

The Birdman's heart batters against his ribs. His friend is still alive and now he must find her, before it's too late, but he's trapped indoors, doing nothing. He scrubs his hand across his face, trying to wipe away his guilt. Tiredness weakens the old man's ability to stand guard; he settles in his armchair, and when he begins to snore, Jimmy makes his decision. The detective told him not to go outside, but his conscience can't be ignored. He grabs a torch from the pocket of Eden's coat, then tiptoes down the metal stairs without making a sound.

Jimmy hurries to the Turk's Head. He needs to see Ella Tregarron, but the pub is in darkness so he shelters in the yard to wait. When a light flickers in the dark, he approaches the window. Ella is sitting at one of the steel-topped tables, a candle guttering at her side; the landlady is crying so hard, her shoulders heave with each sob. Jimmy taps lightly on the window. Tears are still coursing down her cheeks when she opens the door, but she swipes them away with her knuckles. She seems unwilling to meet his eye.

'I heard the police let you go, Jimmy. Thank God you're safe.'

He wants to thank Ella for her advice, offering a smile instead, hoping she'll understand. It only sets her crying again.

'I should never have asked you to take the blame. I must be losing my mind, Jimmy.' Her eyes screw shut to contain the tears. 'It was a moment of madness; I'd never have let them lock you away. It's just that Steve's been acting strange since Alex died. God knows what he's done. He'd never survive in prison, he's not strong enough.'

Jimmy touches her arm, uncertain how to give comfort. Ella rubs tears from her eyes again then retreats to the kitchen. She returns with a bag of scraps for his birds, but her eyes are still full of sorrow.

35

Light is fading when I climb towards the Tolmans' house. Its outline is more striking at night, its huge windows glowing against the cliff face; the building looks like a square-edged lantern, shining in the dark. I point at the path to let Shadow know he's surplus to requirements, and for once he leaves me in peace. I'm glad to shelter in the house's wide porch, escaping the wind, until Deborah Tolman appears.

'How's Mike getting along?' I ask.

'He's on the mend, but he's got half a dozen flesh wounds. One of them's pretty deep,' she says. 'I'll keep him here overnight in case he's concussed.'

'Thanks for looking after him, Deborah. I know it wasn't easy for you.'

'Was it that obvious?'

'Only at first. You soon clicked back into the old routine, didn't you?'

'Healing people used to be second nature.' She

pauses at the foot of the stairs. 'My last job put me off medicine for good; it was for a charity abroad.'

'Where were you based?'

'Syria; I spent four years with Medecins San Frontieres.'

Deborah leads me upstairs without another word, but my attitude shifts in an instant. Her self-possession is the result of working in a battle zone rather than a cold temperament. No wonder the sight of another wounded man bleeding at her feet turned her skin pale. The woman has seen more violence than I could ever imagine.

She shows me to the bedroom where she's caring for Mike Walbert. The farmer is lying down with a bandage taped to the side of his neck, his smaller wounds yellow with antiseptic. His eyes are groggy when he tries to speak, but Deborah lifts her hand to quiet him.

'Ben's just checking you're okay, Mike. There's no need to talk.'

Louise Walbert is clutching her husband's hand. Her big, colourful persona has vanished with the accident; she's still trembling from seeing him toppled. She gives me an anxious smile, her attention soon returning to the patient.

'Can I speak to Martin before I leave?' I ask Deborah.

She nods her agreement. 'He's in the basement, fussing over his grand project.'

I leave her comforting the Walberts and walk back downstairs. Eddie has searched the couple's house already, and it would be hard to conceal a victim in rooms with so many glass walls, exposing every action to the outside world. Secrets seem impossible here, until I reach the basement. The white walls match the rest of the house, yet the room is airless because a huge architectural model rests on trestle tables, consuming most of the space. Martin Tolman is applying paint to one of the sections when my footsteps draw his attention. The architect straightens up immediately, his expression awkward.

'Men my age shouldn't play with toys, but I never lost the habit,' he confesses.

He's created a replica of St Agnes, featuring every hill and bay. The brown fields and stone houses are oddly realistic, the Big Pool a sliver of glass, reflecting the overhead light.

'How long did this take to build, Martin?'

'I started it six years ago, but it'll never be finished. The territory keeps changing.'

My eyes scan the miniature island again: the lifeboat house has been remodelled as an observatory, just as Alex Rogan wished, its domed roof split open to reveal a small telescope, with Naomi Vine's sculptures standing guard on Blanket Bay.

'Impressive, but not quite accurate. You've taken some liberties.'

'Architects have to dream, Ben. It's an idealised version of this place, with an observatory and outdoor art for all to enjoy.'

Tolman has imagined a future only he can control. There's something so disturbing about the tiny islanders roaming across his synthetic empire that I scan the room again, looking for doorways, but there's no obvious hiding place. I shake my head to dislodge my doubts, my confidence shaken by suspecting the wrong man for too long. It's unlikely that a pillar of the community and devoted Christian would drag a victim back to such a spotless lair.

'Do you expect to find Naomi tonight?' he asks.

'You seem very concerned.' The tension on his face makes me take a shot in the dark. 'I know I asked you this earlier, but you didn't give me a full answer. Did you two know each other in the past, Martin?'

His face blanks before he blurts out his reply. 'It happened so long ago, it's not relevant anymore.'

'But you had a relationship?'

'It was nothing serious. We both trained at the Royal College of Art; she was in the year below me.'

'You were students together in the nineties?'

'Naomi studied Fine Art, which was far more glamorous than designing buildings.'

'What was she like back then?'

'Gifted and charismatic. People admired her, but she didn't care. She's always preferred her own company.'

'You fell for her?'

Tolman flinches. I can almost see him concocting a lie. 'We met at a party in Mayfair and spent a weekend together. Her relationships never progressed far beyond one night stands.'

'But you wanted more?'

'That's immaterial. It's all in the past.'

'Tell the truth, Martin. Lies don't work in a place this small.'

He pulls in a deep breath. 'Naomi had no idea I lived here when she bought the old mansion. Seeing me shocked her, I think, but she was friendly enough. She gave me one of her sculptures when I called to welcome her.'

'What did you talk about?'

'I said I was happy here, teaching myself Cornish and getting to know the islands again. She told me she was looking for peace and quiet. That's the extent of it; nothing else happened between us.'

'Does your wife know about your fling?'

'Deborah's easily hurt. Please don't mention a mistake I made in my twenties; I regret the casual way I dealt with people back then. My life's been far more fulfilled since she persuaded me to join the church.'

'Naomi Vine's missing and you two were involved. You didn't give me the full picture when I asked if you had history.'

'It seemed wrong to raise old ghosts. You know I didn't hurt her; I was with my wife all day before her house burned.'

'You'll still have to make an official statement tomorrow, Martin.'

He gives a grudging nod before I leave him poring over his plastic utopia. There's no proof yet that Tolman harmed Alex Rogan or Naomi Vine, but the man is so elusive, it's impossible to pin him down. Maybe he was so infatuated with Vine in their student days that feelings were rekindled. On an island this small it would have been impossible to avoid each other.

Deborah Tolman is putting on her coat when I reach the front door, her face blank, making me wonder if she heard Martin speaking about his old flame.

'Don't go out alone, will you?'

'I just need fresh air,' she says. 'I'll stand in the porch and listen to the sea.'

'Thanks again for all your help today.'

She frowns at me. 'I was born here, remember. The community only survives by supporting each other.'

The medic's face looks gaunt when I wish her goodnight, as if reverting to her old duties has ruined her peace of mind.

Shadow gives me a rapturous greeting when I get back to the boathouse, but Eddie looks frustrated. His search has yielded few fresh clues about the killer's identity, or where Naomi Vine is being held, even though every building on the main island has been checked. It's looking more likely than ever that the killer has cast his second victim into the sea instead of burning her alive.

Liz Gannick's voice sounds tired when she explains

her findings. 'I got fingerprints from the paraffin cans in Vine's shed,' she says. 'I've emailed them to the lab, but I doubt there's a match on the national database.'

'It only holds data from convicted criminals, and no one here has a police record except Adam Helston. We'll need to fingerprint all the islanders tomorrow.'

'Want me to start now, boss?' Eddie chips in.

'We should use the time left to search for Vine.'

'The lab won't give instant results anyway,' says Gannick. 'There's no one on duty till tomorrow.'

My job in London was a breeze compared to this. The station in Hammersmith was packed with state-of-the-art equipment, and expert support was only a phone call away. Things operate differently when you're surrounded by the Atlantic and a three-hour ferry ride from Land's End, yet I've got no intention of giving up. The sky outside is fizzing with stars and Naomi Vine may still be alive.

36

Jimmy has returned to the gates of the old mansion. The place is a ruin, its blackened interior visible through gaping windows. When his eyes scan the down, his breath catches in his throat. The wild expanse of grassland has always frightened him at night since an old fisherman told him that drowned sailors haunted the place. The spiky outlines of cairns pierce the horizon, their tall forms like sentries, watching his every move.

Now that he knows Naomi survived the blaze, Jimmy is determined to find his friend. He's still rooted to the spot when the gale increases its attack. Fresh rain pelts the back of his neck, the wind roaring as it gusts across open fields. He's about to set off for Higher Town when a sound rustles behind him and he's shoved to the ground. The voice hissing in his ear is so gruff with anger he can't tell if it's male or female.

'Fly away home, Jimmy. Stay out of my way.'

He tries to free himself, but his attacker's foot rests on the back of his neck, and he's too afraid to fight.

'If you try to stop me, you'll burn too. Do you understand?'

A stammer of noise escapes from Jimmy's lips, his cheek pressed against cold mud. The killer stands over him, murmuring guttural Cornish curses. When he's finally released his whole body is shaking. Jimmy is still too terrified to move, even when the killer's footsteps splash into the distance across sodden ground.

37

Alex Rogan would have been in his element tonight. The conditions are perfect for stargazing when the three of us leave the boathouse; the clouds are thinning at last, the moon visible for the first time in days. It's only 6 p.m., but Liz Gannick looks tired from sifting ashes at Vine's mansion all day, swinging along on her crutches at a slower pace than usual while the wind pummels us.

'I'll help you search the last few houses,' she offers.

'You've done a twelve-hour shift, Liz. Go back and get some rest.'

She stares at me. 'I won't sleep, knowing that woman could be burned alive.'

'I promise to call if we need you.'

Gannick must be exhausted because her protests soon fade. Shadow gives a low whine when she limps away, always keener on female company than male, but he trails after me and Eddie with his tail between his legs. My deputy has regained his fighting spirit, the thrill of the chase sparking in his eyes. He looks like an excitable prefect when he faces me again.

'Do you think she's still alive?'

'He loves being in control, Eddie. Why end the party so soon? If the killer's following the same pattern we've got until dawn before he sets her alight.'

'I tried to persuade Michelle to stay at the pub but she hates breaking Lottie's routine. She's still worried I'm in danger. She keeps on at me to find a safer job.'

'If you leave me here with Lawrie Deane I'll resign.'

Eddie laughs as we march through Higher Town, but I can't forget that someone on the island is intent on doing more harm. The trap set at St Warna's Well proves that he knows basic electronics, or followed a YouTube tutorial, which barely narrows the field. People here pride themselves on self-sufficiency, learning practical skills as children. The investigation is moving too fast to check everyone's movements over the past twenty-four hours, but we can't slow down while there's a chance Naomi Vine's still alive. Her vulnerability when I broke into her house nags at my conscience. I should have ignored her protests and insisted she stayed at the pub until the killer was found. It bothers me that she tried to make contact, before she was taken. If I'd replied to her text sooner, maybe I could have prevented her abduction.

The houses in Higher Town huddle on either side of the lane, their windows already lit. People seem to be obeying my instruction to stay indoors, with no sign of human activity now darkness has fallen. I hope they're following the rest of my security advice, too, keeping doors locked and seeking safety in numbers. The outline of Gugh is moonlit when we reach the Bar, the causeway still fully exposed. Eddie and I will have time to search the buildings on the tiny satellite island before the ocean surges in again a few hours from now, making the way back impassable. I can't imagine the attraction of living in a place where nature confines you at home every day, but it would appeal to a killer with something to hide.

Gugh looks deserted when we step onto the beach, the outline of Obadiah's Barrow standing tall on the brow of Kittern Hill. Chunks of granite litter the grassland, and there are half a dozen cairns, reminding me that the island belongs more to the past than the present. The Carlyons' home must be 150 years old, yet it's one of the youngest things here; apart from two other properties, most of the other structures date back to the Bronze Age. I leave Shadow with Eddie, who sets off to search Keith Pendennis's cottage and the vacant holiday home on the far side of the hill.

Rachel Carlyon looks relieved to see me when she opens her front door. 'Come in,' she says. 'Search wherever you like; I'm afraid Gavin's outside. I'm not sure where he's gone.'

'I won't take long, Rachel, this is my last property. Can I check upstairs?'

She gives a rapid nod. 'Take all the time you need.'

It strikes me again that the place is a slice of local history. Each room is filled with period furniture, from metal bedsteads to tallboys and mahogany dressers. The decorative wood panelling looks original, and a brass light fitting hangs from an ornate ceiling rose. The couple's reading material would appeal to the killer's regional obsession too: the shelves are lined with books on the artists of St Ives, Cornish poetry from the nineteenth century, and a history of St Mary's fishing fleet. I search each room thoroughly, even climbing into the loft, but there's no sign of Naomi Vine.

Rachel is making me a hot drink when I return to her kitchen. The room contains a scrubbed pine table, ladder-backed chairs and a bench that must have been salvaged from a local church. There are more objects hanging from the walls than I can count: tin jelly moulds, drinking flagons and earthenware jugs.

'Where did you get all these antiques?' I ask.

'Gavin loves flea markets. He's always on the Internet, bidding for things.'

Rachel's words nag at me as I peer inside the couple's pantry. Her husband and Martin Tolman have a lot in common: both men are fixated by a particular vision of their environment. Carlyon wants to return to an earlier time, while Tolman is creating an idealised version of the entire island. It's not yet clear whether either man's obsession is powerful enough to make him murder whoever threatens its existence.

Gavin Carlyon stumbles into the kitchen after I finish

searching his store cupboard for a space big enough to conceal a woman's body. The man looks like a Dickensian villain tonight, dressed in a long black raincoat, frowning at me over his half-moon glasses, a long-handled hammer clutched in his hand.

'I've been securing our fence before this wind brings it down,' he says, dumping his hammer and nails on the table. 'I should apologise for being brusque earlier, Inspector, but your approach felt accusatory.'

'It's my job to ask difficult questions until Naomi's found.'

'We argued over a building; it's not a matter of life and death. I hope she comes back safe and sound.'

'You couldn't care less.' His wife gives a derisive laugh. 'You've hated her from day one, Gavin.'

I've never heard Rachel raise her voice, but her husband's insincerity seems to have snapped her self-control. The air between them buzzes with resentment, Carlyon scowling when he finally replies.

'Your friend wants to destroy the island's character, Rachel. I complained about her wretched statues covering our beaches at the council meeting, then she chased after me, yelling curses in my face. The woman's got mental problems. I thought she might attack me.'

His wife points an accusing finger at him. 'Naomi's the bravest, most creative person here. Can't you see that?'

'She's destroying our way of life.' The man's speech crackles with anger.

'Rubbish, we have to adapt to survive.'

'No one wants St Agnes to prosper more than me.'

'You're not bothered about what happens to Naomi, but you'd go to hell and back to preserve a damned building.' Rachel gives her husband one last stare before stalking out of the room.

'My wife's easily led, Inspector,' Carlyon blusters. 'She admires creative people, while I think that most art is a waste of time.'

'Why didn't you join our search this afternoon, Gavin?'

He runs a hand across his brow. 'I had another wretched migraine, but it's lifting now, thank God.'

Something about the man's manner convinces me he's lying. I'd like to press for details, but there's still no proof that he's involved. A final question slips from my mouth before I can drag it back. 'Would you mind explaining how you got injured at the fireworks display last year?'

The man's arrogance crumbles away. 'A freak accident put me in hospital for a few weeks.'

'Who was in charge?'

'Mike Walbert. The poor man was mortified, even though he wasn't to blame. He was so upset he flew over to Penzance twice to visit me in hospital.'

Carlyon's manner has calmed, but I wonder whether he sees the farmer's injury this afternoon as poetic justice, even though his wounds are superficial. I thank him for letting me search his home, then leave him to it. The property feels as unnatural as a museum, stuffed with historic artefacts, the atmosphere loaded with tension while the couple pull in different directions.

Eddie's enthusiasm is still intact when I catch up with him and Shadow, even though rain is dripping from the end of his nose. 'There's nothing suspicious here. The holiday cottage is still locked up and it doesn't look like anyone's been there, but Pendennis gives me the creeps. His cottage is so clean, the air stinks of bleach.'

'Let's talk at the pub, Eddie. If you don't eat soon, you'll keel over.'

'I had something earlier, there's no need.'

My deputy looks reluctant to slow down, but visiting the pub could help our investigation. We'll hear the latest news, as well as refuelling ourselves. When he follows me across the Bar, the causeway still stands a few feet above sea level. The Carlyons' tiny kingdom will remain open to the outside world for another few hours.

The Turk's Head is doing a roaring trade tonight. A log fire is blazing in the hearth and Ella Tregarron is busy pulling pints behind the bar. Most of the islanders are huddled around tables, the atmosphere noisy. It reminds me of my childhood, when every crisis was fixed in Bryher's only pub. Eddie and I have taken a corner table when Louise Walbert hurries over. My first concern is that her husband's condition has worsened, but she's clutching something in her hand.

'I went home to collect overnight things for Mike and this was hung on our gate.'

The envelope has her name printed on the front and is already open. Everyone in the packed bar is watching us, reminding me that our conversation should be held in private, so we duck into a small function room behind the main bar. The space looks like a throwback to an earlier time, with a swirling red carpet and walls yellowed by tobacco, but at least we can read the killer's message in peace. It's painted on a razor clam shell this time, proving again that his materials come from the island. Thousands of shells like this wash up on its shores each year.

Louise Walbert reads the words out loud: '*Kyn few hi lemmyn, y ferow a verr spys. A aswonnydh omglewans a vadhya yn tan.*'

'Do you know what it means, Louise?'

'Something about fire, but most of it's beyond me I'm afraid.'

'Fetch Ella, can you, Eddie? She may be able to translate it.'

The landlady seems uncomfortable when she peers at the Cornish words in silence, before looking up at me. 'Stan Eden's the one you want, I've only done an evening class.'

'Just try your best, Ella.'

'I think it says: "She lives still, but soon will die. Do you know how it feels to bathe in fire?"'

Louise lets out a dull murmur. 'First Mike gets hurt, then this.'

'Don't walk back to the Tolmans' alone,' I say. 'You mustn't be by yourself until the killer's found.'

Louise is so concerned about her husband, there's no point in scaring her more by explaining that Alex Rogan received a similar threat before he died, and one was found at Naomi Vine's house. The new message makes five in total, including the one sent to my home on Bryher. I can't forecast which of us he plans to attack next.

Eddie and I are still talking to Louise when a woman's scream rings through the wall, making us rush back to the bar. At first I can't see where the noise is coming from, until I catch sight of Sally Rogan at the centre of the room. She's dressed in pyjamas and a bright red dressing gown, her feet bare. My old friend looks even more disturbed than when she attacked Jimmy Curwen. She's yelling at full volume, arms flailing, while she bawls at the assembled crowd.

'Why are you lot in here, drinking? You should be hunting for the bastard who killed my husband. Do you think I can rest till he's locked away?'

Sally whirls from table to table knocking glasses over until they shatter on the flagstone floor, her wild energy mimicking the storm outside. She yells out a protest when I brace her arms at her sides, but soon collapses in floods of tears. I take a step back to let others comfort her, but Sally's outburst makes me wish she was safe in the hospital on St Mary's. The strain of losing her husband is pushing her over the edge.

Zoe appears while I watch the islanders comforting the stricken woman. 'Sal ran outside before we could stop her,' she explains.

'Did you know she suffers from depression, Zoe?'

'It was in remission. She's been stable for years.'

'We'll get her to hospital when the ferries are running again.'

Sally's outburst reminds me of her father's description of her violent outbursts, but my biggest concern is that the killer is leaving messages and booby traps galore, intent on creating mayhem. I scan the pub's interior again, but see only a united community tending a grieving woman, aware that he could he among us right now, watching the chaos unfold.

38

It takes all of Jimmy's courage to rise to his feet. His spine aches from where he was kicked to the ground, his heart still beating a nervous tattoo. The rain is lighter than before, but wind is screaming across the down, its gusts mimicking the cries of gulls. Jimmy knows he should return to Stan Eden's house, yet his need to find Naomi is greater than any desire for safety. He can still see his sister slipping from the sandbar when he closes his eyes, the waves dragging her under. If he'd acted faster she would be alive today, but this time there's still a chance. To find Naomi Vine he must follow his attacker without being seen.

Jimmy's head spins as he walks deeper into the down. Shock is catching up with him and he knows he must rest before continuing his search. He heads for the cave where he sheltered before, its mouth lit by moonlight. The air inside is cold, but at least he's sheltered from the icy breeze. He huddles at the back of the cave, eyes closing with exhaustion, until something moves at the edge of his line of vision. When he crawls towards the cave's exit, fear floods his system again.

He can see the outline of Boy's Rock, spearing up from the grassland like a giant's profile, and a figure moving at its base. Someone in a long black coat is busy collecting fallen branches, then stacking them in a pile, movements slow and purposeful. The killer's new bonfire makes the one that claimed Alex Rogan's life look small by comparison.

PART 3

'Thy rage shall burn thee up, and thou shalt turn to ashes ere our blood shall quench that fire'

King John, (Act 3, Scene 1),
William Shakespeare

39

It's 10.30 p.m. when I finally persuade Sally to go home. She's still muttering curses, grief and anger pouring out of her, when Zoe and two other women from Middle Town escort her home. I remind everyone in the pub to walk home in groups and offer neighbours shelter until the killer's found. Some look defiant while I give out my instructions; people are eager to take matters into their own hands, which could prove disastrous. If the killer is patrolling the island, bystanders will be in harm's way.

Eddie's eyes glitter when I explain my strategy for the rest of the night. Excitement at taking part in a murder hunt is still written all over his face, but right now I just want the culprit found. We need to visit the Walberts' farm first, because it's the last place the killer left a calling card. His campaign is gathering pace; with any luck he's growing sloppy and we can pick up the thread from there. My thoughts race as we cover the ground to Lower Town Farm. Most of the islanders were in the pub tonight, but the Helstons were absent, along with

Martin Tolman, Keith Pendennis and Gavin Carlyon. I'd like to know how all of them have been spending their time. In an ideal world a troop of officers would be at my disposal, but that can't happen until the storm subsides.

Shadow is waiting by the farm gates, tongue lolling after his hard sprint across the fields, as if the killer's deeds are just a glorious game.

'Check the front of the property, Eddie. I'll search the back garden.'

The view from the Walberts' patio explains why the couple have dedicated their lives to farming this patch of land: there's a clear view over Blanket Bay to Burnt Island, then two thousand miles of dark water rolling into the distance. Even at night the view is staggering, with storm clouds racing across the face of the moon. I wish that Mike could help us now, his practical vision always quick to find solutions, but the man has been levelled by an injury I should have prevented. I focus my energy on searching for any small detail the killer may have forgotten, but my torch reveals that the lawn has been swept clean by the raw breeze, and there's nothing on the path except a few tufts of moss. When I check the back door and downstairs windows, the farmhouse is secure.

The killer must have left his calling card then vanished, proving that each attack is planned with absolute precision. It's only when I see the shed door hanging open that my spirits lift. Two cans of paraffin are tucked under a work bench, and beside them a bag full of rags and wax tapers. I could be imagining things, but the killer's intentions still seem to taint the air. He's stockpiling tools in multiple locations, as if he wants to raze the entire island to the ground. I pull on sterile gloves then pour the paraffin down a drain beside the house, in case our arsonist makes a return visit.

Eddie looks disappointed when I return to the front of the building, his smile only reviving when he hears about the fire-starting kit I saw in the shed. It's possible that it was there during today's search, but the islanders were too focused on finding Naomi Vine to notice key details. He falls into step as I follow the track inland, both of us driven to find the sculptor before it's too late. Middle Town looks deserted as we march down the lane, lights on in most properties. The islanders appear to have heeded my warning to return home from the pub and keep their doors bolted.

'Let's search the down again, Eddie. The last message told us she's being kept at a holy site; that whole area's riddled with ancient graves.'

Eddie hurries along beside me, matching my pace, but Wingletang Down is an unforgiving place tonight. A strong wind is still racing in from the Atlantic, gorse bushes flailing in the breeze, the scrubland silvered by moonlight. When we come to a halt outside Naomi Vine's house, the site looks ghost-ridden; if she's still alive, the sculptor will be devastated to see her home reduced to a blackened shell.

'Let's do a quick tour. The killer may have made a return visit.'

Shadow stays close to my side, releasing a low growl. He still seems anxious about entering the grounds, but traipses after me while I scan the path for signs of activity, my gaze catching on piles of leaves blown inland by the squall. I walk further round the building's perimeter before spotting a bundle of feathers lying on the ground.

'Over here, Eddie,' I call out.

My deputy has his phone pressed to his ear when he races towards me. 'Stan Eden says the Birdman's missing. They were in the lighthouse earlier, but he ran off and hasn't been seen since.'

'These feathers belong to Curwen, he carries bundles around in his pockets.'

Eddie drops to a crouch. 'There's an outline in the mud, then footprints as someone ran away.'

'You can see where someone's hands have clawed the earth.'

Rain is blurring the footprints that track across the path and we've made matters worse by polluting the area, making it hard to distinguish between the Birdman's and the killer's prints.

'One of them's got small feet,' Eddie comments. 'Mine are bigger, and I'm a size nine. Those can't be more than a seven.'

I peer down at the imprints, which are already disappearing. It crosses my mind that a couple could be carrying out the attacks, or a man with a small build like Adam Helston. It would be useful to know the shoe size of all the suspects, but there's no time to chase details. At least we have proof that the Birdman was here, the largest set of footprints leading us across the down. The man can't be solely responsible for the killings, because he was locked up when the latest message was left, but he's been too close for comfort since the case opened. I need to find him fast, to understand exactly what he's seen. I focus on the horizon and try to imagine where he's hiding. Moonlight shafts through the clouds suddenly, making the landscape eerier than before, with rock formations raising their sharp heads to the sky. Before we can take another step, a man appears on the path. He's wearing a waterproof coat, its hood obscuring his features; there's a weapon in his hand, raised to shoulder level.

When I step onto the path the man comes to halt, his face still obscured. He's holding a baseball bat uplifted, as if he's planning an immediate attack; Shadow races forwards before I can say anything, paws landing on the man's chest while he gives a loud bark of greeting. Another flash of moonlight reveals his face at last, tense with irritation at my dog's boisterous welcome. I recognise his pallid, time-worn skin immediately.

'Why are you out here, Steve? It's not safe.'

'It's time he gets what he deserves.' The landlord's face is quivering with anger.

'Where were you earlier? I didn't see you at the pub.'

'I was upstairs, until Sally lost the plot. It was the final straw seeing the poor girl like that.'

'The killer may be armed, Steve.'

'I'm not hiding indoors, waiting for him to attack us again.'

'Does Ella know you're out here?'

He gives a rapid nod. 'She couldn't stop me.'

Tregarron's actions make me even more determined to find the killer fast. If we don't catch him soon, more people will end up hurt. I'm about to send the landlord back to the pub when a light flickers at the corner of my eye; a new fire is burning on the western horizon, bright red flames spearing the sky. My advice to stay indoors could be doing more harm than good. I've given the killer a perfect opportunity to roam free without fear of being caught.

40

Steve jogs after us as we cross St Agnes, with the wind at our backs. A vivid glare is still visible up ahead, although the flames appear to be dwindling, the stench of chemicals making me gag as we race uphill to the church. I'm out of breath when I wrench open the cemetery gates, my eyes still fixed on the dull red glow. Eddie is at my side, cursing to himself, while Steve lags behind, determined not to miss the action. The light is coming from a metal trough, half full of sand, lying on the church steps, releasing plumes of smoke and a few spluttering flames.

I understand the killer's game immediately. The island's fishermen keep emergency flares on their boats, packed with chemicals, designed to release a light that shines for miles. But tonight a dozen have been lit to mimic another house fire, sending us in the wrong direction. When I crouch beside the bucket, I see that the flares are rigged to a trip wire like the one at St Warna's Well, but the killer has used a kitchen timer to let him escape unnoticed.

'Clever bastard, isn't he?' Steve mutters.

The landlord is still heaving for breath when I turn to face him, and it crosses my mind that he's the only islander we've seen since leaving the pub. Tregarron could have planted the device himself, but the pub has been searched today, revealing nothing incriminating. The killer has succeeded in luring us back to one of the island's holy sites, just as his message stated. Little damage has been done, apart from scorch marks on the building's wooden doors.

I leave Eddie and Steve to search the graveyard while I step inside. The nave still smells blameless, my lungs filling with incense and communion wine, but this time the space is empty. Nothing appears to have changed since my last visit, until I see a word, spray-painted above the altar: FELLYON

My Cornish is limited, but even I get the message this time. The killer is calling me a fool for chasing in his footsteps without guessing his motives. He's used a decoy to bring me here, while keeping Naomi Vine out of sight. I'm still trying to understand his motives when Eddie calls my name. His voice is so urgent that I feel certain he's found another calling card, but Steve Tregarron is slumped against the church wall, head bowed, his face waxy in the moonlight.

'He's ill, boss,' Eddie says. 'I've told him to rest for a minute.'

'What's the trouble, Steve?'

Tregarron's eyes are unfocused, his voice hoarse. 'Angina. My pills are at the pub.'

'Let's get you home. Can you put your arms round our shoulders?'

Eddie looks tense as we help the landlord to stand. I doubt he's ever seen anyone die before his eyes. He's spent his entire life on minute islands where most people expire from old age, and the greatest threats come from the sea and harsh weather.

We manage to lift Tregarron back downhill in less than ten minutes. It takes careful manoeuvring to carry him upstairs to his flat, but at least he's conscious when we lay him on the sofa. I call out for Ella but there's no reply.

'Where are your tablets, Steve?' I ask.

'Bathroom cabinet,' he wheezes.

Eddie is doing a good job of caring for the landlord when I return to the lounge. Tregarron's hand shakes when he slips a pill under his tongue and Shadow has picked up on the tense atmosphere, whining quietly as we wait for the medication to work. Steve's eyes are still screwed shut against the pain, and frustration hits me that the crisis might have been averted if he hadn't tried to play hero. He takes long shuddering breaths, as if the effort of inhaling worsens his pain, but colour is gradually returning to his cheeks. Now he just looks exhausted, rather than fatally ill.

'How are you doing?' I ask.

'Better, thanks. Sorry to waste your time.' He manages a weak smile.

'Don't worry, but you can't chase around like a maniac in your condition. Where's Ella gone?'

'I don't know.'

'Come on, Steve. I'm not leaving you here alone.'

His face crumples suddenly. 'She'll be with a man.'

'How do you mean?'

'That's how it works. She's never really been mine.'

Tregarron is too weak to explain, his eyes closing from exhaustion, but I insist on calling Ella's number. There's no reply after two attempts and it dawns on me that the island's mysterious landlady may have become the killer's third victim.

41

Jimmy waits for the figure to disappear over the horizon before picking across the wet grass, the wind tugging his clothes. His mouth dries when he sees dozens of branches stacked inside a circle of elder bushes, ready for another bonfire. He glances around, but the down appears empty. There's no sign of the figure he saw gathering firewood. The ragged grassland contains only the massive rock formations he's known all his life, rising from the landscape like waking giants. Jimmy reminds himself that he can't let another life slip away, his borrowed torch scanning the ground in frantic circles. An owl's call convinces him that he's moving in the right direction, its shriek as piercing as an infant's cry.

He walks slowly around the granite pillar of Boy's Rock. Track marks are revealed when moonlight pours down suddenly, showing where a boulder has been dragged across the mud. It takes effort and determination, but he shifts the stone by a few feet, then steps back, puzzled. A hole in the ground has been exposed, wide enough for an adult to squeeze through, the earth rubbed smooth around its mouth. He kneels down to look inside but the darkness scares him. The gap seems to contain only black air and the bitter smell of wet earth. Jimmy shines his torch into the opening, but fear prevents him from crawling inside.

42

Wednesday 9 November

My phone rings after 1 a.m., while Eddie and I are helping Steve Tregarron. I regret picking up immediately
because the DCI's hectoring voice whines in my ear.

'You had no intention of calling back, did you, Kitto?'

'The killer set another fire tonight, sir. Luckily no
one was injured.'

He makes a loud tutting sound. 'Check the islanders
are safe then start again tomorrow. I won't have you
risking any more lives.'

'This is our last chance to find Naomi Vine.'

'Stay indoors till sunrise, Kitto. If you disobey me
it'll be a disciplinary matter. Do you hear?'

'Loud and clear, sir.'

I hang up before Madron can issue another pointless
order. The man is so risk-averse he's prepared to let the
killer revel in his moment of power. Eddie joins me in
the hallway of the Tregarrons' flat a few minutes later.

His boyish face looks calmer now that the landlord is recovering. He agrees when I explain that we can't continue our search until Ella returns. The landlord is too weak to be left alone, even though he claims that his chest pain has stopped.

Eddie stays with Steve while I go downstairs to wait. I switch on a single light behind the bar then ring Ella Tregarron again, but the pub's door creaks open before the call connects. The landlady's expression is anguished, her black coat and boots mud-spattered.

'Where have you been, Ella?'

She almost jumps out of her skin. 'Jesus, you frightened me. I thought the place was empty. I was looking for Steve; the old fool left here swinging a baseball bat.'

'You took one hell of a risk.'

'I was afraid he'd get himself killed.'

'We brought him back just now. He had an angina attack.'

'Not another.' Her voice is tense with fear as she peels off her wet coat. 'Where is he?'

'Upstairs, resting. His pills are doing the trick.'

'Thank God.'

'Did you see anyone else out there?'

'Jimmy Curwen near Boy's Rock, but he hid before I could reach him.' She hesitates before speaking again. 'Sam Helston was down on Blanket Bay.'

'What was he doing?'

'Staring up at the church. I don't think he even saw me.'

'How come your clothes are filthy?'

'I slipped on the mud.' She glances down at the brown splashes on her jeans.

I take a breath before speaking again. 'Steve thought you were with another man.'

Her expression is weary as she drops into a chair. 'He's always been jealous, but it's worse than ever. I only have to chat to a customer for him to lose the plot . . .' Her voice fades into silence.

'Were you having an affair with Alex Rogan?'

She shakes her head. 'I had a stupid fling with a summer tourist, years ago, soon after we got married. I've regretted it ever since. Steve was convinced Alex fancied me, but that's rubbish. The bloke was in love with Sally.' There's fear in her face, as well as denial.

'You think Steve hurt him, don't you?'

'My husband's the best man I know.' Ella's voice falters when she speaks again. 'But jealousy's a kind of madness, isn't it? I was scared he'd lost control, and now I feel terrible. I was stupid to doubt him.' Her tone grows strident, as if she's trying to convince herself. 'Let me see him, please; the angina leaves him exhausted.'

'Give me your phone first, Ella.'

She releases a bitter laugh. 'So I'm the killer now, am I?'

'You were warned to stay indoors. Anyone breaking the rule gets the same treatment.'

Ella tuts loudly before dropping her mobile into my hand. She hurries away, leaving me to scan her call list, but the phone has only been used twice today, to contact Julie Helston and Rachel Carlyon. Steve has rung her frequently over the past week, keeping tabs on her whenever she leaves the pub, but the only other male caller is Mike Walbert. I drop the phone back onto the bar: a five-minute conversation with one of the island's elder statesmen is hardly incriminating, but the reasons for her husband's jealousy nag at me. Steve is ageing fast, while she retains her beauty. The man seems torn apart by the idea of losing her.

Tregarron discovered the first body and spent tonight proving his desire to catch the killer, yet he appears a broken man. It's possible that he's hidden Naomi in an obscure place then faked an angina attack to put himself in the clear, but instinct tells me it's unlikely. I can see why he would target Rogan, but Vine has given him no cause to attack, unless he's begun to hate the incomers his business needs to survive. If Ella was telling the truth, the Birdman is hiding somewhere on Wingletang Down and Sam Helston is also roaming free. There's a chance that Helston's the killer, but the man has no history of conflict, despite his short fuse.

Eddie appears while I'm mulling over the new information. 'Steve's recovering, thank God,' he says.

'Are you all right? It upset you, seeing him so ill.'

He scowls at me, lack of sleep finally negating his politeness. 'I just want this over; the killer's running rings round us.'

'Let's find him then. We need to go back to Wingle-tang Down: Ella saw Curwen there and the killer may be drawn to it too. I think he'll start his next fire well away from any houses, like on Burnt Island, to avoid being seen.'

When I look up again, Liz Gannick is in the doorway. The forensic chief's childlike form is kitted out in waterproofs again, her expression determined. She points one of her crutches at me like she's wielding a shotgun.

'I'm sick of doing nothing. I'll come with you.'

I point out that I'm the SIO, but Gannick ignores my objections, reminding me that I need a good partnership report. Her attempt at blackmail doesn't convince me, because I doubt she'd damage my career without serious provocation, but I let her join us anyway. Her pace may slow us down, but her expertise could bring fresh insights.

43

Jimmy keeps his back pressed against Boy's Rock. He wants to enter the narrow tunnel to look for Naomi, but the dark terrifies him and his torch batteries are failing. He remembers his mother singing him to sleep as a boy, until the darkness felt as comforting as an embrace, her rose perfume scenting the air. But there's no kindness in the atmosphere tonight, only fog rolling in from the sea.

His breathing quickens when he finally lowers himself through the opening, falling seven or eight feet before landing in a tunnel. The space is so confined he's forced to crawl along on hands and knees. He tries to call Naomi's name, but a whimper emerges from his lips instead. The air is toxic with chemicals and silence, and his torch beam narrows to a chalk mark, spiralling across muddy walls until it suddenly expires. Darkness paralyses him until something touches his hand.

A raw scream comes from Jimmy's mouth when the sensation happens again; this time he feels a brush of fur and the sharp points of tiny claws. Rats are trying to flee, terrified by his sudden invasion. He gropes forward but finds only empty walls, his palms scraping over rough stone. A sound in the distance panics Jimmy again. If the killer finds him, he'll have nowhere to hide.

He crawls back through the tunnel to the point where he entered. It requires all his strength to scramble up the vertical shaft once more, its walls slick with rain, then lever himself until his weight falls onto the wet grass. He wants to lie still and recover, but an owl screams out a warning from a low copse of trees. Jimmy rolls under some bushes, spikes of gorse scratching the back of his neck. Soon a new torch beam scours the earth, then a pair of muddy black boots pound across the grass at eye level while he tries not to breathe.

44

It has finally stopped raining when we set out again. My team makes an odd spectacle: a lumbering giant, a small woman clipping along on silver crutches, a young cop who resembles a choirboy and a wayward dog. The killer's messages are too unclear to offer a good starting point. All he's demonstrated so far is his desire to protect the island's unique heritage. We've witnessed his fury that its ancient language has died out, and that local buildings are being bought by outsiders who don't respect St Agnes's past. But the field of suspects is still too wide. The killer remains one step ahead and he loves humiliating us.

All I can do now is patrol the territory around the suspects' homes. The people highest on my list are still Martin Tolman, Sam Helston, Jimmy Curwen and Gavin Carlyon. Any of them could have waited until their wives were asleep then set out to create mayhem, and all have an axe to grind. Tolman lied about knowing Naomi Vine in the past; there's no guessing what other deceptions he's concealing. If Ella was telling the truth, Helston has been spotted tonight near the church where the flares exploded. The Birdman has been too close to the case, ever since his coat was used as a shroud for Alex Rogan's body, and Gavin Carlyon has expressed his dislike of Naomi openly. He seems obsessed by protecting the island from further change. There's an outside chance that Steve Tregarron was reduced to madness by jealousy, but the man's illness looked genuine, unless he's a talented actor.

'What's your strategy?' Gannick asks.

The forensics chief looks happier now she's back in the game, her sharp gaze scanning my face for showing doubt. I make an effort to keep my voice upbeat when I reply, aware that signs of weakness will slow us down. I've seen plenty of murder investigations founder when the SIO loses confidence.

'You and Eddie can sweep the down while I visit Sam Helston. I don't care how many people we disturb tonight, as long as Naomi Vine comes home alive.'

Shadow barks loudly as though he's endorsing my view, then streaks away across an open field. The creature is enjoying his midnight ramble while the rest of the island sleeps, but I'm too preoccupied to care about his antics. The lights are out in every house I pass in Middle Town, apart from a pale glow from the lighthouse gallery. It feels comforting that Stan Eden is keeping watch tonight, just as he protected fishermen at sea, even though the old man can do little to help.

The wind has dropped by a fraction when I head for Lower Town, but I can still hear the sea pounding the shore. The sound is inescapable on such a small island, with every house close to the incoming tide. On a good day it's reassuring, but tonight it sounds brutal; waves are still attacking the land with unnatural force as the squall blows itself out. Shadow hovers at my side when I reach the Helstons' farm, releasing a low growl. The front of the house is in darkness, so I walk to the back of the building and see Sam through the kitchen window, sitting alone, head bowed. Helston is collapsed on a chair, too tired and wind-blown to remove his coat, a bottle of whisky at his elbow. The man doesn't look like an archetypal killer, tiredness rather than excitement written across his features. He gives me a furious look when I tap on the window.

'You again,' he mutters, opening the back door by a fraction. 'Leave us alone, for fuck's sake.'

'Let me in, Sam. We need to talk.'

He lurches back to the kitchen table, but Shadow is oblivious to his bad mood: the dog approaches Helston cautiously, then rests his muzzle on the man's knee. I expect the farmer to brush him off, but he buries his hand in his fur. Some of the tension lifts from his voice when he speaks again.

'Your dog follows you everywhere, doesn't he?'

'It's not personal. He'll chase anyone for food.'

Helston manages a grudging smile. 'Do you want a drink?'

'I'd love one, but Naomi Vine's still missing. You've been outside tonight, haven't you?'

He rubs his hand across his face. 'I couldn't sleep. I hate being cooped up here.'

'Why?'

'The farm's a bloody millstone.' He stares down at his hands. 'It's been in my family for generations, but Adam's not interested. He wants to learn building skills then be a property developer.'

'Do you think he started the fire last summer out of frustration?'

'Christ knows, the boy's so close-lipped no one can reach him.' He slops another inch of whisky into his glass. 'It's breaking Julie's heart. My wife used to be the life of the party, back in the day. Now all she does is sew those bloody things.' He points at a basket full of ragdolls, their beaded eyes open a little too wide, each one wearing an identical smile.

'It can't be easy, watching her only son spread his wings.'

'She's hardly laughed since he got into trouble. She used to dream about Adam taking over one day and how we'd be able to take breaks. I've tried to make him stay, for her sake, but we can't keep him prisoner.'

'If you let him go he's more likely to come back.'

'You're kidding,' he replies, with a dull laugh. 'He'll enjoy the high life and forget we exist.'

'Tell me where you went tonight, Sam.'

'Across the north shore to Blanket Bay. I had to make a decision.'

'About what?'

'I'll tell Adam he's a free agent tomorrow. He can be Liam Poldean's apprentice or join MI5 for all I care. We'll sell the farm when I retire.'

Helston's story almost convinces me, apart from a lingering belief that the man's bitterness about losing his heirloom may have turned violent. I've seen him go for his son, fists raised, barely able to keep his anger in check.

'Does Julie know you were outside?'

'I doubt it, she sleeps like the dead.' He leans down to rub Shadow's head again, booze making his movements unsteady. 'Let me help you find the killer. You'll never catch him on your own.'

'Get some rest, Sam, and don't take any more walks tonight.'

He gives Shadow another pat before I leave his property. I wait until the door closes before searching his barn and outbuildings again for signs of Vine's presence, but all I see are empty pallets waiting to be filled with next season's daffodils. I feel almost certain that young Adam Helston has nothing to do with Rogan's murder, or Vine's abduction. The crimes smack of a slow-burning, sophisticated fury, a million miles from the boy's impulsive protest at being trapped in the family business.

I circle back to the down along the coast path, but there's no one around. I can't see anything suspicious in the sea caves or on the shore. By the time I find my colleagues, they're at a standstill. Eddie reports that every cave on the down and the area around Vine's

ruined mansion has been searched, with no sightings
of Jimmy Curwen.

'Let's go back to Boy's Rock,' I say. 'That's where
Ella saw him.'

'We've covered it already,' Gannick insists. 'The
killer's collected enough firewood there for one hell
of a blaze.'

'Then it's worth a second look.'

I can see why they're reluctant to go back. The area
around the rocky outcrop is covered by sopping wet
grass, rainwater soaking my jeans. I use a fallen branch
to clear a path to the granite mound. It's only when I
pull back some bracken at the foot of the rock that a
narrow opening appears in the ground.

'Jesus, how did we miss it?' Eddie mutters. 'Do you
think she's down there?'

'It's possible,' I reply. 'He kept Alex Rogan hidden
and we're running out of options. I'll go down and
take a look.'

'I can do it, boss,' says Eddie.

'It's easier for me.' Gannick turns in my direction. 'If
it's booby-trapped, I know how to defuse it.'

My brain scrambles for an instant, trying to imagine
Madron's reaction if she got hurt, every safety protocol
broken. It's the conflict on Eddie's face that seals my
decision: he's torn between wanting the challenge and
thoughts of his baby daughter.

'I'll try first,' I reply.

The opening won't accommodate my hulking shoulders.

For a few seconds I hang suspended, like a cork stuck in a bottle, before hauling myself back onto the grass.

'Let me go down.' Gannick's eyes glitter in the starlight as she lays down her crutches. The woman seems eager to prove that her life is charmed.

'Don't rush, Liz. Keep stopping to check for tripwires.'

'I was planning to jump with my eyes closed.' She gives me a withering look. 'Let's move, shall we?'

Eddie and I keep tight hold of her wrists, gradually lowering her into the hole until she reaches the bottom. Her voice echoes back, letting us know she's safe. Minutes pass too slowly while she's hidden underground and I can understand why the killer would leave Naomi Vine here. He must believe that the down is sacred territory, pockmarked by ancient graves. After five minutes I kneel beside the opening and yell Gannick's name. When no reply comes, it takes effort to stay focused. If the woman's injured, Eddie will have to go down to find her. His face is tense as the seconds tick past, but there's still no sound.

Shadow is standing by the hole, ears pricked, whining softly. Before I can stop him, he dives into the opening, only his bark reassuring me that he's reached the bottom without breaking his neck.

'He's got a death wish,' Eddie mutters. 'We'll never get him back up.'

'Don't be so sure, he can take care of himself.'

I make the statement more in hope than expectation. Shadow's high spirits often grate on my nerves, but he's smarter than he looks. My theory that he'd make a good search and rescue dog is about to be tested to the limit. I can still hear him barking below ground, but the sound weakens as he disappears from reach. Ten minutes later he barks again, and this time Gannick's voice echoes from the opening, filling me with relief. The dog scrambles above ground, making the climb look like child's play. He wags his whole body to shake mud from his fur, then favours me with a long gaze, as if he's proved a point.

Liz Gannick is breathless once Eddie and I drag her back into the open air. 'Remind me never to go pot-holing. It's a bloody labyrinth down there; I'm lucky Shadow found me.'

'What did you see?'

'Tunnels lined with stone, some sections are five feet tall.'

'Underground graves,' Eddie says. 'Archaeologists mapped the passageways years ago, but no one's allowed down there now.'

'The killer doesn't follow rules,' Gannick replies. 'Take a look at this.'

She shows us a blurred image on her mobile, tinted red by flash light. The photo shows cans full of chemicals, piled against a muddy wall. The killer has stashed enough explosives to ignite a small town, but that doesn't explain where he's hidden Naomi Vine.

45

Jimmy follows in the killer's footsteps. Fear nags at him, but he's determined not to let it push him off course. His gaze stays fixed on the figure up ahead. The killer's slim outline is wrapped in a black coat that billows in the breeze, a woollen hat pulled low over his hair, face obscured by his raised collar and scarf. Jimmy's tension only subsides when he senses that the figure he's trailing is also afraid. The owl releases another piercing call, and the killer swings round in panic, forcing Jimmy to hide in the long grass.

It's easier to stay out of sight once he reaches the eastern shore, hope rising that Naomi Vine is still alive as his lungs fill with saline air. Moonlight shifts across uneven waves as he follows the figure over the beach, the tide beginning to turn. He stops frequently, concealing himself behind boulders, as they reach Covean Beach. Jimmy sinks below the dunes, hoping for a direct view, when the person up ahead comes to a halt, but the light is too poor. All he can see is the ocean unwinding into the distance, breakers whitened by flashes of moonlight. The figure stands motionless, watching waves crash onto the shingle, oblivious to the scouring breeze.

Once the killer moves again, his movements are jerky with panic. He stoops down to light a match then walks away. Seconds later Jimmy hears a cracking sound, then the sky ignites; he sees an explosion of colour through cracks between his fingers, white heat surrounded by blood-red smoke. Jimmy waits until the brightness fades before rising to his feet, but now the beach is empty. The killer has disappeared from view.

46

Liz Gannick is still describing her underground adventure when a new light flares to our east, then another on the western horizon. Eddie swears to himself while my gaze switches to a third fire in the north. The killer is giving a pyrotechnical display for his own private amusement, surrounding us with a circle of flames. It's impossible to tell whether he's set a trail of fake explosions, or if one of them has claimed Naomi Vine's life. The killer is so organised, he's probably used timers again to stay out of reach. My only certainty is that he's nowhere near the fires that mark the horizon; there's a chance he's returned to the scene of his first crime.

'Let's go back to Burnt Island. The site's got a special meaning for him.'

Our progress is slow as we return to Higher Town, and it's obvious that Gannick is exhausted. I can't fault her bravery, but once we get back to the Turk's Head, I pause by the fire doors. This time there's no need to insist she stands down until morning.

Gannick offers a tired smile. 'Call me if you want to drop someone down another hole.'

Something catches my eye as Eddie and I march back towards Middle Town. The lights are on in Liam Poldean's cottage while the other houses are in darkness, and instinct makes me take a detour to his property. The man is fully dressed when he greets us, even though it's almost three in the morning. He ushers us into his living room, where an old western is playing on his TV screen with black and white cowboys picking fights in a packed saloon. Poldean's good humour is missing for once, no sign of a smile on his face.

'You're up late, Liam.' I comment.

'My youngest has got a stomach bug. I've run up and down the stairs a dozen times while he pukes his guts up.'

'Sorry to hear it. Have you seen anyone out-side tonight?'

'I've had my hands full, I wasn't looking.' He shakes his head blankly.

'Is your boy okay?' Eddie asks.

'He'll survive. Val told me to give him Calpol and watch his temperature.'

'You're sure no one's been through the village?' I ask again.

'Just Sam Helston a few hours back. It looked like he was in a hurry.'

'Thanks, Liam, that's helpful.'

His face gathers in concentration. 'Stan Eden was

309

at the lighthouse earlier, but there's been no one else.'

My eyes catch on a pair of boots by the front door, glistening with mud. 'Have you been outside, Liam?'

'Only to check our flat roof – the wind's lifted the guttering.'

I have to hide my disappointment when we go back outside. I sense that Poldean would never leave his kids unattended, his calm manner making him an unlikely killer, but it's frustrating that he's given no new information. I was hoping the killer might grow reckless enough to take shortcuts through the village, rather than following the paths that wind between fields. I already knew that Sam Helston had been out for a midnight stroll, and that Stan Eden likes to guard the whole island.

I catch sight of the old lighthouse keeper hurrying towards us, clutching two metal cylinders to his chest. Eden looks uncomfortable when we draw level, his white hair making him appear ghostly in the moonlight.

'I've never seen anything like it,' he splutters. 'Those fires were as clear as day from the viewing gallery.'

'Where did they start?' I ask.

'Browarth Point, St Warna's Cove and Tolgillian.' His gaze meets mine as he raises the flares he's carrying. 'I found these outside the lighthouse.'

'Take them home, please, Stan. It's not safe outside.'

He shakes his head fiercely. 'I've kept watch here all my life. I won't stop now.'

There's no time to argue, so I offer him a duty

instead. 'Can you stand guard by Boy's Rock? We know he's been there tonight. Call us if you see anything suspicious.'

The old man hurries away without a backwards glance, still clutching the killer's latest gift. Eddie and I stand alone in the middle of the village, the time left to find Naomi Vine alive slipping away. I visualise the sculptor in her studio, attractive and defiant, as we jog towards Burnt Island. She struck me as too independent to accept help, despite her nervous temperament. If she's still alive she'll be fighting every step of the way. I'm not surprised that Vine made a deep impact on Martin Tolman, but I can't prove that he's harmed her for remaining out of reach.

The tide is approaching as we hurry across the sandbar to Burnt Island. I still believe that the killer may return to the original murder scene for his next act of violence. It's the most beautiful, pristine part of the island, cut off from humanity for most of the night, and it was Alex Rogan's favourite place for stargazing. I understand why he loved it so much when we reach the peak. The sea has finally calmed and the clouds have blown away, as if the island was the most peaceful place on Earth. Clear silver light spills across the rocky expanse, right down to the shore, but there's no evidence of the killer. Eddie's mobile rings just as we're stepping back onto Blanket Bay, his face tense with concentration. After the call ends he sways on his feet, until I reach out to steady him.

'What is it, Eddie?'

'That's not true. It can't be.'

'Take a breath, then explain.'

'He's got Lottie.'

My grip on his arm tightens. 'What do you mean?'

'Michelle was in bed. He broke the window and grabbed the baby from her cot.' Eddie's talking too fast, forgetting to breathe between words.

'Go and make sure Michelle's okay. I'll search the north coast.'

'I can't stop, for fuck's sake.' His jaw clenches tight before he speaks again. 'He's got my daughter.'

'You're needed at home; I'll call you with any news.'

Eddie sets off at sprint towards Lower Town. The news about Lottie has sent a shot of adrenaline through my system: I remember her smell of talcum powder and innocence as I sang her to sleep. Shadow is at my heels as I chase past the Big Pool towards Porth Killier. He barks in protest when I stop to draw breath, as if he'd prefer to carry on splashing through rock pools indefinitely. My own lungs are heaving and the time has come to stop hedging my bets. The sun will rise in a few hours' time and Naomi Vine's chances of survival will end, along with those of Eddie's baby. I can't keep on pursuing every false lead. I need to find out where they are without any more mistakes.

I run through the list of suspects in my head. Plenty of people on the island dislike change, but few are unhinged enough to steal a two-month-old baby from her cot. Martin Tolman lied about knowing Naomi Vine in the past, but had no clear motive to attack Rogan, or harm a child. The Birdman is still at large, and Sam Helston's anger could have turned against all newcomers for undermining the traditional farming life of his family. It's still possible that Steve Tregarron set tonight's chain of explosions then feigned illness to make himself look innocent. The man's jealousy may have driven him so far beyond reason, he no longer cares who he hurts.

I'm still considering which suspect to pursue when a thread of light shines in the distance, flickering like a beacon, and my decision's sealed.

47

Jimmy peers out from his hiding place, catching sight of a new fire burning at the northern end of Covean Beach. He keeps his eyes fixed on the flare as he heads towards it, his heart lifting when the dark figure reappears. This time there's a parcel in his arms. The killer pauses by the high tidemark, staring out at Sackey's Rock, its sharp outline blurring as the tide rushes home. Jimmy hides behind marram grass on the dunes until the man starts moving again. His mouth is dry with panic when the figure steps onto the Bar, the waves swirling at his feet.

This is where his sister drowned. Jimmy's mother always told him to avoid walking out to Gugh as the waters rose, in case the sea swept him away too. But tonight he must ignore her advice. He waits until the black-coated figure reaches the distant shore, never once glancing back at St Agnes. Jimmy forces himself onto the ridge of sand. He concentrates on each step, afraid of slipping into the deep water that lies on either side.

He feels weak with relief when he reaches Gugh. Keith

Pendennis's house lies directly ahead, all of its windows dark. He looks up at Kittern Hill, where the figure halts by the Carlyons' home. Jimmy watches him shift the parcel he's carrying over his shoulder, his pulse quickening when he sees an infant's pale face. The killer is carrying a baby in his arms. The figure hurries on past Obadiah's Barrow, its outline glittering with starlight. Jimmy is afraid the man will drop the child on the ground. He catches sight of a shadow running uphill, then ducks behind a drystone wall to avoid being seen, waiting five long minutes before emerging again. Now the man is unlocking the door of the holiday cottage at the top of Kittern Hill, but a few minutes later he reappears, his arms empty this time, then vanishes into the darkness. Jimmy scours the horizon, losing track of his outline.

Jimmy waits until his nerves settle before rising to his feet again. He normally loves visiting Gugh at low tide, to count the kittiwakes' nests on its high granite cliffs, but tonight he's terrified. He edges through the dark towards the holiday cottage, checking whether the man is lying in wait, but the property seems deserted, no sound except waves crashing against the rocks below. The door handle won't budge, yet he can't stop now. Naomi Vine may be waiting inside to be set free.

He stands by the window, peering into the empty house. Moonlight illuminates a small kitchen, with chequered lino and white units. It's only when Jimmy looks again that his mouth gapes open in shock. The green shirt Naomi Vine was wearing lies crumpled in the corner, a red handprint marking the wall, beside a smear of blood.

48

I can still see the thread of light, but Shadow has streaked away, looking for better adventures. When I drop down onto the sands at Porth Killier I catch sight of a figure by the shoreline, his powerful torch beam skimming the shingle. This is the source of light I've been chasing, but the man ignores my presence, keeping his head down while he inspects every grain of sand. Shadow flies across the beach like a speeding bullet, barking at high volume. The man spins round in panic as my dog snaps at him, refusing to back down.

'Come away, Shadow,' I yell out.

The dog's behaviour calms by a fraction as I approach, but he's still keeping guard, not letting his prisoner move a muscle. It's only when I'm within touching distance that I recognise who I've been following. It's Martin Tolman. The man's face is obscured by a cap and thick scarf, protecting him from the breeze. He looks relieved when I catch hold of Shadow's collar and drag him away.

'Your dog's got a fighting spirit,' the architect comments. His voice is mild, but his expression's fearful.

'What are you doing here, Martin?'

He shifts away from me. 'I couldn't sleep, which is rare. My nights here are usually easy.'

'You're in trouble, aren't you?'

Tolman looks like he might try to run, but soon changes his mind. Shadow would tackle him in seconds, and there's no hiding in a place like this. 'I don't know what you mean.'

'Where's Naomi, Martin?'

A dry laugh rattles from his mouth. 'I'd never harm her, believe me.'

'Spit it out, for God's sake.'

'I didn't give you the complete story, that's true.' Tolman's gaze remains fixed on the sea. 'I was afraid Deborah would overhear us.'

'Tell me now or you're under arrest for abduction.'

'I ran into Naomi at an exhibition in London, ten years ago. It was like a grenade blowing my perfectly ordered life apart.' He drops down onto a boulder, as if his legs can no longer support his weight. 'I hadn't seen her since college, yet my feelings hadn't changed. I was infatuated; it all came rushing back. She cared for me too, but nothing's permanent in her eyes. I left my first wife and kids for her, which was a terrible mistake. A few months later she ended it.' The raw pain in his voice makes his speech grind to a halt.

'Keep going, Martin.'

317

'I went to France to build a new life, but she followed me. The relationship lasted another year, until she walked away again.'

'So this is revenge?'

He shakes his head vehemently. 'She's not to blame. Her childhood was dreadful; first the care home, then endless foster parents. That's why she can never settle.'

'You got involved again after she moved here?'

'I think she tracked me down. She believed I'd end my marriage to Deborah, like the first time, simply because she'd changed her mind.'

'You wanted her so much you killed Alex Rogan. Did you think they were having an affair?'

'I've done nothing wrong.' Tolman's voice drops to a murmur. 'If I knew where she was, I'd set her free. I can't bear the idea that she's in pain somewhere, out of reach. That's why I'm out here, searching. I owe her that much at least.'

'What about your wife?'

The architect flinches. 'Deborah's been my salvation. She's given her life to helping others and stopping their suffering. I can't throw my marriage away.'

'Why not tell her the truth?'

'It would hurt her too much. Naomi asked me to leave Deborah, but I refused.'

'Yet you slept with her anyway.'

'Once, soon after she arrived. If Naomi makes up her mind she's impossible to refuse, but her work's like a calling. It always comes first.' His words falter again. 'A relationship with her is like confronting a whirl-wind.'

'If she's alive she won't be thrilled that her home's been destroyed.'

'She'll be devastated,' he replies. 'Naomi's not robust anymore. When we were young other people's opinions didn't matter, but now a bad review leaves her wounded for days. That's why I'm afraid for her.'

'How did she react when you ended the affair?'

'She said we could be friends, but I've only seen her in public since.'

'Was she afraid of someone? Whoever's taken her has got Eddie Nickell's baby, too.'

'My God, that's terrible.' His eyes blink shut for a second. 'Naomi doesn't trust Gavin Carlyon. She believes he hates her for bringing change to St Agnes.'

'Go home now, Martin, and lock your doors. We'll talk tomorrow.'

He steps closer, eyes glittering like wet flint. 'My wife would fall apart if she knew I'd been unfaithful.'

'I can't promise to hide it.'

'Please don't destroy my marriage over a mistake; Deborah will be the one that suffers.' His gaze is imploring.

'My priority is finding Naomi, before it's too late.'

The architect's speech leaves me confused. There's so much distress in Tolman's voice, he could be the perpetrator or a victim, caught between competing demands. His shoulders are hunched as he heads across the beach, with Shadow still snapping at his heels.

49

Jimmy's fear drops away as he rattles the back door of the cottage. His hands are cold as he tries to pry a window open, fingers slipping from the wet glass. He scans the hillside again for a sign of the figure he's been tracking, but there's no movement. Even in darkness he senses that the house is empty. He can see the neat and tidy living room through a gap between the drawn curtains, a gingham cloth covering the table, ready to welcome the season's first holidaymakers.

He's so exhausted that he leans against the wall, his face dropping forwards into his hands. He wants to return to the comfort of his birds, but a faint sound breaks the silence. It could be a gull bawling high overhead, but the noise is coming from another ground floor window. He tries to open it, but the plastic frame is slick beneath his fingers, a blind obscuring the opening. Jimmy stands beside the glass until the sound comes again, and this time it's unmistakable. An infant's thin scream drifts through the air; the baby he saw must be locked inside the property, and Naomi Vine may be trapped too.

Jimmy's instincts propel him back across open land to the

first house he sees. Concern for Naomi gives him enough courage to rattle the door knocker until footsteps rattle down the hall. Gavin Carlyon is wearing nightclothes when he appears. He frowns when Jimmy points at the brow of the hill, agitation making his movements wild and uncontrolled. Carlyon stares at him, then pulls his dressing gown tighter round his throat.

'You're not making sense. The police say it's not safe outdoors, you'd better come inside.'

Jimmy shakes his head, then gestures towards the cottage again, but Carlyon grabs his wrist. The man's grip is tight enough to burn when he pulls him over the threshold.

50

Frustration hits me when I reach Covean Beach. I've wasted valuable minutes with Tolman, but the man is so secretive he may yet turn out to be the killer, tortured by his affair with Naomi Vine. Now it's too late to cross the Bar, the causeway slipping below the waves, and the killer has planned his campaign to perfection: Gugh is the perfect murder site because the islet will be cut off until dawn, minimising his risk of being caught. Rescuers would need a powerboat to cross the fast-moving waters of the strait.

'Fuck that,' I mutter under my breath.

The point where the sandy ridge slips below the waves is still visible; with any luck I can wade across, but Shadow splashes into the water behind me.

'Stay there,' I yell at him. 'Don't follow me.'

For once the creature obeys, which is lucky, because the currents are so rapid he'd soon be swept away. He stands at the water's edge, whimpering, as I follow the Bar from memory. It's easier than I expected after

322

making the journey many times as a kid. When I reach the midway point, waves are lapping at my knees but the sand still feels solid under my feet. I take care to place my weight on the ridge, then look ahead to get my bearings.

The ground slips away suddenly, leaving me up to my neck in icy water. I breathe out a string of curses, and Shadow is barking non-stop in the distance, but I've already drifted too far from the causeway. My only chance is to swim the hundred metres to the shoreline, my teeth chattering as I thrash against the tide. Currents are pulling me north, and moonlight is bouncing off a huge expanse of ocean. If I don't reach Gugh soon, I'll be dragged into the shipping lane with the freighters sailing to America. Panic makes me plough through the water fast, but the gap widens. I try backstroke to increase my speed, yet the shore is too distant.

It seems to take me forever to reach Gugh's north coast and collapse on the beach, heaving for breath, the cold breeze slicing through my wet clothes. My hands are shaking as I drag my phone from my pocket. Water gushes from its plastic casing, and my biggest mistake hits home. I should have called Eddie before setting off; now I'm stranded here until morning – unless one of the island's three occupants can lend me a dinghy.

The chill hits me again when I climb Kittern Hill, my clothes still dripping with brine. I could skirt round the island's shores, but this is the quickest route to the

323

Carlyons' home. Halfway up, I look back at St Agnes in time to see another flare ignite, but my confidence holds. The killer can release fireworks all night long: I've searched every square inch of St Agnes, even looking underground. Naomi Vine must be hidden here, if she's still alive.

The islet's only holiday cottage rests on the brow of the hill. It belongs to an elderly Welsh couple who have visited each summer since I was a boy. The killer despises all of the island's visitors and may have chosen the cottage simply to destroy their cherished possession. The building is well-kept with gleaming paintwork, not a single roof slate out of place, but something flickers behind one of the ground floor windows, making my pulse quicken. The property is always vacant at this time of year.

I come to a standstill when it dawns on me that Rachel Carlyon must have a key – she cleans all of the local holiday properties. Something shifts in my chest when I remember her fixing the light in the shop, deftly replacing a blown fuse; she could easily have attached flares to kitchen timers, because of her skill with electrical devices. Maybe she shares her husband's hatred of change, her friendship with Naomi Vine no more than a sham. That would explain why one of the footprints by the old mansion was smaller than the Birdman's; it could have been made by a woman. Questions rattle round my head when I approach the cottage. The back door is unlocked and I try to enter without making a sound. I press one of the light switches but there's no power, leaving the room still in darkness when the front door slams.

I run into the hallway to find the space empty, apart from the sickly smell of air freshener, and there's no movement on the hillside. The man I'm pursuing has an unnatural ability to vanish, but he can't leave Gugh unless he's an Olympic swimmer. We're both stranded here until sunrise. I'll search the property fast, then go after him again. Just as I head down the corridor, I hear an infant's piercing scream and adrenaline floods my system. Lottie's here somewhere; the bastard may have injured her. Instinct makes me pull my torch from my pocket, but seawater has killed the battery. I'm shoving it back into my pocket when a shaft of pain burns through my temple, white light flaring in front of my eyes until I hit the ground.

51

Every bone in my body aches when I come round. My skull's throbbing and it sounds like a dentist's drill is whining inside my ear. My cheek is pressed against cold, wet carpet, but when I try to move, nothing happens. My brain is working too slowly, limbs refusing to follow orders. There's a reek of chemicals that I can't identify. All I know for certain is that my clothes are saturated and the sea's cold has penetrated my bones.

I try to work out what happened from my injuries. Pain courses through my back and hip, and even though my thoughts are muzzy, the penny drops. The killer has given me a dose of Rohypnol. I force my eyes open, but thick, black air hangs in front of my face. My days undercover taught me that Rohypnol is the gangster's drug of choice and the rapist's best friend. It can leave victims catatonic for hours, but the darkness tells me I can't have been out for long. The killer must have misjudged the dose – my bulk has saved me from losing hours to oblivion, but hasn't spared me the drug's numbing effect on my muscles.

It takes concentration to lift my thumb a centimetre from the floor, yet the movement fills me with relief; at least it proves I'm not paralysed. When I inhale again, the acidic smell of petrol is overwhelming. I try to identify its source, but it's everywhere. Panic crawls across my skin. He only needs to strike a match to turn the place into a fireball. I wrench my eyes open again, refusing to yield to sleep, then something shifts in the dark.

A narrow beam of moonlight spills from a tiny skylight window overhead, revealing white walls, a desk and filing cabinet. The sky is lightening, but it's still dark when the moon slips behind the clouds; dawn must be an hour or two off yet. I see a woman curled up on the floor a few metres away. Naomi Vine's vivid red hair is the last thing I register before blackness returns. The woman may have been lying on the sodden carpet for hours; I can't even tell if she's alive or dead. It will be impossible to help her until my body's working again. If the killer comes back before I'm strong enough to fight, Naomi and I will burn together.

52

Jimmy waits alone in the Carlyons' kitchen. The room is so warm that tiredness threatens to send him to sleep, so he rises to his feet. He twists the door handle but it refuses to give. His birds must feel like this, trapped in their wire enclosures until their wounds heal, but he can't understand why Gavin has locked him inside the room. The man said that it's for his own safety, but he has never shown any care before, looking through him like he doesn't exist. The clock on the wall is ticking too loudly, while Naomi Vine waits to be set free.

He counts the objects on the walls to stop himself going mad. There are old pictures in wooden frames, silver teapots on a narrow shelf, beside pieces of bone china and the type of copper pans his grandmother used for making jam. Everything seems to have been borrowed from another age. Jimmy is about to give up when he spots an old-fashioned phone, like the one his parents owned. The handset rests on a cradle, above a circular dial. He calls 999, the number his father taught him, in case of emergencies. A woman's calm voice asks which service he wants, but he can't make a sound.

He's still clutching the receiver when Gavin returns, now fully dressed, with a blanket over his arm.

Carlyon crosses the room in a few strides, unplugging the phone from the wall with an angry gesture.

'For God's sake, Jimmy, why call someone when you can't even speak? Sit down before you break something; it took me years to build up this collection. Sleep in the armchair till morning. It's too dangerous outside until the killer's found.'

The man's coal-dark stare is furious, making Jimmy cower in the corner of the room. He does as he's told until Carlyon leaves the room once more with the phone tucked under his arm.

53

The silence is so complete I can hear Naomi Vine breathing. The sound is too shallow, as if she's running a fever, but at least she's alive. We're lying in a large, well-equipped office. There's a blackout blind over the side window, the only illumination coming from the skylight overhead, whenever the moon emerges.

My head's still pounding, but at least my vision's clearer; the intermittent moonlight mean I can assess Vine's injuries. It looks like she's been used as a human punchbag: one of her cheekbones is broken and her left eye is puffed shut. She must be freezing too, only wearing a vest top and jeans, her feet bare. Her hands and ankles are bound together with rope. I can't tell whether she's asleep or drugged. Her slim figure looks so frail against the dark carpet, a rush of anger worsens my headache. The killer is prepared to hurt anyone from outside the island, even if they've done nothing wrong.

I try to call Vine's name, but release only a gush

of air. This must be how Jimmy Curwen feels: my thoughts are clear, yet my tongue feels as heavy as lead. I'm still trying to form a sentence when a tapping noise comes from outside. It sounds like footsteps, but could just be the house settling as wind gusts in from the sea. I have no choice but to wait until the killer reappears, with dawn less than an hour away. The anger inside my chest is rising to a boil, but my body feels leaden. I'll have to accept whatever the killer deals out, until my limbs start moving again.

The gathering light reveals that Vine is waking up, moaning quietly to herself. I'd almost lost hope of finding her alive. The sight of her hands twitching on the sodden carpet fills me with relief, even though I'm powerless. I can't guess how much the sculptor has suffered since she was taken, but she's still fighting. There's a spark of rebellion in her eyes when they finally open, even though the room is a tinderbox, waiting to catch fire.

54

Jimmy pulls a bundle of feathers from his pocket and strokes it against his cheek, the softness settling his thoughts. There's no key in Carlyon's back door, but one may be hidden somewhere, if he searches hard enough. He pulls open a drawer tentatively, finding it packed with tarnished silver cutlery. The house is so full of antiques it feels like he's being dragged into the past, but Naomi needs him to stay in the present. All he finds is a hoard of old-fashioned crockery, until he searches the highest shelf of a cabinet by the stove.

His fingers close around some fragments of stone. They look like grey pebbles collected from the shore, until he studies them more closely. Letters have been scratched across their surfaces. Jimmy only understands a few of the Cornish words his grandfather taught him when he was young.

Mor, sans tan. Sea and holy fire.

None of the rest makes sense, until Jimmy remembers the carvings on Burnt Island. The stones slip from the Birdman's fingers as his panic rises. There was so much anger in Carlyon's face when he locked him in this airless room.

He must be the one keeping Naomi Vine trapped inside the holiday cottage.

Jimmy jumps down from the stool, his movements faster and more desperate. If he can find a way out, he can still free her, then return to his birds.

55

My mouth feels like it's packed with cotton wool, my skin tingling as sensation returns. I try to speak, and the words spill out in a dry whisper.

'Are you okay, Naomi?'

She whispers through the growing light. 'I've been better.'

'Injured?'

'My face hurts like hell and my hands are numb.' She scrapes her wrists over the carpet, trying to loosen the rope that binds them.

'Who's doing this?'

'I don't know. His voice sounded familiar, but I can't be sure.' She takes a long, sobbing breath. 'Someone put a hood over my head at my studio; he drugged me. When I came round, I'd been tied up . . .'

My sympathy builds as her words ebb into silence. The woman has endured harsh punishments just for being an outsider. 'Try to remember, Naomi. Details will give him away.'

'He wants to kill me. I know from the way he laughed;

he loved hearing me scream. He was babbling away in Cornish.' Her voice is flat with exhaustion.

'Go through it, step by step. Could it have been Jimmy Curwen?'

'No way. It was the Birdman who tried to set me free.'

'Curwen helped you?'

'I was tied to a chair; he couldn't undo the chain so I sent him to get help. Then the man came back and blindfolded me again. I can't remember much except waking up in a tunnel somewhere.' Her voice quakes as she remembers. 'I thought I'd die down there, but he dragged me out.'

'It's over now. We'll get out soon, don't worry.'

She gives a hollow laugh. 'How, exactly? I'm tied up and you're paralysed.'

'People are searching for us.'

'You're just humouring me; we'll die here. Where the fuck are we anyway?' Panic resonates in her voice.

'A cottage on Gugh. He carried you across the Bar.'

'He must be insane.'

'You said his voice sounded familiar. Who did you think it was?'

'It was muffled, like he didn't want me to guess. I thought it was Martin.'

'Martin Tolman?'

'His tone sounded the same, but I could be wrong.'

She seems too exhausted to say more, her voice fading, but my thoughts are working over-time. Jealousy could have driven Tolman to harm Naomi, and he tried to conceal his past with her, but why would he kill Alex Rogan?

'I can't take much more of this,' Naomi whispers.

'We can't give up. Michelle Nickell's baby's been taken too.'

A loud sigh hisses from her mouth. 'Why would Martin do that? What kind of monster would take a new-born child?

The air fills with the sound of Vine's sobbing, and I can see her body trembling as the light increases. I can't even comfort her, and my mind strays back to the missing baby. I try to roll onto my side, my legs jerking forward a couple of inches before the paralysis returns. My strength is slowly returning, but we may have minutes, not hours, before the killer comes back.

56

Jimmy is running out of options when he opens the pantry door. The cupboard is lined with jam jars, packets of flour and biscuit tins, but a small window lies directly ahead. After a few attempts he manages to wrench it open. It takes effort to force his body through the opening then drop to the ground. He lands heavily on his side, but he's so elated the discomfort barely registers. A kittiwake squeals, high overhead, welcoming him back.

The Birdman presses himself against the wall of the house, in case Carlyon sees him, but the place is in darkness. It's only when he draws a deep breath that pain threatens to drag him under. Jimmy's shoulder is burning, his left arm hanging down at an odd angle. The stabbing sensation is so deep, he can't move, even though he should be fetching help. Keith Pendennis's cottage lies at the foot of the hill, but his vision is blurring. Jimmy leans against the wall, trying to breathe steadily, waiting for the pain to subside.

57

I can see the objects around me better now that dawn's pink light is sifting through the window overhead. The owners of the cottage keep their winter fuel here, a wood-box packed with logs in the neatly equipped office. The carpet glistens with moisture, the stench convincing me that the killer has upended several cans of paraffin, in case he needs to act fast. He would only have to drop a match through the window for the room to become an inferno.

The light reveals Naomi Vine's injuries more clearly, too. The woman has ugly bruises running from her hairline to her jaw, as if the killer has beaten her head against the concrete floor, but at least she's stopped crying. The keening sound has been replaced by silence. I can still barely raise my arms, even though pins and needles jabbing under my skin prove that my system's recovering.

'Tell me about Martin, Naomi.'

Her good eye suddenly blinks open, the other still

swollen shut. 'I could be wrong about his voice. Why would he hurt me like this?'

'He told me about your relationship, but I think he lied.'

She turns her face away. 'He was too controlling right from the start, I had to end it, even though I cared for him. I never should have started seeing him again. I thought he'd grown up, but his jealousy was even worse.'

'How do you mean?'

'He hated me going out, even with girlfriends. I begged him to get counselling but he didn't listen. I hated walking away, when he'd given up so much.' Her voice is low and mournful.

'What happened when you moved to St Agnes?'

'It was a shock to see him. Martin still had feelings, but I told him we could only be friends. I managed to avoid him until recently.'

'How do you mean?'

'He saw Alex Rogan leaving my house. Martin was furious; he accused me of having an affair.'

The picture comes into focus suddenly. Jealousy could have driven Martin Tolman to kill the astronomer, then abduct Naomi for throwing his orderly life into turmoil. Her voice sounds distraught when she speaks again.

'I made him leave, but the row got to me. I'd never seen him so angry. I moved here to work, not to dredge up the past.' There's a fresh glint of anxiety in her eye when she studies me again. 'Is my house okay? I hope it's not damaged.'

'Don't worry about that now.'

Her face crumples as she reads my expression. 'What happened?'

'There was a fire, I'm afraid some of your work's damaged.' There's no point in telling her the place is in ruins.

The woman flinches, then her face suddenly calms, as if one more loss is immaterial. Her explanation has added to my concern: Tolman could return soon, to finish what he started. When I glance down, the ropes around her wrists look looser than before, from where she's been dragging them across the floor.

'Can you free your hands yet, Naomi?'

'It hurts like hell. The skin on my wrists is raw.'

I'm about to make another suggestion when a new sound whispers through the air. It's so faint, I can hardly hear it, but when it comes again Naomi's gaze meets mine.

'What's that?' she asks. 'It sounds like a cat mewing.'

The noise is stronger now. The thin wail of an infant, flooding my system with relief.

'Lottie must be hidden somewhere near.'

Naomi reacts instantly. Pain makes her cry out as she forces her damaged wrists to flex, but she works with renewed energy, and soon the rope drops to the ground. She scrabbles at the fastenings around her ankles, clearly desperate to find the baby, something falling from the pocket of her jeans as she toils. The pain in my temple worsens as feeling returns, my skin twitching as the drug leaves my system. I can flex my muscles, but still lack enough strength to sit up. I feel a pang of envy as she rises onto all fours.

'Jesus,' she mutters. 'I've been on the ground so long, my head's spinning.'

'Take it easy, Naomi.'

She ignores my suggestion, weaving unsteadily as she crawls over to some cupboards. Paper and envelopes spill out as she searches, until she opens a large drawer. Vine's expression is startled as she faces me again, with the baby in her arms. The child is wrapped in a stained white blanket, her face pink and furious as she bawls at top volume.

'She must have been asleep.' Vine gazes at Lottie, as if she's witnessing a miracle. 'What the hell can we do? There's nothing to feed her.'

'At least she's alive.' My thoughts flick to Eddie and Michelle waiting at home, desperate for news. 'My phone's screwed, but the microchip will still be working. They'll be able to track it here soon.'

Vine pays me no attention. She's hunched against the wall, focused on comforting the baby. There's no sign of fear anymore, which increases my concern. The child has lowered Naomi's defences, making her forget the dangers we're facing.

58

Jimmy is half-blinded by the pain from his fall. It's still coursing through his muscles, but he can't wait any longer. If he
stays near the Carlyons' property, Gavin will catch him and
lock him up again. He stares down the hill at Keith Pendennis's
house. The man's fierce reputation scares him, but there's
nowhere else to turn.

He runs towards the property, with every jolt triggering a
fresh burst of pain. Jimmy uses his right hand to pound on
the door until Pendennis appears. The man is bare-chested,
thick ropes of muscle stretched across his torso, yet Jimmy
holds his ground. He points to the top of the hill, eyes pleading
with Pendennis to follow. At least the man is paying attention;
there's no sign of the sneer Carlyon wore.

'What's wrong, Jimmy?' he asks. 'Are you hurt?'

Pendennis leads him inside the house and makes him sit on
a kitchen stool, then runs his hand over Jimmy's arm, making
him cry out.

'Your shoulder's dislocated. Look out of the window for me,
see if you can spot any birds.'

Jimmy's vision blurs while Pendennis grips his wrist. There's a wild surge of pain, then he can move freely again, but his panic intensifies. Morning light is flooding across the ocean and time is running out.

59

'What the hell can we do? The door and window are both locked.' Naomi stares at me, clearly desperate for answers. It feels like I've been on a three-day bender, even though my mouth tastes of paraffin instead of booze. My main focus is on the baby. Lottie is still lying in Naomi's arms, her cries weaker than before.

'Don't give up, Naomi. You have to stay strong.'

'I need an escape plan, not a pep talk.' She gives me a dead-eyed stare. 'I'm the toughest person you'll meet, believe me. This beats lying underground with rats crawling over my skin.'

There's anger in her voice, but her face is tender when she comforts the baby, all of her movements gentle. Naomi's terror appears to have vanished. Her experiences must have numbed her senses.

'Did anything else happen, around the time of Rogan's murder?' I ask.

'A piece of stone arrived in the post, with old Cornish

words scratched on it. I never found out who sent it.'

'Why didn't you say?'

She winces as she rubs the raw skin on her wrists. 'I didn't know it was important; I threw it away.'

'Even though you knew Martin was learning the language?'

'Don't blame this on me. It's not my fault.'

Her voice is rising to a shout and something about her reactions fuels my concern.

When my gaze drops to the floor, I see that the small object that dropped from her pocket is a key. My thoughts shift suddenly, like the wind changing direction. I have to catch my breath before speaking again.

'I did some research into your background, Naomi. It sounds like your childhood was pretty rough.'

She clutches the baby closer to her chest. 'People have had worse. I spent years in a kids' home full of monsters and paedophiles, but I survived.'

'You must have longed for a proper home.'

'Of course.' Her voice is strident with anger. 'I thought I'd get one here, but it didn't work out.'

Blood is pumping through my system, my head slowly clearing, yet I don't move a muscle. 'Martin's got nothing to do with this. No one's coming for us, are they?'

Naomi's gaze flickers when she looks at me again.

'You tied those ropes round your wrists. That's why you could undo them so easily. It was you who put a brick through the Nickells' window, and stole their child.'

'That's a mad thing to say.'

'You wanted to frame Martin for killing Rogan. Your whole abduction, to get even. I bet it hurt like hell, wounding yourself. Did you run into a wall?'

'How could I injure myself like this? I'd never do something that stupid.'

'You took a man's life and destroyed your own home to make your ex look guilty. It must have kept you busy, chasing round the island, setting flares.'

'That's rubbish.'

'Your world's fallen apart. Tolman rejected you, your sculptures are less popular than before. Buying that old mansion took all your money, didn't it? I bet your finances are at rock bottom. This would give you a massive insurance pay out and put him behind bars.'

'Shut up, for fuck's sake.'

'No one on St Agnes would hurt you or Alex Rogan. The islanders welcome visitors; without them, they wouldn't survive. But it beats me how you dragged a grown man up the hill on Burnt Island.'

She gives a mocking laugh and her manner changes, pretences suddenly dropping away. 'I didn't have to force him, believe me.'

My breath catches in my throat; until now I've been following a hunch, but Naomi has just confirmed my theory. I hold my breath when she lays the baby down beside me. If I push too hard, Lottie will suffer worst. When Naomi grabs one of the paraffin cans, I barely have time to shut my eyes before liquid pours over me, saturating my hair, skin and clothes. Its burning tang makes my throat convulse.

'Think of the baby, for Christ's sake,' I say, choking out the words.

'Remember, I've got a lighter in my pocket.' She delivers a hard kick to my ribs.

'You'd never escape in time. Is that what you want, after seeing Rogan burn?'

'We'd all have lived if you hadn't guessed. I gave you just enough Rohypnol to put you out of action for a short time. You'd have recovered and I could have carried on with my work.'

'You've left DNA evidence all over the island; they'd only need to fingerprint you to join all the dots. I want to know how Alex died.'

'Shut up and let me think.'

I'm praying that Eddie has figured out I'm trapped on Gugh and has sent a rescue party. Naomi's face is rigid with tension as she considers her options; she's pulled her lighter from her pocket, gripping it in her hand.

'You want the baby dead too?'

'I'm not going to jail. I've spent enough time locked up in places where no one gives a damn.'

Lottie is gurgling quietly to herself, one small hand clutching the edge of her blanket. Her only chance of survival rests on me keeping Vine distracted.

'Why not explain it to me, Naomi? It doesn't make sense.'

'I don't have to justify myself.' She's growing more agitated, running her thumb across the switch on her lighter.

'At least put Lottie outside where Eddie can find her.'

'She's coming with me when I die. Her pure spirit will cancel out my mistakes.' Her gaze goes out of focus, her injured face crumpling. 'Martin wanted us to have a family, but I missed my chance.'

'You could have found someone else.'

'No one will honour my legacy now, because of you.' She spits out the words, then lifts the lighter in the air, ready for us all to burn. I have to work hard to force a smile onto my face.

'Not yet, Naomi. This is our last chance to talk.'

Vine's hand hovers in the air, then she kneels beside me, her face inches from mine. I still lack the strength to lunge for the key, so I listen to her murmur, with a rising sense of horror. There's glee in her tone as she describes the fire that ravaged Alex Rogan's body.

60

Jimmy tries to explain that Naomi is in danger, but Pendennis just shakes his head. The old boxing coach tells him he must have his shoulder strapped, to prevent muscle damage. Jimmy soon tires of his droning voice, getting to his feet when the man's back is turned. He blunders outside, running up Kittern Hill, with Keith Pendennis trailing behind. The dawn chorus is deafening as gulls and terns swoop inland, but their song is hard to interpret. Does it mean that his friend is dead or alive? The cottage looks peaceful when he finally comes to a halt and Pendennis turns to face him.

'It's empty. Whatever scared you has gone away.'

Jimmy points at the house again, but the fitness coach shakes his head.

'Only Rachel Carlyon has a key.'

Jimmy stares at him for a moment, then picks up a stone and hurls it at a ground floor window. The older man reacts fast when the pane explodes into fragments: he grabs the Birdman's arm, bracing it at his side.

'What the fuck are you doing? That's someone's property. You'll have to pay for the damage.'

Jimmy tries to wrench free, determined to enter the cottage, even though his wounded shoulder is burning. He uses all of his strength to free himself, but Pendennis pins him down.

61

The sound of glass shattering brings panic to Naomi's face, and time is running out to save the child. I roll forwards to grab the key, knocking the sculptor off her feet, the lighter still clutched in her fist. The mad gleam in her eye lets me know she's past caring whether we live or die.

'We can still walk free, Naomi.'

'I told you, I'm not going to prison.'

My movements are shaky as I lunge forwards. She flicks her lighter before I can knock it from her hand. A wave of flames race through the air as the vapour ignites. I grab Lottie from the floor while Naomi waits for fire to wash over her. She seems happy to die, but I won't give her the pleasure. The woman kicks and punches as I haul her across the room. The space is already filling with toxic smoke that presses in from the walls; my limbs are still so weakened by Rohypnol that the key drops from my fingers.

I reach down to find it, but flames have already

engulfed the floor. There's a searing pain in my arm as I shield Lottie against my chest. It's getting hard to breathe, the smoke making my eyes stream. Vine has changed her mind now the fire's blazing. She's clawing my back, no longer willing to play Joan of Arc. She'd happily walk over my carcass to escape this place alive. When I throw myself at the door, the hinge stays intact. The wood finally splinters as I ram my body weight against it for the third time.

My first concern is for the baby, but I haul Vine into the living room then slam the door to contain the fire. Lottie is limp in my arms as I strip off my shirt, the fabric still aflame when it hits the tiled floor. I yank the blanket away from Lottie's face. Her eyes are shut and I can't tell whether she's breathing; she must have inhaled too much smoke, her small lungs struggling to cope. I'm still crouching beside her when the Birdman claws his way through a broken window, oblivious to my presence, his gaze fixed on Naomi Vine.

62

Jimmy ignores Pendennis's shouted warnings. He hurries across the room, Naomi's thin frame blending with the memory of his sister as he takes her hand. Her clothes have burned to tatters, raw wounds on her skin, but her chest is rising and falling steadily.

Kitto is yelling at him, and smoke is gushing into the room. From the corner of his eye Jimmy can see the cop breathing into the baby's mouth, but he stays focused on his task. He wets a towel under the kitchen tap. Vine cries out in pain as he wipes her face with small, dabbing movements, as if he were tending a wounded bird. His mind fills with relief when her eyes open, even though her expression is pained. She'll survive, and he won't have to dream of her, like his sister, lost under a sea of flames. Jimmy is so focused on nursing her that he barely hears the policeman yelling at him.

'Get out of here, while you can.'

The man's urgent tone brings Jimmy to his feet. He helps to lift Vine through the broken window, not caring how much his shoulder hurts. He's still smiling with relief when the pure morning light touches his face.

63

Fear hits me like a sledgehammer when we get outside. The baby's skin is pale blue, her eyes closed, even though I've been breathing air into her lungs. Someone shouts my name but nothing matters except keeping Lottie alive. I press one finger against the side of her neck and feel nothing, until a weak pulse beats against my skin. She makes a choking sound, then colour floods back into her cheeks.

'Thank God for that.'

I cradle her against my chest as Keith Pendennis approaches. He looks incredulous when I explain that Vine is the killer; we must stand guard until she's locked in a holding cell on St Mary's. The woman lying on the wet grass looks too frail to harm anyone, her lower legs covered in burns, a dark line of bruises marking her face. The reality of her situation seems to have hit home at last. She's curled in a foetal position, eyes screwed shut to avoid picturing her future.

When I rise to my feet, Shadow is tearing up the hill,

with Eddie sprinting behind. My deputy's face looks stricken when he sees me clutching Lottie.

'She's okay, but we need to get her to hospital.'

He seizes his daughter from my arms and relief floods through me when the child releases a thin wail. If she can cry, she must be breathing more easily. By now the pain is starting to register; the skin on my forearm has blistered away from my hand to my elbow, but I'm lucky to be alive. If I'd spent more time in that locked room, none of us would have escaped.

I'm still in a daze when I see Liam Poldean and Mike Walbert crossing the channel in a small boat loaded with fire-fighting equipment, but it could be too late to save the cottage. Smoke and flames are already gushing from the ground floor windows; there's little chance the volunteer fire crew can contain the damage, especially as the tide is still too deep to bring the water tank across from St Agnes with Mike's tractor. The police launch is anchored by the shore at the foot of the hill. Lawrie Deane and Keith Pendennis carry Vine down to the waiting vessel, while Eddie tends his baby. Someone wraps a silver blanket around my shoulders once we reach the boat, but the cold air feels soothing after the flames, the pain flaring through my nerve endings.

The boat heads for Hugh Town at its highest speed, a long strand of wash churning behind us. At last the wind has dropped, the storm finally relenting. The sea is bathed in clear light as we ease into St Mary's Sound. When I look back, Jimmy Curwen is watching us leave, but he's not alone; a swirl of gulls dance above his head as he walks blank-faced towards Liam and Mike's boat. It hits me again that I made a serious mistake; Jimmy would never set out to hurt anyone, unless they were attacking the creatures he considers to be his closest friends.

I can't absorb all the information Eddie gives me as the boat scuds over the waves. He's gazing down at his daughter, but it sounds like he spent hours going from house to house, until Shadow led him to Covean Beach. The dog is curled at my feet, half-asleep, as if it's all in a day's work.

Naomi Vine is blank-faced when she's carried to the ambulance on Hugh Town quay, refusing to say a word. I'd rather not share the confined space, but I won't leave her unguarded after the trouble she's caused. Normally I'm allergic to hospitals, but it's good to arrive in a clean environment, where the air smells of disinfectant instead of paraffin. I've known the doctor who examines me all my life. Ginny Tremayne gave me all my inoculations as a kid, and doled out free condoms at my secondary school with an amused look on her face. The medic's salt-and-pepper hair is drawn back in a loose ponytail when she inspects my wounds.

'You'll need some Novocain before I dress that burn, Ben. It'll make you feel a bit woozy.'

'No, thanks. I've had enough drugs to last me a lifetime.'

A look of concern crosses her face when I explain

about my dose of Rohypnol. Tremayne examines my eyes with a torch pen then makes me recite the alphabet, before checking the state of my tongue. 'No lasting damage, but that burn needs cleaning fast. Are you sure about the local anaesthetic? It'll hurt like hell otherwise.'

'I'll grin and bear it, Ginny.'

'I thought you were too smart to be macho.' She gives me a gentle smile. 'Curse all you like, the room's sound-proofed.'

She takes ages swabbing my wound, then covering it with gauze. I've been sitting in the chair so long, pain and exhaustion have levelled me, but Naomi Vine's mad speech is still ringing in my ears. I need a full confession to lay the case to rest.

'Can I go now? There's work to do.'

Tremayne gapes at me. 'You'll be here two days at least. I'm treating you for shock, and that wound needs to be kept surgically clean or you'll need a graft. You don't want that, do you?'

The doctor's manner is so firm there's no point in arguing, so I let her lead me to one of the minute hospital's rooms, resenting her instruction to lie down. I'm certain there'll be no rest with the buzz of voices outside and the clatter of feet marching down the corridor, but my eyes close anyway, a tidal wave of sleep washing over me.

When I surface again, it's from a vicious nightmare. I dreamed that the sky was lit by huge fireworks, while St

Agnes burned, but my real surroundings are calm. The room is in semi-darkness and a figure is seated by the door, his overcoat neatly folded on his lap, not a hair out of place. DCI Madron pulls his chair closer when he sees my eyes opening.

'You've slept all day, Kitto,' he says quietly. 'Your fan club's been here, bearing gifts. Your uncle brought you a radio, Zoe Morrow left some brandy, and there's a book from Liz Gannick. Maggie's just outside, chatting to the nurses.'

'There's no need for fuss, sir. I'm fine.'

'You even slept through the nurses changing your dressings. They're pleased, by the way. The scarring should be minimal.'

'How's Lottie?'

'The baby needed some oxygen, but she's fine. Eddie and Michelle took her home earlier.'

'And Naomi Vine?'

'The morphine's loosened her tongue. I've taken a statement from her already.'

'She killed Rogan and staged her own abduction to frame Tolman, didn't she? It satisfied all her needs. She wanted the boathouse as her gallery and to punish her ex for rejecting her.'

'It looks that way,' Madron replies with a slow nod.

She arranged the meeting the night before Rogan disappeared, said she'd had a change of heart about his observatory plans and had decided to finance the whole thing. She even made him promise not to tell his wife until they'd thrashed out the details, so it could be a big surprise for the community. He mentioned that he was going to the mainland that night at her house, which gave her the perfect opportunity. She lured Rogan onto Burnt Island, then shoved him into the fire while he was drugged.'

'How did she get him there?'

'She pretended to be so excited about the new observatory she wanted to plan the rebuild immediately, fed him a line about Burnt Island being the best vantage point, and begged him to take a quick look with her first thing in the morning, before his boat left.'

'And Jimmy Curwen had nothing to do with Rogan's death.'

'He must have dropped his coat at the scene. I imagine he wanted to put out the flames.' Madron looks down at his hands. 'The burning body would have been a terrible sight.'

'Why did she want to punish her ex so badly?'

'She'll need a full psychiatric assessment, but a specialist on the mainland thinks she's got narcissistic personality disorder. Naomi attacks anyone that gets in her way. Martin Tolman and Alex Rogan was obstructing destiny, in her view. Her campaign began soon after she arrived on St Agnes. Apparently she took an immediate dislike to Gavin Carlyon; she tampered with the fireworks before last year's display, which explains his injury. The youth courts will have to retract Adam Helston's arson conviction, too. I imagine his parents will be thrilled to hear that their boy never started the

fire at the Walberts' place, and they'll sue for a big compensation claim. She set light to their barn as practice
for greater things to come.'

'What about the Cornish messages?'

'That was clever, wasn't it? She wanted us to believe
that an islander hated outsiders enough to kill them, so
she bought a book of local words and phrases on the
mainland. The language became one of her obsessions.
She hid the stones and seashells she used at the crime
scenes at the Carlyons' house, in case her own property
was searched.'

'Did Rachel know?'

'She's claiming innocence. Vine says she stole the
keys to the holiday cottage from Rachel's house, but
she could be lying. The woman seems to have had a
hypnotic effect on some of the islanders.'

Madron pulls his chair closer, and for once the anger
between us drops away. 'You did well, Kitto. Your
approach was unorthodox, but your commitment's
exceptional. Eddie's got you to thank for bringing his
baby home alive.'

'I made mistakes, took too long getting there.'

'You race at things, Kitto. It wouldn't hurt to slow down.'

'Why do you criticise me all the time?'

His smile fades. 'Did you ever hear about my oldest son?'

'No, sir.'

'Tom was young and impetuous, like you, immune
to advice. He was training to be a pilot, but he died in
a motorbike crash before his thirtieth birthday.'

'I'm sorry to hear it.'

The DCI shakes his head. 'I chose the right man for the job. Liz Gannick tells me you're a natural leader; she's hinting that her partnership report will be favourable.'

Madron says a brisk goodbye then exits the room, leaving me closer to understanding why he always finds fault. I take time remembering his low-key praise. Words of encouragement slip from his mouth so rarely, I should have made him write them down so I could get a tattoo.

I fall asleep again, only waking when a nurse slips into the room. She barely speaks as she removes the gauze, then dresses my burn again, before leaving me alone. My thoughts keep returning to the extraordinary measures Naomi Vine took to frame her ex-boyfriend. Someone must have told her about the underground tunnels on Wingletang Down, where she kept her arsenal. I still don't know where she acquired all the flares, making it seem like the whole island was under siege, but she must have made plenty of trips to the mainland.

It's after midnight when I rise to my feet, too preoccupied to sleep again. I walk into the corridor, dressed only in hospital-issue pyjama bottoms and a white surgical robe. Lawrie Deane is dozing on a bench outside the room next to mine, where Naomi Vine is being kept. He looks startled when I wake him. The news that I want to speak to the woman who almost killed me seems to amaze him, but he lets me go ahead.

Vine's appearance has changed since we lay opposite each other on a stretch of filthy carpet. Someone has washed her hair, every speck of grime cleansed from her skin. Apart from the frame over her legs to protect her burns, and her bandaged cheek, she looks like any other forty-year-old woman. Only her intense expression reveals that she's mentally ill. I lower myself onto the chair, a few feet from her pillow.

'It's late for bedside visits, Inspector.'

'I've been thinking about what you did.'

'I've got no regrets.'

'Why did you kill an innocent man, who was just about to become a father?'

'He wouldn't listen to me. The boathouse would have made a perfect exhibition space, with a viewing platform, so people could see my sculptures arranged across the beach. They would have looked so beautiful, right at the point where the ocean meets the land.' Tears well in her eyes.

'Alex wanted something better. His telescopes would have shown people the entire solar system.'

'That man was only chasing glory, and he was a coward at the end. You should have heard him squeal as his flesh melted away.'

When she begins to laugh, I know she'll never go to prison. She'll live in a psychiatric institution for the rest of her days. I can still hear her cackling as I return to my own room.

64

Jimmy's hands are still shaking when night-time falls. Ella insisted on fussing over him, murmuring apologies while she bandaged his shoulder, but he can't forget seeing Naomi Vine on the floor, her skin blackened by fire. Ella says that she'll go to jail, but he prefers to remember the sculptor in her studio, turning metal into living forms, and the gifts of food she pressed into his hands.

When Jimmy checks the clock on his wall it's 10 p.m. Time to feed his birds. He carries a bag of seed and bottles of water downstairs, pausing to look up at the lighthouse when he reaches the yard. A dim light shines down from the gallery, reminding him that Stan Eden is keeping the island safe. But when he turns around, someone is waiting in the shadows, and the fear he's suppressed resurfaces.

'No need to run away, it's only me.' Martin Tolman steps into the light.

The Birdman makes a small, bowing motion, even though the look on the architect's face is unnerving. Tolman provides a roof over his head, but the man's tense expression makes him fear his home is at risk.

'I hear you tried to save Naomi Vine. That was a brave thing to do; I'll always be grateful.' Tolman walks closer, his gaze unblinking. 'Have you ever visited the bird sanctuary on St Mary's?'

Jimmy nods his head slowly. He was taken there once as a boy. The place filled him with wonder: seeing the creatures recovering inspired him to build his own cages and tend his wounded gulls.

'My friends run it now; they need help looking after the birds. The job's only part-time. It doesn't pay much, but you could survive on the wage. Would you be interested?'

Jimmy stares at Tolman in disbelief. All he's ever wanted is a job, like the other islanders, to buy medicine for his birds and feed himself without begging.

'Is that a yes, Jimmy?'

The Birdman nods his assent rapidly.

'That's good news. I'll come back tomorrow to make arrangements.'

Tolman says a quiet goodbye, leaving Jimmy reeling. Since his parents died, he's longed for independence, and now it's so close he can almost touch it.

The creatures are calm tonight when he crawls inside the enclosure to lay out fresh straw. The Atlantic gull can finally stand, but it shrieks in protest as he carries it outside. Jimmy cradles the bird against his chest, admiring its glassy black eyes and the yellow markings on its fierce beak. He whispers a few words, then opens his hands. The gull spreads its wings, before beating them wildly.

Jimmy tips his head back to watch the bird lunge into the air, then soar above the roofline, heading for open water.

364

65

Thursday 10 November

I've been signed off work for the next three days. It's late in the morning and a stream of visitors have marched up the path to my cottage, most of them hungry for details, even though I can't disclose anything until the trial ends. It's a relief to be alone for the first time in days, apart from Shadow, who's lying on the sofa beside me, sleeping off his escapade. Naomi Vine is still clogging up my headspace, but she's safe in the medical centre at Penzance prison. Tomorrow she'll receive a full psychiatric assessment. I can guess the results already; anyone who's prepared to kill a man, torch her own home and attempt two more murders for the sake of a building is unlikely to be declared sane.

Madron has kept me out of the loop while the case winds down, but details have filtered through anyway. Gavin Carlyon has filed a complaint about his accusations being ignored, and now that Vine has been arrested his claims seem justified. His wife is still pleading ignorance about the materials stored at their home, but I'm not convinced; Rachel was so gripped by hero-worship, she would have done anything for her glamorous new friend. Now that the danger's over, I feel a degree of sympathy for Naomi Vine. The sculptor's life imploded after her parents died, the care system doing more harm than good. A combination of factors caused Vine's breakdown, but the misery she suffered as a child must have contributed.

I stare down at the book I'm reading. The final chapter of *The Great Gatsby* lies open before me, but all I can see are parallels. Gatsby had the world at his feet: talented, good looking and charismatic, yet he threw it all away, like Naomi Vine. I gaze out of the window instead of finishing the story. The storm has cleared at last, wisps of sea mist lingering on the air, the atmosphere calm. Hell Bay stretches out in a long arc, with breakers rolling across the shore. It's soothing to watch the tide chivvy shingle further up the beach, but unfinished business nags at me. It could just be exhaustion from the strain of the case, but the feeling won't shift.

My gaze falls on the watch Maggie gave me before the case started, its silver casing undamaged by the fire. I take it from my wrist to examine it again, wondering how many hazards it's seen during its fifty-year lifespan. The inscription on the back makes more sense to me now: '*Time waits for no man.*' If I'd stayed in that locked room a minute longer, all three of us would have died. I hold the watch to my ear and listen to its tick, slow and regular as a resting heartbeat. I normally avoid considering the future, taking each day as it comes, but that approach has to change. Being alone has lost its appeal, so I'll have to make phone calls and start taking risks.

I'm about to return to my book when Shadow jumps to his feet, ears pricked. The creature can identify every islander by their tread, reacting differently to friend or foe. He looks thrilled to greet whoever is crunching down the shingle path, tail wagging madly as he races along the hall. Eddie enters without knocking, as if it's the most natural thing in the world. My parents were so relaxed about friends visiting they never bothered to fit a doorbell.

'Anyone home?' he calls out.

'In the living room.'

My deputy looks different out of uniform. He's wearing jeans and a sweatshirt, his blond curls uncombed for once. I notice that he's clutching a large shopping bag.

'Michelle's sent you some lunch,' he says.

'I thought you were on duty.'

'The DCI gave me permission to visit.'

I roll my eyes. 'Why's everyone queuing up to nurse me, for God's sake?'

'Count yourself lucky. It's shepherd's pie and some kind of chocolate cake. I'll stick the beers in the fridge.'

'Now you're talking.'

I sit in the kitchen while Eddie loads a ceramic dish in the microwave. The dog fixes me with his blue-eyed, insistent stare until I feel obliged to scoop some of the pie into his bowl, then the meal passes in a flurry of conversation. Eddie provides more details from the case when I press him. Apparently Liz Gannick found so much evidence on the petrol cans left at the Walberts' house and the stash of explosives, Naomi Vine's guilt would have been proved, once her prints were taken, even without her confession. Incinerating her home to destroy the main evidence of her crimes wouldn't have saved her from a prison sentence.

'I still don't get why she tied herself up, then waited to be found.'

Eddie shrugs his shoulders. 'She knew the Birdman would call eventually, because he was her only regular visitor. She wanted to make it look like Tolman had attacked her, but the Birdman couldn't alert us, so she waited hours then ran out of patience. She was so unhinged, she let light to the place.'

'Rogan lost his life because of her broken love affair.'

'She was obsessed. Naomi knew Tolman was learning Cornish, so she did the same. She didn't care how many people she damaged.'

'How's Sally doing, Eddie?'

'She's calmer now the killer's locked away, and her dad's staying at her place.'

I stare at him in amazement. 'How come? Neither of them wanted to back down.'

'Louise Walbert frog-marched Keith to Middle Town. It was sticky at first, but they've agreed to forget the past. He's planning to live there till Sally's had her baby. Keith's talking about running the Dark Skies Festival, in Alex's memory, to give Sally something positive to focus on.'

The news fills me with relief. At least one of Alex Rogan's dreams has been fulfilled: his wife has buried the hatchet with her father before their child arrives. We're halfway through the meal when I notice that my deputy's awkwardness has vanished; he's using my first name, body language relaxed despite recent traumas. My mistaken belief in the Birdman's guilt at the start of the case has destroyed the pedestal he placed me on, which is an almighty relief. It's only when he's about to leave that his expression grows solemn.

'I heard the news about Zoe getting married.'

'Rumours spread fast, don't they? She's making me fly over to Mumbai for the wedding next July.'

'I thought you two might end up together. You're always happy when she's around.'

'And a miserable git the rest of the time?'

'That's not what I'm saying. You're the kind of bloke people trust; that's why we asked you to be Lottie's godfather. I hate thinking about what might have happened if you hadn't carried her outside.' His words fade, while he pushes the idea aside.

'Naomi didn't set out to hurt Lottie. She just wanted

something pure to hold, and she'd dreamed of having a kid when she was with Tolman. She's so deranged she thought no one would guess she'd staged the whole mess herself.' I drain my bottle of beer. 'I still think one of your old schoolmates would do a better job as godfather.'

Eddie shakes his head firmly. 'Lottie needs the best man on the islands.'

'Flattery will get you nowhere.'

I swallow hard before speaking again; I don't want to take on a responsibility I may not be able to fulfil, but I can't forget seeing his baby fighting to breathe. Words slip from my mouth before I can silence them.

'The answer's yes, Eddie.'

He punches his fists in the air. 'Thank Christ for that; Michelle told me not to come home till you agreed.'

I say goodbye when the meal ends. There's an awkward moment in the porch as he gives me one of those man hugs that are halfway between a handshake and a wrestling manoeuvre, finally crossing the line into friendship after a bumpy start. Once the door shuts behind him, the sense of unfinished business that's bothered me all morning finally lifts from my shoulders.

Half a dozen well-meaning texts have arrived since Eddie's visit, including one from Zoe, inviting me round for the afternoon. I could carry on lounging on the sofa, but Shadow is dancing at my feet, telling me that I've spent too long feeling sorry for myself.

'Come on, monster. Take me for a walk.'

My dog vanishes into the mist once I step outside, but we always reach the same destination eventually.

Author's Note

St Agnes is one of my favourite places in the Isles of Scilly, and I hope that some readers may feel inspired to visit the remote destination for themselves. But I must explain to anyone that does make the journey: this novel isn't a guidebook. The story blends imagination and reality. I have taken liberties with the island's geography, to add danger to my tale, but I've also tried to conjure the magic of the place. There is no old mansion house on the island, and although you will find Neolithic gravesites on Wingletang Down, the tunnels are make-believe. St Warna's Well exists, but is smaller than in my description. The island's tiny dimensions and population of just eighty-two permanent residents are accurately described in *Burnt Island*. St Agnes does have a decommissioned lighthouse, which has had its light removed and is now a private residence, but there are no cottages at its feet.

The Turk's Head is a great place for fine beer and locally caught fish and chips, but it does not have rooms for hire. The island's post office is a treat to visit, with lovely staff and a good selection of locally produced food. You will find a decommissioned lifeboat house on the island, and a tiny, beautiful church with stained-glass windows that reflect the island's fraught relationship with the sea.

All of the Isles of Scilly have experienced maritime tragedies; dozens of local fishermen have been lost to vicious storms over the centuries, yet the beauty of the ocean remains. I've never felt closer to the sea than on St Agnes. The quiet is so complete, you can hear the tide from every part of the island, until the sea's whisper feels as natural as breathing.

Acknowledgements

Many thanks are due to the brilliant team at Simon and Schuster: Jo Dickinson, Rebecca Farrell, Jess Barratt, Dawn Burnett, Rhiannon Carroll and the excellent sales team. I receive so much support and encouragement from you all, my job feels easy.

Many thanks to Stephen Wright at Two Cities, for commissioning the series for TV, which has been a huge boost. Thanks are also due to my literary agent Teresa Chris and my TV agent Katie Langridge for believing so passionately in this series from the start.

Thanks to the kind staff of the Turk's Head and the Post Office on St Agnes for answering questions about island life and whether or not someone could drown at high tide if they fell from the Bar. Thanks also to Nigel at Paulgers Taxis on St Mary's for an excellent guided tour, and Rachel Greenlaw for her hospitality at her lovely apartment, Cowrie. In a typical piece of Scillonian generosity, Rachel took me out for coffee and offered me a week's free accommodation on the first day we met! Thanks to lovely Linda Thomas at Porthcressa Library for describing winter storms in the Scillies, and how the off-islands can become isolated for days during a bad squall. Pete Hicks, St Mary's lifeboat cockswain, spent time describing sea conditions around St Agnes, which helped a great deal. I am also very grateful to Sam Rogerson, Cornish Language and Culture Support officer, for translating the Cornish passages in the book for me. *Oll an gwella, Sam!* Your help was invaluable.

Thanks as ever to all of my writing pals: the Killer Women, the 134 Club, Penny Hancock, Clare Chase, Valentina Giambanco, Mary-Jane Riley and Miranda Doyle. My husband Dave Pescod is a brilliant and tireless critic, and still my biggest cheerleader after twenty-three years. Thanks also to stepsons Jack, Matt and Frank, for encouraging me to keep writing. What lovely, thoughtful men you have become!

Special thanks are due to my mother, Wendy Rhodes, for being so full of joy when she heard that the series had been optioned. Your texts and kind words keep me writing, Mum. Cheers to Honor, my sister, for being generally fabulous.

Finally, thanks to Twitter pals Peggy Breckin, Julie Boon, Jenny Blackwell, Louise Marley, Janet Fearnley, Hazel Wright, Christine South, Polly Dymock, Angela Barnes, Rach Medlock, Sarah LP and hundreds more. Your kind messages of encouragement inspire me to produce the best stories I can dream up, to keep you all entertained.

*Go back to the beginning
with DI Ben Kitto and read his first
investigation on the Isles of Scilly ...*

HELL
BAY

After ten years working for the murder squad in
London, a traumatic event has left DI Ben Kitto grief-
stricken. He's tried to resign from his job, but his boss has
persuaded him to take three months to reconsider.

Ben plans to work in his uncle Ray's boatyard
on the tiny Scilly island of Bryher where he was born,
hoping to mend his shattered nerves. But his plans
go awry when the body of sixteen-year-old Laura
Trescothick is found on the beach at Hell Bay.
Her attacker must still be on the island because
no ferries have sailed during a two-day storm.

Everyone on the island is under suspicion.

Dark secrets are about to resurface.

And the murderer is ready to strike again.

AVAILABLE NOW IN PAPERBACK AND EBOOK